Books by Ann Cornelisen

TORREGRECA

VENDETTA OF SILENCE

VENDETTA OF SILENCE

VENDETTA OF SILENCE

a novel by

ANN CORNELISEN

An Atlantic Monthly Press Book

Boston—Little, Brown and Company—Toronto

LIBRARY OF CONGRESS CATALOG CARD NO. 76-161421
T10/71
FIRST EDITION

ATLANTIC–LITTLE, BROWN BOOKS
ARE PUBLISHED BY
LITTLE, BROWN AND COMPANY
IN ASSOCIATION WITH
THE ATLANTIC MONTHLY PRESS

Published simultaneously in Canada
by Little, Brown & Company (Canada) Limited

PRINTED IN THE UNITED STATES OF AMERICA

To My Mother and Father

AUTHOR'S NOTE

All the names of characters in this book were invented by me. If, by some evil genius, they coincide with names of real people, I hope it will be understood that was not my intention. As for the story — at the request of my publishers and my lawyer, I have agreed to call this a novel. Perhaps it is more comfortable to think of it as such.

VENDETTA OF SILENCE

ONE

I

Occasionally in Italy, and always when it seems least likely, a foreigner is allowed beyond the portcullis of exquisite courtesy that protects the patrician family from intrusion. You cannot woo them. You either are or are not *simpatica,* an elusive quality, everything and nothing. I no longer try to explain my good fortune: I simply belong to the Brancatis and have for the last sixteen years, ever since Gabriella, the matriarch of the family, decided to allow me to rent a small furnished flat at the back of their Roman palace. She was very frank. She had told her administrator No Women. She wanted a foreign man, preferably an elderly bachelor, she said in her precise English, but perhaps . . . She examined me more closely: I was aware my gloves were not as clean as they might be. "The war left us in a muddle. You Americans could have done so much for Italy. Instead . . ."

To my unpracticed eye she seemed to have weathered the upheaval with grace. Monolithic walnut doors had glided to behind me with the soft oily suction of a bank vault being closed. A young footman in a red and white striped jacket had skimmed soundlessly, tracklessly over the marble floors as he led me through drafty salons hung with tapestries and family portraits to her sitting room. There in the warmth of an ever-burning fire and surrounded by Venetian chests and cabinets cluttered with photographs of resolute military gentlemen and wistful ladies in what appeared to be long satin tank suits with trains, she ordered her world. In time I understood. Nothing was quite as she had known it. Old retainers had died to be replaced by their nieces and nephews who were glad to have work but were unwilling to view their functions with the gentle reverence Gabriella had come to expect. Now accounts were rendered to her in millions of lire, instead of prewar hundreds or thousands. At thirty lire, even a newspaper sounded an investment and had nothing good to report: Communist party gains; expropriation of land from large owners; Trieste.

To smother an amorphous sense of anxiety that ruined leisure, she kept herself busy. She remodeled forgotten corners of family palaces. She checked daily by telephone on the social engagements of her daughters-in-law and the physical condition of their offspring. She had season tickets to those fashionable afternoon concerts at the *Accademia,* where even Brahms and Stravinsky are filtered to distant tinkling serenades by the velvet, taffeta and feather baffles of ladies' hats. She played canasta and bridge, and when all else failed, she bullied "Miss Emily," her English companion of thirty years. Soon, though she had dozens of other tenants she might have taken in hand, she was correcting my erratic grammar, then my accent – "Vowels are *so* important in Italian, my dear" – and before I quite understood what was happening to me, had recommended a dressmaker, caused a cleaning woman to appear at my door, arranged for me to buy a car at a noble discount, and claimed first right of rejection over any young man so bold as to ask me out for dinner. "In Europe a woman must never appear to be without family protection. You had best bring him along for a glass of sherry." Few measured up to her standards, fewer still braved a second encounter, but none ever doubted that he was responsible to the Marchesa Gabriella Brancati di San Cosimato for my safety.

At first I was puzzled. Why should she be so very kind to an unknown foreigner, particularly an American? So many of us, overcome by what has been called "elective affinity," had settled in Italy that we no longer intrigued anyone. On the contrary, we shared a tactless habit which should have alienated us from Italians *and* Americans. One evening we reveled in telling our hosts, with that abundance of harrowing detail Italy never fails to provide, that nothing in their country worked properly. The next, we were the cicerones of civilized life, explaining patiently to "tourist" friends that only crass nations did not nap after lunch, swilled gin cocktails, and ate their dinner in what we now knew to be the late afternoon. On the face of it we should not have generated much *simpatia,* but fortunately *simpatia* is not the slave of a rigid formula.

Gabriella may always, as her friends claim, have wanted a daughter. She has five sons, a feat which she feels has much to do with the Italian woman's innate sense of duty, and little or nothing to do with genetics. (She dismisses Mendel on a double count: He was both Austrian and a monk.) Her sons have left her for their own lives, which is, she says, as it should be. Three of them live in Milan and run a complex family business; the fourth, Renzo, is a lawyer who handles a multitude of dynastic problems; and the fifth, Guido, manages the family estates. They are such exceedingly handsome men with long, fine-boned faces and Irish-blue eyes that one expects nothing more from them than perfect tailoring and charm. The deception is not intentional, but must be useful at times, for each in his own field is quite ruthless. Gabriella herself is an example of their skill. She would direct; they allow her to advise and she is content. She has no reason to scold them. They are intelligent, even astute. They are devoted to the young women they have married; so is she. Guido, whom she would like to spoil, is not married, but he refuses to live with her. He is always somewhere in the country, just out of reach of balls and charitable bazaars and Sunday afternoon tea with relatives. His mother is resigned. She smiles and says a wife will change him; meanwhile she has discovered the joy of spoiling grandchildren and is not, I am quite sure, in need of a substitute daughter.

In spite of my arrogance, impatience, my instant American

(that is, perfect) solutions and my tongue, which, though it resisted the beauty of Italian, clattered me into disastrous situations – in spite of all, Gabriella persisted. I am so grateful. She is one of those rare and delightful women who never complain of loneliness or ill health or the strange misdirections of the world. She can be counted on *not* to tell you the physio-dynamics of her latest liver attack or her daughter-in-law's most recent typical bit of selfishness. She is absolute in her judgments of right and wrong for others and slightly more lenient with herself. Once she has decided what she must do, no earthly force can block her. She is proud, intelligent, impatient and, I think, lonely, a stern combination summed up as determination in men and strangely enough coldness in women. Many years before I was willing to analyze myself as cruelly as I analyzed my friends, she may have recognized some of the same traits in me.

If so, it was too late to change them, but she has mixed a great many shades of gray into a world I had painted black and white, and I am happier for them. My only regret is that we almost never agree about anything, most especially Italy. She did not and does not approve of my interest in the South, her South which I took for my own, nor can she accept my identification with southerners. If I say, "We need water," she answers sweetly, "We, dear? But in America you have plenty of water." She counters my rare explosions about twentieth-century feudalism or any other Italian ism with, "That is all very well for you to say. You do not understand." But she knows I do and she is proud of the years I spent working in the South when I should, she thought, have been absorbed in something "more appropriate." She adopted me for better or worse – which is it, I wonder? – and when I am not around to hear her, she lectures her friends about the tragic inequalities of southern life, about women who are old and defeated at forty and men who were born that way. She tells them stories of things I have seen and she has not, and talks of reforms which she now insists cannot wait even one more month.

Six or seven years ago when I decided to write a book about the South and was searching for a peaceful place in which to do it, Gabriella offered me a small Brancati house in San Basilio Saraceno, high in the Lucanian Apennines. No one had lived there for more than fifty years. Each fall Guido spends a week in the house while he goes over the harvest ledgers with his overseers and visits the farms under their control. Twice he has taken friends there to hunt, but after a few days of seeing nothing larger than baby sparrows, they have left in disgust. Under the circumstances money has not been wasted on repairs and the fact that the house was livable at all is a compliment to the masons of another age and to the sporadic attentions of the factor's wife.

I spent four happy summers there – long summers from May to mid-October – in the kind of peaceful isolation only such places can provide. San Basilio is, indeed, the perfect place to write a book. It is one of the most remote, most relentlessly uncomfortable townships in the civilized world. It offers no distractions – no late parties, no concerts, political discussions or love affairs. It is a still and lonely place. The shade of a tree is a blemish on the landscape, and a tentative trickle of water, meandering along its wide rocky highway of clay, is a fruit as seasonal as persimmons. I know San Basilio's limitations and delights. It is a purdah of the mind and body where the sight of a passing car and its implied contact with the outside world are enough to occupy the imagination for an entire evening.

The road itself is not new. For more than two thousand years it has skirted San Basilio's mountain to snake off toward the capital to the northwest and the Adriatic to the east, but early and late the Basilisks have not been travelers. They have farmed their stony fields with unreasoning tenacity and then huddled together in a warren of stone houses little more than huts that spiral in ever wider circles around the Duke's palace. When the Basilisks requested his protection, they did not receive it. They have been the victims of every passing army, every entrenched despot, and in all ages, victims of the weather. Still, to them, the road leads nowhere. Some unwritten Mosaic law decrees that life is to be fought there; no outside world exists and so no need to dream.

At first I fascinated the Basilisks. What might I be doing? In their world work is physical. The mind, like wisdom teeth or the appendix, is an inconvenient mistake of nature that flares up when the body is idle. Reading and writing are only palliatives: I seemed to do nothing else. They were courteous, but curious. They asked questions. Are you rich? Do you know my cousin in Broccoleeno? Aren't Italians the best lovers? Would you like an Italian husband? For a while they, like Jane Austen, seemed to think it a truth universally acknowledged that a single woman in possession of a good fortune (good enough, that is, that she need not "work") must be in want of a husband. The Basilisks do not lack imagination, but even they could not believe their own fantasy for long. There are, after all, more logical places to shop for a passionate Latin bridegroom. But what was I doing? Once the Carabinieri questioned me so persistently about my "activities" that I realized I was suspected of spying, which would be a truly futile occupation in San Basilio. At various times I was supposed to be buying or selling, or perhaps both, antiques, surplus American cheese, and babies. By the end of the first summer they had given up and categorized me for all time: "She is the Marchesa's friend." That one phrase explained any idiosyncracy.

Actually the Basilisks accepted my presence in San Basilio more easily than Gabriella. Each fall when I reappeared in Rome talking about those minor events that loom large in village life, she would listen patiently and, when she could stand no more, interrupt me, always with the same objection.

"Don *This,* Don *That!* Is it a town of priests?"

"Mother, you know it's not," Guido would object, but Gabriella was not to be stopped.

"Well, if all those *other* Dons are so important, they must have some sort of title – Baron or Count or just plain Doctor. You could call them something else. Really! So many Dons and Donnas, my head reels. It's worse than Spain."

Finally the book was finished and with it, Gabriella assumed, my San Basilio cycle. But one book leads, somehow, to another; there is always so much that was left unsaid. I have spent the past two summers back in San Basilio. My intention was to write a book I have long had in mind, about the tangled medieval lives of southern Italian women. I thought that all I needed was time to sit down and write it. I found, soon enough, that a woman's sympathy for other women, even her understanding, is not enough for the book I had embarked upon, nor was an abundance of time in itself sufficient for a task that appeared each day more complex.

Anyone who writes risks intellectual death by drowning in the murk of his own mind. After he has dredged about in the silt for exactly what he thinks and then for exactly the words that express it, he can settle further into the gumbo he discovers *is* his mind, or he can surface and look around, preferably at something very different, but at least at something external. What I saw was San Basilio. What I thought I saw was material for a novel – not quite what I had planned originally, though two of the same women were involved. While I waited and hesitated, I made notes.

Notes are the writer's natural detritus. Cryptic phrases – "the crossword puzzle windows of abandoned factories" or information of unknown origin – "In 187– the government officially denied any problem with brigands in the South. The forces of order had killed 1,632 in the last year (!)" – such tidbits, written on scraps of paper, lurk in the side compartments of purses, in bathrobe pockets, diaries and half-read books, waiting to be rediscovered. More sustained efforts usually reach a folder on one corner of my desk where they languish until, in a flurry of preguest neatness, I wedge the folder in a bookcase and forget it. In all probability that same fate awaited my embryonic novel.

The first few chapters were written as such. Then came a period when I was too busy to go on as I had begun; besides, what was happening was unclear. I resorted to notes, often detailed, which I planned to expand and reorganize – sometime. For certain things – whole episodes, conversations, reflections — there are only my diaries which have never changed form over the years: the oddments that have interested or amused me in any one day typed hastily on coarse yellow paper and stuck in a loose-leaf notebook.

I had imposed one limitation on myself: the story was to be told as it happened; no omniscience, no decorative caulking; the defects of judgment and the lacunae all there. But people in life, unlike characters in fiction, do not sprint obediently around an arbitrary track to an arbitrary finish. Mine, in fact, balked and decided they were in the wrong race altogether. Slowly, quietly, for to be abrupt is to be conspicuous, they slipped away to disappear in the shadowy monotony of their days. They were relieved; an official decision had dissolved the situation and with it what little responsibility or guilt they may ever have felt. They chose not to act, not to know, and I realized that only I needed an ending which I could believe to be true. Ten months ago I was given that ending. I am convinced it is true, but I have no proof.

I left San Basilio early last fall because Gabriella was ill. The doctors said heart strain, put her to bed, and ordered her to rest. She is not a person who rests on command. Renzo and Guido hoped that my return (and probably my stories of Don This and Don That) would distract her. I found her in her bedroom, which she now called her *camera ardente* — her mortuary chapel — banked in flowers and almost invisible under cascades of lace and ribbons. Books and letters and tapestry with snarled hanks of wool were strewn over every surface. The cushion of my chair even concealed a pair of vicious knitting needles. Gabriella looked tired and I wondered, not for the first time, exactly how old she was. I knew better than to ask; age is not a subject she appreciates. As a young woman, if she was too angular for beauty, she must have had a certain equine distinction which the years have only accentuated. And, of course, there are her eyes, the same Irish-blue eyes she passed on to her sons (so much for her non-Mendelian genetics). Now under each there was a half-moon of violet, slightly puffy skin which I had never seen before and which in a face so white and thin and bony were sad reminders that time does pass. She was also very nervous and very, very peevish.

She informed me that I looked tired and also untidy. My description of the long trip did not excuse me. And the novel? Had I finished it? She wanted to see it. I explained that it was finished in a sense, that it would never be reworked and was actually just another bundle of papers to be put away. Still, she would read it. She mistook my silence for stubborn refusal and was so irritated that she flushed and her breathing became a series of short strangled pants. Agitation, she explained, was bad for her heart. She need hardly have bothered to play on my sympathy; I know too well the frustration of being in bed while the world goes on without you. I promised to bring my bundle of papers and did later that same evening.

For a week every time I went to her *camera ardente* she could talk of nothing else. Her delight was to invent endings and test them on me. Except to say she would have to read to the last page, I did not comment. One afternoon it was Guido whose lap was full of papers. He asked if I were sure there was no way to publish it, perhaps with the names changed. When I shook my head, he dropped the subject. He resents pressure himself and so does not apply it to others. Unfortunately Gabriella is of a different cast of mind. She had decided the "novel" should be published and intended to keep after me until I relented. For support she called on Renzo, who saw the project as an excellent tonic for his mother's boredom and therefore something to be furthered, even at my expense. He was mild, but insistent: there was a great deal, beyond the story, that should be brought to light; was I allowing my aesthetic dissatisfaction to influence my judgment? I shrugged and tried to change the subject. I did not want to explain my real reasons, especially to Renzo who has always accused me of the blackest pessimism – the kind that expects every chair to collapse, every mattress to be stuffed with bedbugs, every shoe to conceal corns. He would not be distracted. Then, as now, I cannot do less than justify myself.

First, I have no proof of what I believe to be the truth, none, that is, acceptable to a court. In a small community incidents multiply by fission. One detail can be the parent of a whole generation of incidents, which in turn split and take on a being of their own. Anyone who wants to reconstruct events is presented with thousands of amoeboid pieces which seem only vaguely related. Trial and error and the unscientific use of probability may put the puzzle back together, but at best is a slow process of introducing a likely shape to a likely hole and if the colors do not match, finding another likely hole where they do. I *think* I have the pieces back together, but the natural gap between opinion and absolute certainty is wide enough for some doubt.

Second, in southern Italy lawsuits are the regional sport. For the poor they are a gamble, the only one open to them: some crumb of property may be gained when before they had nothing. Brothers sue brothers over a half-acre of hillside so bare even goats spurn it. Sisters rush to court for the equitable division of a one-room house and husbands sue in-laws for dowries which never existed. For the Powerful, who are not necessarily rich, lawsuits are the one sure means of exerting pressure for the advantageous settlement of some totally different question, or, if by chance there is no question pending, they are like other short-term speculations, good investments. In San Basilio even the Bishop has joined the lists, charging the retired sacristan of the cathedral with the theft of a pair of candlesticks. We all know the quarrel is actually over the sacristan's employment insurance, just as we all know the Bishop gave him the candlesticks after an itinerant junk dealer offered less than a dollar for them. But the justice of the accusation is not the issue; the pressure it exerts *is*. If no morsel of property offers itself for controversy, then there is always defamation of character, or invasion of privacy, either guaranteed to stir things up where privacy is unknown and defamation of character, along with the weather, absorbs ninety-five percent of normal conversation.

A strange hobby? Not at all. Southerners are simply more

practical than the rest of us. They make the most of a raw material we, in our dullness, do not recognize as such — the hundreds of unemployed lawyers willing to try suits for contingency fees. Who is exploiting whom does ultimately become a problem, but there is no denying that, in an isolated community, the law as a sport has certain obvious attractions. Little or no expense is involved and yet it offers the ultimate in pleasure — revenge — with an outside possibility, no less exciting for being outside, that a pot of gold may be dangling at the end of all that red tape. Italian court calendars are notoriously clogged. With subtle handling suits can drag on for ten years, ample time to set in motion the fringe annoyances that elevate this type of law from mere litigation to judicial art.

It is, as I said, all a matter of pressure. The filing of a lawsuit releases a blizzard of queries. Drowsy bureaucrats of agencies as various as the Automobile Club and the Vice Squad will investigate your past and your present. It is their duty to certify that you are *in regola,* which, given the complexity of Italian administration, is unlikely. The Judiciary Police arrive with a sheaf of unpaid parking violations; the total now amounts to ten times the original and they urge payment before your furniture is confiscated. The Census Bureau, which somehow overlooked you eight years ago, sends an inspector to count toilet bowls and doorknobs. Several days later his natural collaborator, the tax collector, presents his accusations. Your bank suddenly is not satisfied with the money in your account, but must know the source thereof. The Commissioner of Police sends an ominous invitation to present yourself before ten o'clock yesterday with all your documents (and you sense, a change of underwear). In the meantime your neighbors, most of them sworn enemies after squabbles over *their* dirty garbage pail or *your* noisy New Year's Eve party, have been quietly interviewed by the Public Security Police on the subject of your "habits," by which they mean your morals. Yes, the pressure is the point. It is applied to force a settlement and these are the preliminaries. The implication is clear: matters can only get worse. How strong are your nerves? How pure your innocence? No one would invite such torture without fair assurance that it would serve some purpose.

Four months have passed since I first presented this defense to Renzo. I was determined in my objections which were exactly those a shrewd Italian lawyer could understand. Reluctantly he admitted the practical wisdom of the argument and has, against his will, been my ally in convincing his mother. With the inversion of opinions which plagues my relationship with Gabriella, she is now as positive that nothing should be published as I am sure it should. In time she will understand and forgive me.

I am guilty of allowing the months to pass while I hoped vaguely that "something" might happen. Nothing has. Finally the tumblers of my mind have clicked back into place. What happened in San Basilio was sudden and violent. The outside world noticed, briefly, then turned to more important events. The Basilisks, absorbed by their own schemes and fears, would accept any compromise to be free to scheme without fear, and I unwittingly have joined their vendetta of silence. I see now that I have been a southerner-by-adoption for so long that I reasoned negatively from their conviction of futility. I believed, as they do, that nothing can change: we drift on calm waters rather than risk inevitable drowning in our own waves. I was right that the police will not move without the proof I cannot supply and that the Basilisks will proclaim their innocence in a barrage of lawsuits against me, but I am avoiding the only *real* point: two people have been forced to give up their freedom, and so their lives, because of what I am certain is a mismating of the pieces of our puzzle.

Many years ago the powerful in Lucania focused their attention on me briefly and decided I was a traitor to "our class." I was impatient with their pretensions and their elaborately uncomfortable imitation of gentility and their inhumanity, more vile than most because it is conscious, convenient and so vociferously Christian. The other ninety percent, those tentative men and bleak stubborn women, accept with bitter dignity that they have been blackballed from the world and that their ration of life, so magnanimously passed down, is just enough that they do not die, never so much that they have energy or time for revolt. They are wary. They trust no one. They neither expect nor believe in compassion. They have kept me an outsider and in so doing have made me one of them. We cannot share isolation. It is by definition a solitary state, but we, the isolated, recognize each other as we plod alone. We nod, smile wanly, and exchange the gritty bits of humor we have panned from the slow stream of our days. When we part, we know we have one illogical thing in common: a belief in some eventual justice.

But the future is always postponed in San Basilio and I am impatient. I am not the only person who suspects what happened there: I simply risk less in asking for justice. I do believe change is possible and whatever means necessary to bring it about are valid. Officially I can do nothing, so I have decided to publish what happened, exactly as I wrote it, or gathered the material I intended to transform later – some unfinished chapters from the novel, random notes, essays, diary entries, letters – all of it!

If I can churn the affair back up to the surface of the Basilisks' lives, they will act in self-defense, and every action is revealing. Sooner or later they will give themselves away. If they are tempted to sue me, they should remember that they cannot embarrass or threaten me into settlement. They will have to prove me wrong and risk public display of all they wish to hide.

I still believe in eventual justice, but why should we wait any longer? Southern Italians have done nothing else for centuries. Beginnings are always feeble. If a few ripples on that gummy, stagnant pond can free two innocent people, then we might try a wave or two.

Rome
February 1971

TWO

I

In San Basilio all of life is centered, as it has been for a thousand years, in the Piazza, in an acre of slick yellow cobblestones enclosed by three massive palaces and a row of squat crumbling arches, the remnants of an ancient aqueduct. Where bishops and dukes once held court and meted out their various judgments on man, there is now a consortium of authority. Of the Duke only his audience throne remains in the deep niche carved from the wall of his palace. Above the stone tuffet a jet black stencil of Mussolini's head with a stewpot helmet and jutting chin is just another symbol of forgotten regimes. To be sure the Bishop still lurks behind the batiste and damask hangings of the palace windows. Apparently they blur his vision, for the modern world, so hazily perceived, is to him the embodiment of Sin. He denounces it with a lulling, tidal regularity, interrupted by periodic squalls of ill humor during which he fulminates, not at the individual sinner, but at a sin encouraged by the quixotic marriage of Italian State and Church, that collective and most pernicious of all sins – Secular Power. Across the way, undisturbed by this ebb and flow of disapproval, judges and tax collectors, mayors, prosecutors and denizens of the school system sit almost buried in the forms, seals and code books of their sovereignty. Below, those being administered lounge in front of political party headquarters or doze in gloomy cafés or gossip with that most particular barber who "integrates his resources," as they say, by renting two rooms above his shop — with or without ladies — to traveling men marooned in San Basilio. Life goes on in slow motion. The Basilisks are spectators who wait patiently for some improbable drama to unfold. So far nothing has titillated them since 1870 when, in a cautious rush of Unification fervor, they voted to change the town's name from San Basilio del Vescovo — St. Basil of the Bishop — back to the earlier, more heroic San Basilio Saraceno. Here change is a slow corrosion like rust in a very dry climate.

Every evening and Sundays at noon the Basilisks collect in the Piazza to watch each other. Only those eccentricities established by years of repetition are accepted without comment. Privacy is unknown; effusion required. There is one exception. Don Ferdinando and Donna Giovanna Sanseverino enjoy royal immunity. They smile or bow or ignore everyone in the municipal cloister as they please. A path opens in front of them. Women murmur "My respects, Don 'Nando. My respects, Donna Giovanna," and the men touch their hats. For forty years their public appearances were limited to Sunday mornings and an occasional evening stroll when — tall, thin and hung rather than dressed in conservative gray clothes — they jerked down the Corso and across the square like fragile mechanical toys in need of rewinding. At their most jovial they did not encourage intimacy. Years ago when I was first introduced to them in mid-Corso, my impression was that they clung together more in defense of their own detachment than in affection. Donna Giovanna turned enormous, affronted brown eyes on me; Don Ferdinando stared straight ahead. Silence. In desperation I mentioned their charming villa beyond the curve.

"Charming, indeed! But simply because it's empty do not imagine that I want to rent it," Don Ferdinando replied to a question I had not asked, minting his words in a high irritable voice. "I'll never rent it. Good evening." He nodded, wheeled his wife around and together they joggled off toward the

Piazza. So began a bowing acquaintance that impressed the Basilisks, but was never more than a ritual courtesy.

On one of the afternoon walks that were my only relief from the social asphyxia of life in town, I had discovered the apricot house. From the town, of course, I had seen it, a speck high on a spur of land whose tip sloped gently downward toward the valley floor in a wide fertile delta of terraced fields, but whose side banks were as neatly perpendicular as the cuts in a tufa quarry. Trees, mere tufts and plumes at that distance, buttressed the house against the sheer drop on either side, but still it looked a cold, bleak aerie, the ideal site for a watchtower or even a fortress. The first time I stopped at the iron gates to peer down the short avenue of cypresses, I saw the overgrown garden, and beyond, San Basilio on its long plateau of land across the valley. With distance came perspective; once more it was an enchanted world. In the glowing chiaroscuro of late afternoon I imagined a cascade of miniature bricks, jumbled beyond ordering, where children had played at building towers and castles and then run off leaving their make-believe behind. Time and the tricks of brutal southern light taught me that more than a telescopic view of the town, the garden offered tranquillity. The spur was wider than it had seemed from a distance. There was room enough and more for a maze of straggling hedges, once perhaps a topiary of meticulous symmetry, and a dilapidated summerhouse, thatched with gray-brown bamboo fronds that clattered in the wind. From an invisible bower came the lazy plop of water falling into a pool and down where it seemed land must end, hidden by trees, was the apricot house with window pediments that curled up over the windows to break, where they might have met, and flow back on themselves. A face with eyes that winked and brows that quirked leered at me from the façade and a gentle, tantalizing smile came and went with the shadows. There is no logical explanation for the formless apprehension such houses rouse in me, but I long to be safely inside looking out.

Whenever I was in San Basilio there were few days that I

did not stop at the iron gates for a brief look at the garden, the apricot house and the shimmering mosaic of the town beyond. I felt no conscious regret; it is simply the only house I have ever wanted to own. One evening early last spring lights from the house spread shutter patterns across the garden and smoke from the chimney crept through the cypresses to wrap me in the tart winter smell of the country. I was curious to know who had softened Don Ferdinando's resolve. The answer amused me: Donna Giovanna's nephew, Marco Santoro, *tanto bello, tanto buono* – so handsome, so (good) kind. Here birth into the gentry endows a man with more than worldly security; he is exempt from human requirements. If, by chance, he is both handsome and kind, he becomes a *stupor mundi*. From the litany of praise Don Marco clearly was such a man; the apricot house had a worthy tenant.

Then one morning last August, as I drank my coffee in a café and watched the men in the Piazza, speculating about how many years they could loiter in the same positions before they petrified, a querulous voice broke into my thoughts.

"I should like a word with you – in private – if such a thing is possible in San Basilio." For a moment I did not recognize Don Ferdinando. He was more than thin; he was skeletal. His skin was ashen and a white hoop of shirt collar stood away from his spindle neck. I asked about his health. "I'm quite well enough for my age, thank you. Now, would tea be all right? Say at six today? My wife will be delighted to receive you. Good day." He disappeared as quietly as he had come, leaving me conscious once more that, for him, words were in short supply and to be hoarded like a small boy's pennies.

Exactly at six I was shown into a vast gloomy drawing room of Palazzo Sanseverino, a room so crowded with lumpy plush furniture, marble busts and tables draped in fringed scarves that, for a moment, I thought I was alone. Don Ferdinando stood up and called me to a corner where he and Donna Giovanna huddled over a brazier of burning coals. She, at least, had not changed. She murmured a welcome and fixed me again with those hurt brown eyes as though waiting to be snubbed in her own house. While he fussed about arranging me in the embrace of a rump-sprung chair, he punctuated his offers of cushions and shawls with short blasts against the atomic bomb, which is credited locally with changing the patterns of the weather, and against the inconvenience of palaces in general and Palazzo Sanseverino in particular: it was the dankest, most inconvenient of a dank and inconvenient genre. When we were drawn up facing each other like monarchs ready to treat, there was a sudden embarrassed silence that sent us headlong into discussion of the cataclysmic manifestations of the weather – without its stunning variations social intercourse in San Basilio would indeed perish. We drank tea, avoided the battered lavender and green cakes, which were more decorative than edible anyway, and finally, when we were again running out of pleasantries, Don Ferdinando announced that this was a business meeting. Donna Giovanna picked up her knitting and withdrew into her own thoughts.

Don Ferdinando had a proposal to make. They were moving to Naples to live with one of their sons – their reasons, he emphasized, did not concern me – therefore they wanted to sell certain odd parcels of property. One was the apricot house: not the broad terraced fields that sloped down to the valley, just the house and the garden. Everyone knew, he told me smiling gently, of my affection for the place, of my walks there and how I stood looking through the gate. I would find it completely in order. Did I know that light and water had been put in last year and the whole house, inside and out, painted for Donna Giovanna's nephew, Marco Santoro? As for payment, they wanted only a token and my promise that, should I ever sell it, the buyer would not be a Basilisk.

"It would give us great pleasure to think of you there," he said almost wistfully and then leaned back and smiled, pleased with himself and the effect of his little surprise. Good sense battled with temptation until my silence piqued him. "Well? Say something!" he barked.

"Won't your nephew want the house?"

The thick stillness that only an insult can produce settled like fog in the room. Donna Giovanna's head jerked up from her knitting; Don Ferdinando's skin turned waxy. "Not unless you believe in ghosts," he snapped. I must have looked startled; I honestly was. He shook his head, as though to clear it. "You must have been away." He stopped, sighed, and then looked at his wife for a moment before going on. "Marco was killed, run over by a truck. Just six weeks ago. Now then . . ."

2

Letter from Gabriella Brancati to A.C.

Gabriella seldom writes to me. When she does, it is always in English and almost always about something that has displeased her. Over the years I have learned that a short note means instant annihilation; in a longer letter her affection helps her argue around the subject until she understands my point of view so completely she forgives me. Whether long or short, her letters are prompted by love. Infuriating as they are at times, her agility with a language that is not hers is impressive, particularly to someone like me whose written Italian occasionally reaches the heights of a not very bright fifth grader's composition.

Santa Caterina in Val Gardena
27 August 1969

Mia cara Anna,

Ever since your *espresso* I have been waiting (ten days now) for further announcements. A "token payment" for a house suggested a marriage agreement to my old-fashioned mind. Now Guido tells me that your *Don* Ferdinando, whom you quite mistakenly assume I know, is an elderly gentleman of means and influence with a wife, children and grandchildren of his own. I need not have played "butcher-baker" after all. You are not to marry this rural unknown and the "arrangement" is respectably unromantic. Instead I have every reason to be offended. *If* you wanted a house in Italy – and it seems high time you admitted you are not leaving *next* month as you have thought for the last sixteen years – as I was saying, *if* you wanted a house in Italy, why did you never mention it to me? Peasants are determined to live in cities now. I own dozens of abandoned stone houses, surrounded by cypresses, overlooking towns, lakes, mountains, factories – even one perilously near an airport should that appeal to you. They are scattered around Tuscany and Umbria, which in time you would find sufficiently bare and unpopulated to appeal to your sense of wilderness. You could have had any one of them to remodel and I daresay in all cases your neighbors would have been more congenial. My last word on the subject: we will make a systematic tour of my houses and see if there is one that strikes your fancy, just for those times of year when even you admit your Lucania is impossible.

If I sound cross, I am, but I do understand your desire to have some place, no matter how small, that is really your own. Judging from the men in my family, it is an exclusively feminine instinct. I hope your "apricot house" will make you happy, and I know quite well you are not going to give it up simply because I would prefer you nearer and more comfortable.

You must find a servant girl who is clean and dependable. Properly trained servants are essential to comfort, so I would *suggest* (Guido says I must learn to suggest rather than command) you bring her to Rome for a few weeks. She must be taught to cook delicately and to serve if you are ever to entertain. Few people, even those who claim they adore jaunts into the country and simple living (I am not one of them) actually enjoy great globs of heavy, baked pasta laced with sour provolone and sausage, and the peasant girl with the rough hands and thundering boots who keeps handing your greasy fork back to you with instructions to keep it for the fruit may be picturesque, but . . . No matter what you say, *our* southerners are known to care little for cleanliness. A question, I am sure, of usage, lack of water, etc. and etc. – we need not argue that point again – but a short time under the gentle tutelage of Miss Emily and I am sure the mysterious benefits of bleach in your sheets, starch in your blouses and muriatic acid for porcelain fixtures will all be revealed to her. Miss Emily will be quite free in the first weeks of November and would enjoy flexing her disciplinary muscles I am sure. She has that wonderful British directness about essentials. She is firm without offending, and no issue is ever personal. I say this only because you have never seen her in her executive capacity. She is so un-Latin and such a delight to have, though at the moment she is driving Cook quite mad about "good English puddings." Who would want such a thing I cannot imagine, even if Cook could calm the retchings of her stomach long enough to produce one!

The weather has been chill and the trippers bolder than ever. The other day a family with three small rather dirty children asked to come inside to wait out a rainstorm! I am not sure there are many more years of pleasure left for me here.

After my reentry (now that is a bad translation from Italian – it sounds very much as though I had spent the summer in orbit around the moon) I will plan our inspection trips, so that we will both be comfortable enough to argue constantly.

I do send my very dear love and for all my grumbling understand about the apricot house. Come home soon. We all miss you.

Gabriella

3

Two weeks after my tea at the Sanseverinos' I moved into the house with a bed, a desk, several chairs and some kitchen equipment. In time the rest would arrive from the various storerooms of my life, but I was too impatient to wait. I wanted to enjoy the gilded September days and then flee, like a tourist, at the first howl of autumn winds.

A young peasant girl named Teresa Ferri came every morning to clean. My days began with the piercing nasal chant of her singing in the kitchen. Anyone else might have thought it a mournful awakening, but I knew she was happy: at last she had the only job she was fit to do. She worked hard and was very quiet, except when she forgot and consoled herself with the Miserere common to all lonely women.

When I first remember her seven years ago, she was a wistful, thin little girl, all eyes and bones, who peeked at the world from the safety of dark doorways. The other children would not play with her; they only taunted her about her twisted foot, calling *"'a zoppa," "'a zoppa"*— the lame one — and then skittered off, knowing she could not chase them. She would walk away from them with her odd, but not ungraceful, slide-and-glide gait as though she had important matters to settle elsewhere. On one of these retreats she was crying and walked right into me. I put my arm around her shoulder and asked what was the matter.

"Nothing," she mumbled.

"Were they teasing you?"

She nodded.

"Don't let them worry you, *piccinin*. You'll see. In a few years it won't make any difference."

She shook her head. "Papa says I'm no good for anything. I can't work. He . . ."

Through the neighborhood the bellow of a deep, rough voice echoed. "Teresa! Teerray! I'll smack you hard. Teerray!"

She flinched, pulled away from me and stumbled, running and hopping toward a building across the way. There, on a balcony, a brawny man in an undershirt and trousers stood, scowling down into the dusty courtyard. This first glimpse of Bruno Ferri reminded me of an old photograph: Mussolini, the harvest hand, addresses the peasants during an impromptu (but well-recorded) visit to the wheat fields.

After that Teresa often waited for me by my car. Once, I remember, I said how pretty her hair looked. Her eyes shone. "Did your mamma wash it for you?"

"Haven't got a mamma," she whispered.

And so bit by bit the story came out. The same midwife who crippled Teresa had been unable to save her mother. She lived with her father, stepmother and five half brothers in a rundown apartment, one of the first of its kind built just before the war as "peasant housing." When she finished the fifth grade, she was to take care of her brothers, do the chores, cook, launder and all the rest. "Papa says that's all I'm good for, and still he gets mad at me."

Over the years she has grown long and lean, more a gypsy than a Lucanian, with high cheekbones, burnished, golden skin and large sparkling eyes that flash defiance rather than beg for gentleness. Now those children who teased her are disconcerted by her composure and call her *"presuntuosa,"* though she is proud of nothing except possibly her shiny red-brown hair which a tortoise clip holds neatly in place at the back of her neck. Hers has been a lonely life. Girls her age are getting married: she is her father's housekeeper and has been beaten too many times to object to his arrangement of her life. Now behind her gentle dignity there are the first signs of bitterness: the acid answers, the silences, the dreams — *If I could be like others.* But she knows she is not like others. She resents her two shapeless dresses and the pointed run-over shoes that Bruno Ferri, insisting they are "good enough" for her, has resoled with strips of old rubber tire. She resents her stepmother, her brothers, her father's laws, her own twisted foot — everything that makes up her life. Soon she would be crippled in mind as well as body. When I offered her work, I counted on her father's greed. He released her to earn money and for once she was happy.

Teresa took over the ordering of the house. It is not large: a sitting room, a dining room with a simple kitchen behind it on the ground floor; two bedrooms and a bath between on the floor above. She waxed the red tile floors, washed windows and scoured the kitchen, but she was not satisfied with the bathroom. In the remodeling Don Ferdinando not only added pipes and taps, he replaced an array of waterless marble fixtures set in counters — a basin, a tub and a cabinet-throne — with porcelain duplicates. Teresa said it looked like a sausage factory, and unknown to me she attacked a hide of whitewash that covered the counters, scraping and chipping until she uncovered small white tiles with intricate Byzantine patterns in deep blue. It is never on view, but is quite the most attractive room in the house.

Together we cleaned out the fireplaces, one of the unexpected delights of each room, and scrubbed the mantels with pumice to remove the sticky brown patina that years of woodsmoke had left on the white marble. We must have worked a week in the sitting room, putting rods up, then curtains, cleaning and relining bookcases and the triangular cupboards set in the corners between the chimney and the wall, unpacking books — the seemingly endless tasks that are, of necessity, taken care of before a woman, if not a man, can feel settled in a house.

Slowly the sitting room changed, softened. There was light,

but not glare. Sounds did not boom from wall to wall to floor and back. Someday, I decided, it would be a very comfortable room. Then I realized that Teresa stood in awe of what I thought was comfort; she wanted to treat the room as a museum. I suppose it was the first rug she had ever seen. She would not walk on it with her shoes. She either kicked them off to cross it barefooted or skirted it, tangling with electrical wires and tripping over tables. No one was to sit on the upholstered chairs; rush-bottoms were good enough for my visitors. But best of all she loved a walnut desk with a thread of fruitwood inlay around the drawers and fruitwood shields set in at the keyholes. I put it near a window so that I can watch the town and almost every morning I found her crooning over it. She was convinced that a daily coat of wax would eventually make its dull, ink-stained top shine.

"How much would a desk like this cost?" was a regular question.

My answer had to be vague; I would lose face if I told her the truth, that it is 1890 government issue bought for three dollars from the San Basilio post office when the ministry supplied the modern ash and green Formica horrors so generally admired. Instead I talked to her about the things still to come: chairs, a refectory table, a sofa perhaps. No, she liked the room as it was, that is, she liked the furniture, not the pictures. She saw no value in old prints of San Basilio, and an abstract oil of the "Sassi"* done with a palette knife was so incomprehensible that, after she dusted it, she hung it upside down or sideways as often as right side up. Each morning before I was up she cleaned the sitting room. Her technique was a general disinfestation, as though I had entertained a band of lepers in her absence. When she finished, she closed the shutters and windows, sprayed DDT liberally over *everything* and then shut the door with such finality that even I felt an intruder.

* The Sassi of Matera are the cave-dwellings where, until recently, some fifteen thousand people lived.

I had expected to work in the garden myself, maybe an hour a day. I was in no hurry about it. The idea of a permanent excuse to be outside appealed to me, but there must be something about me that attracts tyranny. One morning just after I moved in, a ragged little man appeared in the garden. There was nothing furtive about him. He ambled around, stroked the bushes and mumbled to them. He was waiting, rather the way a stray Italian cat waits in front of a strange door until someone's legs come in sight and he can rub against them. He, of course, ends up in the most comfortable chair, yowling for a saucer of milk, which was not at all what this little old man had in mind. Please, he would like to potter in my garden. He was a very good gardener, very quiet, very dependable. Anybody would tell me. His name was Sabato – Saturday – and I have since found out he is truly Saturday's child. During the war he and his wife were "refugeed" from the Abruzzo and plodded south, carrying their possessions in burlap sacks on their shoulders, heading for an unknown cousin in San Basilio. Their arrival and the tales Sabato told with gleeful embellishments stimulated the Basilisks' imagination and with it their hospitality. Sabato and Maria became *"I Nostri Profughi,"* our refugees, the only ones and so petted that they never returned to the Abruzzo. Sabato, "In Recognition" though of what no one has ever been able to tell me, was appointed assistant cemetery keeper, a job which he enjoyed until a year ago when an overzealous government clerk turned up the fact that he was seventy-four years old and due for a pension. Except for that bit of bad luck, no one would ever have known, for they tell me he looks exactly as he did twenty-five years ago. His face is creased and eroded, like the cutbanks he has spent his life hoeing, and almost the same color, an orange-gray, relieved by a square moustache that straggles down over his upper lip and muffles his comments. It is an elastic face. He arranges his expressions to fit the occasion. He can be the archtype doltish peasant, a modern Piers Plowman, limp and subservient, ready to pull at his grizzled forelock and murmur *"Sissignore,"* or – and I believe it to be his true personality –

he can be exuberantly gay or sad, or even exuberantly neutral. In any humor he is stubborn.

When I realized that he was spending all the daylight hours in my garden, I insisted he name a salary. He refused. Each figure I proposed, he rejected as more than he was worth. We have now agreed on a symbolic ten thousand lire* a month which he considers a sop to my conscience and not so high that he has to accept my suggestions. We do not, it turns out, agree on gardens. To Sabato shade is the thief of untold square inches of soil that might be used for *real* crops, like cabbage, cauliflower or artichokes. He would cut all the trees, but is too shrewd. Instead he is slowly pruning them to the life-death limit. By next spring stunted branches will claw the sky and if he has gauged his torture accurately, will produce only a fuzz of yellow-green leaves. He admires bushy ferns trimmed into make-believe armchairs and divans – a complete garden salon. He will not agree to the removal of a row of canna. They add dignity. Aren't they planted outside all police stations? We have reached a compromise. He is very patient with me. When I leave, he will do as he pleases. Until then he spends his days hoeing. I hear the rhythmic twack-twack of his *zappa,* but only recently have I understood his system: he hoes and rehoes everything that can be seen from the road; the rest is unimportant. A jungle of nettles and acanthus, or rambler roses that grow in great tangled mats can be ignored, if they are out of sight. Each morning at dawn I hear hoses being dragged around and as soon as water has gurgled into the storage tanks above my head, there is the soft hiss of spraying from the garden below. Precious, precious water! I face another bathless day, which means nothing to Sabato who has not indulged in such perilous ablutions since 1938 when friends threw him in the sea as a joke. He assures me baths are weakening, though his concern is probably more for the viscosity, and therefore the sale value, of the contents of my cesspool than for my health. No matter. This aged pixie has taken charge of me and

* Approximately sixteen dollars.

my garden and is determined he will do his best to cultivate us both.

He has his own old-fashioned notions of the world's order. As he says, he was born before the days of luxury, that is before universal schooling. He can neither read nor write and Italian will forever be the argot of the rich. He speaks a private dialect, a lilting amalgam of Abruzzese and Basilisk. Sunday is a day of rest. He has his weekly shave and, dressed in the black suit and uncreased fedora which will do Sunday duty until they accompany him to his grave, he goes to the Piazza and waits with the men of the town for the day to pass. The other six days he works. One of his chores is to champion his *padrone*. He hoes for him, prunes for him. He protects him, flatters him, even circumvents him when necessary. I, as the *padrona* of the moment, am made to feel a duchess. Every morning and every evening Sabato sweeps off his battered work hat and bows to me. He cleans the gutters and rakes the paths. He prunes, plants and guards the gate. He even hauls the ashes from the fireplace and lays new fires with wood he procures from mysterious "abandoned" woodpiles. In these few short weeks Teresa and Sabato have organized me so well that I feel obliged to explain and apologize for any deviation I may make in their plans for me.

Suddenly one afternoon the preliminaries were over. The house itself was in order; Sabato reigned in the garden. Only a minute storeroom jammed full of old newspapers, kindling wood, a chipped basin and ewer, odd chair legs and we knew not what remained to be sorted, but Teresa considered that her province. She would clear it out with Sabato's help. I should retire to the garden and contemplate my chores for the next morning. It was to be my first day at work.

From my bench I watched the plum dusk creep over San Basilio. The end of a limpid day. The town had glittered in three such sharp dimensions that I imagined a radiant fourth shimmering in the blue of the valley beyond. No. Time cannot shimmer, only light. Is it, perhaps, the fourth dimension of Lucania where time has no meaning? Can people be phototropic? They seemed to be, those Basilisks who scurried about, collecting their children and livestock, and then slammed doors shut on the world darkening around them. From below the horizon the last glow of the setting sun, diffused through the clouds, melted into the smoke from a thousand chimneys to wrap the town in lavender mist.

I heard the latch close behind me and then Teresa's crunch and drag along the gravel path. She stopped, trying to decide, I think, whether I was asleep there on my bench. I turned and asked if there were anything wrong.

"No. I just wanted to say we finished the storeroom. Now Sabato has plenty of space for his wood. I put some papers on your desk. They might be important. I don't know, but I thought you ought to see them before they were thrown out."

"Newspapers?"

"No. Handwritten," she hesitated. "Some have figures. Some are notebooks. I thought you'd better see them first. Good night."

"Good night, Teresa," and as I listened to her slow, almost reluctant step along the drive, I pondered the mystic attraction any handwritten paper has for the uneducated. They cannot be selective. These were probably old shopping lists or the first drafts of a grandchild's schoolwork, but the squiggles of a human hand must not be disposed of without proper consideration. Teresa would never treat such worthy documents lightly. The gate rasped home and almost in answer the church bells tinkled and clanked irritably, as only southern bells do, in the twilight call to Angelus. I too went inside and slammed my door against the night.

My desk, which had been unnaturally hotel-room bare, was now a discouraging sight. Teresa's pile of marbled ledgers and loose papers had slithered sideways and collapsed into a disorderly fan. An invisible magician seemed to be offering a card, any card. My first was a plumber's estimate. The second, printed on spongy paper that had turned a deep tan, was dated September 1937 and was a notice about arrears in the payment of the goat tax. The third, a letter in spidery script, started *"Pace e Bene"* and went on to extol the charitable works of an order of nuns: on the back of one page was a shopping list. After all, Donna Giovanna had asked me to burn everything in the storeroom. I flipped up the cover of one ledger by a corner so worn that the layers of cardboard had separated into a cottony *mille feuille.* The acrid odor of mildew rose from the pages: "These being the accounts of the following farms in the Pizzuto Valley" and a list of some ten separate holdings. Inside faded brown ink marched along watery green lines. At the end of each was a neat figure. One day's salary seemed to be 2.5 lire, hardly a modern rate. Altogether there were eight ledgers, four pairs, for even Don Ferdinando adopted the traditional defense of two sets of books: one told him the truth and one told the Finance Inspectors what he would have them believe. Italian taxation is a game of fiscal chess. Don Ferdinando would be a methodical player, maybe even a cunning one, but he did not need these ledgers. I piled them in the kitchen by the sink and found a bag to hold most of the papers, which I did not bother to read.

When it was almost full and only a few receipted bills were left on my desk, I uncovered two notebooks, school composition books with thin covers of black waffled paper that had been "plasticized" to make them child-resistant. I think I opened the first one because it was so obviously modern and might be something of mine that had been caught up in the jumble. That sounds like an excuse and it may be. Under "Subject" in a small, precise, almost cramped hand was written "Marco Santoro #1." Nothing else. Not too surprisingly the second was labeled in the same hand "Marco Santoro #2." I wish now that I could claim a deep moral struggle, even one I lost, between the Right to Privacy and the Communality of Trash, but it would not be true. I was curious about Marco Santoro, this nephew of the Sanseverinos, who had been my predecessor in the apricot house. Without a second thought I turned the page of the first notebook and began to read. I read idly at first and then slowly, very carefully, stopping occasionally to wander back into my memory for some half-forgotten, half-misunderstood incidents that linked up with what he had written. Now I cringe at the thought of my intrusion into another's life. Guilt has set in — finally — and I do not know what to do with Marco's notebooks, his diaries, for that is what they are. They seem important to me and I am not quite sure why — yet.

THREE

I

Marco Santoro Notebook #1

September 1968

Forty-eight hours of San Basilio have proved something I would never have believed possible: I can hate a place on sight. Vague as my expectations were, they have all been disappointed. The land is barren – flaxen stubble in rolling mounds of gray clay, rocky crags, naked and sinister in the distance. In the spring, they say, it is a paradise of silky green wheat shoots. Of course one must live through the winter to see it. In contrast to the vastness of the country, the town is an anthill swarming with people who scurry back and forth on useless errands. They are never too busy to do a favor; in fact they pester you to invent chores. They have been taught this is ingratiating. The children are wizened, their faces old and knowing. The elderly are only more corrugated by the sun and maybe more desperate because they can think of nothing within their powers to do but complain. And the Piazza? The marrow of town life? With its air of stolid fusty propriety it reminds me of a wayside station waiting room: first class to the right, second to the left. An aura of stopped drains and tinkling bells. Here a pack of gaunt, droop-lidded dogs and the men who own decent clothes gather at dusk to await the coming of night. While the hounds slouch around tracking improbable, zigzag scents, the men whisper slyly behind their hands as though some clerical Banquo were lurking in the gloom, invisible but ready to eavesdrop on their weather forecasts and sexual speculations. They stop to gawk at any outsider. Last night they gawked at me and at the Regional Director of Schools who marched across the Piazza followed by a posse of clerks carrying his briefcase, overcoat, umbrella, three strings of figs and a live hen held upside down by a cord looped around her legs. The driver of the state car parked outside the arches rushed into the Piazza and danced about offering help. As the car pulled away, the men huddled closer and hissed their comments like geese.

No, the vitality is all below the Piazza, trapped in the maze of stairstep alleys that twist through the Serraglio and the Cavea, as the main quarters are called. Names like Crusader's Gate and King Frederick's Way alternate with Wash-House Street and Street of the Latrines, which does lead outside the Turk's Gate to a windy stone pile that served (or is it, serves?) as a neighborhood accommodation. Down below there is too much life, too little room. That is the way of the South. I wandered back and forth, lost most of the time, looking in doorways, marveling at how six, eight, even nine people and a mule can live in one room. The stench, the noise of those streets and the men who cower in the shadows – while their pompous lords strut in the Piazza, talking about the deceits of the *"popolino."* In this year of Our Lord 1968 man can be proud of such places as this.

At the Naples station the other day I saw boxes of peanuts labeled "packed in a vacuum"– that is life in San Basilio. Fortunately people have never been my solace. Once school begins and the boarders come, there will be plenty to do. Uncle has arranged for my afternoons to be free. He plans to tutor me in the duties his sons have escaped. I must take over, and furthermore enjoy, the management of my own property. He thinks that I am finally the member of the family who can share his code. I cannot, but if it is companionship he wants, I will go through the motions of learning to spy on the overseer, even, I suppose, to collect rents from peasants whose crops have failed. I cannot watch the dissolution of an old man's world without offering some comfort though my conscience . . .

They have given me a house well outside town called the Villa del Re Sergianni after some real or imagined visit Queen Giovanna's lover made to San Basilio. Five hundred years are only yesterday here. Uncle apologized about the distance, not knowing me well enough to understand how I value the peace of isolation. After the fall rains begin, no one will bother me here.

The night I arrived Aunt Giovanna gave a reception. The men's suits smelled of naphthalene; the women were so lacquer-smooth, so creaseless that they must have spent the day dressing. Laura, the blond Albanese in tight blue taffeta and opalescent nail polish, batted her eyes and sighed out questions. "How can you stand it so far from town?" "Not even a scooter?" "Wouldn't your uncle . . .?" "Don't you feel buried here after . . . ?" "Strange, isn't it, with your family, your *presenza* [a coy way of saying she thinks me handsome. Brazen little thing! Apparently she considers no man ineligible] strange you are teaching at such a minor boarding school, isn't it?" My spine tingled: she was sketching the blueprint of a scandal in my past. I was so solemn, so pedantic about the scholar's passion and the sociological aspects of southern history, I was so unaware of her invitation to criticize San Basilio, that she gave me up for a dullard and released me to join the men. They urged another glass of syrupy "bitter" (bilious stuff!) on me and then went back to their affectionate recollections of my parents whom they remember no better than I. "Ah, yes. He was a great man — so wise," they intoned and turned their heads. Then in unison, "She was so beautiful — so kind." All heads swiveled again: a sad mock Grecian chorus. Uncle called me to the door and introduced a pudgy young man with headlight glasses and a pursed mouth. Avvocato Evangelista had brought a message from the Bishop, something about the rent on the Christian Democratic party headquarters in the Piazza. Uncle had to remind me that we own it and asked that I discuss the matter with this young lawyer the next morning. The first, but surely not the last, of Uncle's evasions. Evangelista agreed, but made no move to go. Instead he looked over Uncle's shoulder at the roomful of people and commented, as he straightened his tie, that we were having "quite a party." Clearly he meant to stand firm until invited in and eventually he was, but I missed the face-down. Aunt Giovanna had called me over to whisper in my ear. Would I take her two steps in the *passeggiata?* Uncle does hate it so. I have offered to be her cavalier every evening, if she finds the promenade amusing. She was so grateful I thought she was making fun of me. Then I understood: she is lonely – so am I.

Finally all the people drifted away to the Corso where they bowed to Aunt Giovanna and me with such deference, when we appeared, that no one would have thought that only minutes before we had been munching biscuits and banalities together. These evenings will be public performances, not exercise and fresh air. As we paced up and down Aunt Giovanna murmured a nonstop commentary on the lives of everyone we passed. I must have mismatched the lot because, in my mind, the most innocent faces are connected to the most appalling behavior. Or is that a truism? Aunt Giovanna's knowledge is encyclopedic and her judgment astute. Closed in, as she is, with Uncle and the servants, I wonder she collects so much information. Lawyer Evangelista, *Don* Pancrazio as he wants to be called, she dismisses as an *arrivista.* His father, a shoemaker with a bit of land, could not afford university fees, so Pancrazio set about raising the money himself – and did, by dressing as a monk and begging in the streets of Naples. Law and politics have a natural affinity and our young man started early. To date he has been a Communist (what had looked advantageous, he now scorns as "the Party of the *Cafoni*"*), a Socialist, but only briefly (they did not see fit to

* There is no exact English equivalent for *cafone* (pl. *cafoni*). A clod, a clot, a lout, a hick: they all have something of the meaning. It is a curious word with a split personality. When used by peasants in reference

include him in their list of candidates), and now for two years a Christian Democrat. Aunt finds it interesting that his brother, a missionary priest somewhere in the far reaches of India, has flown home for these political changes of heart. In each case rumors of discrepancies in party accounts have remained rumors. No official comment has ever been made, though everyone praises the missionary brother as a man of true Christian spirit and open pocketbook. Evangelista's political career, like his legal practice, has prospered under the new Bishop. And that brought us around to the Bishop. Why should he soil himself with such company? When condescension and the weather both travel from north to south, there is only one answer: he is Sicilian, ergo a member of a particular Italian subspecies corrupted by Arab blood and nurtured on the sweetmeats of power. Not to be outdone, apparently, he calls the Lucanians troglodytes; his mission is to civilize them. Today a holy war is an exhilarating spectator sport.

This morning the Bishop received me. He is very Sicilian – Sicilian as we expect them to be – physically small and swarthy with languid camel-eyes; verbally platitudinous; and mentally shrewd. He will not tolerate discussion, and questions stiffen his manner of deliberate compassion. Clearly to insist is to flirt with heresy, for the eyes narrow and just as he turns away to stare at the crucifix on the corner of his desk, his listening attitude, you see the dull gleam of speculation. A very stubborn and sometimes arrogant man, our Bishop. One who will be obeyed. The Ecumenical Council has not disturbed him, at least externally. Watered silk and jeweled cross held their own with the gilt of the furniture. In another diocese his desk chair might have been the episcopal throne, and behind it, unctuous and inclined to perspire, stood Pancrazio Evangelista.

---

to themselves, it has an affectionate, slightly ironic sense. They can say – *Chi nasce cafone, muore cafone* – He who is born a lout, dies a lout. Anyone other than a peasant who speaks of a *cafone* is using it perjoratively. The sneer is obvious. [A.C.]

Automatically I dropped down on one knee to kiss the Ring and was left there with nothing better to look at than the Bishop's puffy white hands laced across his scarlet sash. His inspection of me was supercilious: I did not please. Finally he twitched a finger, which I took to mean my release. Evangelista and I acknowledged each other without enthusiasm, and the Bishop began what turned out to be a monologue. He reviewed the disorder of the diocesan organizations. Pagan chaos, he called it, in an "underdeveloped area." And the people! They are like wild animals who would jump from the jungle into the modern world with all its sins and temptations. His task was as humble as that of any missionary in Africa. All the more difficult because nothing in his experience had prepared him for such a crusade. Sicily, naturally, has a different culture, older, more subtle. Tradition and some innate sensitivity of the people make the governing of a diocese there simpler and of course more of a comfort to a bishop, but with God's help and the true missionary spirit, even Lucania can join the civilized Christian world. This was all leading to something, but what exactly I did not grasp. Eventually he came to the point. Uncle had requested I be free in the afternoons. Much as it distressed His Excellency to inconvenience Uncle, he must insist that I, like every other teacher at the Convitto, give a certain number (no more definitely stated) of afternoons to the diocese. Since I am young and well connected locally, he has decided that I could be of great assistance to Evangelista, who is the new president of the Men's Catholic Action Committee. Evangelista smirked piously, then bowed. I too must be a knight in the Crusade.

He murmured on and on, his words an opiate to his own thoughts as well as ours. I could not object, but I did ask what activities they were organizing. He is the Bishop of the four "C's": Confession, Chastity, Communion and Concerts. I must discover what a "Christian Crusade" has to do with his refusal to allow a band to play popular music in the Piazza for the Festa. *That* is one of the main projects at the moment. The Bishop has decreed that no township in his diocese need expect his support or approval (read contribution) if popular music becomes part of the local celebration. For a hundred years "concert bands" have been oomph-pa-pa-ing from lacy gazebos studded with lights, and they must continue to do so even if people will not come out to listen. This is a civilizing step. Backward? We must ward off decadence, lead people in the paths of righteousness, save them from their base appetites – by prohibiting "rock" music. There is a touch of the Inquisition about him. "The Church is not a refuge for aged females! The men are to come to confession and then take Communion. I want them there, even if they have to be forced . . ." By the end of the interview he was quite irrational. As we left, Evangelista commented in a low, holy-places voice that the Bishop is a great man, a very great man. We must rouse the men of the diocese to his support. That much is clear.

Today was my thirtieth birthday, but there was no one here to care or remember. This is a cruel place and lonely, where talk of Christianity, old or new, is futile. Here no man cares for his neighbor. Care is to be used on one's self; that is the immorality of San Basilio, the vacuum that holds us like peanuts. As the new peanut I have been given a nickname – the Obelisk – which, I suppose, refers to my height.

The boys have come – bony, dull-eyed, full of resentment. We are taking each other's measure. They thought it odd that their history teacher assigned a composition. I want to know about their backgrounds. Each was to write the history of his town and then describe what he liked most about his summer vacation and what he missed about home now that he is back at school. I was asking prickly pears to sprout olives; they rewarded me with prickly pears.

"My town has not had any history since Garibaldi, or any water either," wrote one. Pessimism may have seemed the quickest way out. "Not that I like school," he continued, "but I do not like vacations either. Home means work." There is one dreamer in the class. He must be the only one who is not secretly planning to be a football player or a cyclist. His town has been invaded by every romantic figure in history: Richard the Lion-Hearted, Columbus, King Arthur, Charlemagne and in about that order. Most were bored and matter-of-fact. "I guess my town never had any history the Duke of Salandra did not want it to have, but I am not sure because nobody talks about it." He, like many others, was unable to answer directly what he missed about home. "It is not that I miss anything, but I never felt alone there. Here I feel alone all the time." And they look alone and frightened, half crouched to defend themselves, or are they ready to attack the first who falls? Their grammar is execrable. Some slip away into dialect almost immediately. The best have memorized "proper style" from their elementary teachers and will for the rest of their lives start every letter, love letter or job application *Venco a scriverti guesti poghi ricchi per farti sapere . . .* (I come to write you these few lines to let you know . . .) . The misspellings are as sacrosanct as the adenoidal phonetics which produce them.

My colleagues at the Convitto are a clannish, suspicious lot. Most are local and, though they snipe at each other irritably, like members of a scholastic Mafia, they present a united front against "outside" interference. The priest-professors are sullen with me, omnipotent with the boys. They teach with the dogmatic arrogance of the half-educated and the rest of the time are uncertain whether to be jealous or wary of the lay professors, who are too lazy to care anyway. Only one, Nicola Benevento, does not treat class hours as daily penance. He is a lugubrious young man, a Basilisk with a long thin face and a sardonic smile that suggests he takes nothing seriously. He is a male Cassandra, or so he would have you believe, prophesying disastrous school-program reforms the Director will introduce as "didactic innovations in the academic process." Each is more ridiculous than the last, and they all turn out to be 1860 methods decked out in 1960 jargon. Nicola calls him King

Bomb* and predicts his next bomb will be an articulated rationale of whipping, its proper use, its advantages as a teaching aid, its salutory effect on the adolescent male psyche. He exaggerates, but not much. We meet for coffee in the morning before classes. Then he gives himself away. He talks of nothing but the boys: what he would like to be able to teach them and how; the equipment we need and cannot have; the ways of getting through to them. Teaching fascinates and frustrates him. He is discouraged, but not too discouraged to appear brushed and shaved in a clean shirt and a neat, if worn suit. A contrast to the others who look as though they had come straight from an all-night debauch in a wine shop.

This morning it was cold and foggy. When I arrived in my room the janitor had lighted the stove and smoke was puffing out from every joint in the rusty, serpentine tube that exits through a broken windowpane. I tried to shove one elbow joint with its accordion sleeve more firmly into the pipe and the whole structure shuddered, wavered a moment and then clattered to the floor. The boys loved it. We laughed until the smoke made us weep. While the pipe was being remounted, I took them out into the street and kept them warm practicing footwork and dodging techniques. My history of the Papal States is more interesting to them now that I know a bit about soccer.† I have tried unsuccessfully, to imagine which of them will decide to enter the priesthood, as, after all, they pledged to do when they came to the Convitto. They seem unlikely mediaries between God and His people, but only God can decide. God and the Family Finances.

Just now I went for a walk in the garden. It is cold and still except for the trees that crackle. San Basilio was a brooding shadow against the not quite black sky. I had been standing, listening to the silence frost has forced on all those people

* *Re Bomba,* King Bomb, was the nickname given Ferdinand II of Naples, the most overanxious of the despotic Bourbons of Naples, when he bombed his own people. [A.C.]

† In Italy soccer is followed as avidly as football in the United States. [A.C.]

across the way, when something made me turn toward the gate. I sensed, rather than saw, someone there and called out to ask if anything was wrong. Before I could reach the gate, a voice, a low voice but definitely a woman's with an intimate quality that sounded off-key in the black cold of the garden, had assured me she did not need help. It was disconcerting. She called me by name and was amused at my surprise. Her face was only a shadow. I think she wore a light scarf around her head, but I am not even sure of that. She apologized for her intrusion. She walks every evening and particularly likes the San Basilio she sees from my gate. She said something I have thought, but never put into words: The town is beautiful from here, so beautiful one falls into a dream of what it might be – and is not. The idea that anyone would harm her on the road amused her. Her laugh was a gentle, mocking chortle, as though she were enjoying a secret joke. Then she was gone. I never saw her face, but the voice goes on singing through my mind: a cello, sad but gay – a joke – a phantasm. I hardly know.

Uncle's private orientation course is to send me on a survey of the houses he owns in town. Thank God I own land! I am to report on conditions, but it is only an exercise. He sees no need to improve them. When I say the houses are dangerous, he waves me aside. *They* would reduce a new house to worse in a month. That is just the way they live. One- and two-room stalls without water, forty-eight thousand lire per annum.* Seepage from the alley above gums the walls, the floors wobble, the roofs show daylight. I will *not* get used to it. The men rage bitterly against the government, the Church, Minister Colombo and the Bishop for not providing new houses, but about Uncle they are as patiently resigned as he is about them. If I mention Communion or the mass they shrug. Religion does not interest them. "Let the women go," they answer. "We're damned if we don't go. If we do, we're sinners and damned just the same. What's the use?" The deadly simplicity

* Approximately eighty dollars. [A.C.]

of peasant reasoning! One asked me if God could "twist wheat out of stones." When I shook my head, he was triumphant. "You see! He's no better than me."

The Bishop sent for me this morning. Subject: Uncle's determination to collect the rent for Christian Democratic headquarters in the Piazza. Uncle says they pay or leave. The Bishop would make it a matter of Christian Charity, Uncle's contribution to church activities. They maneuver to keep me in the middle; I referred them to each other with the excuse that I am not a competent mediator.

The Bishop hinted that Lawyer Evangelista has found me less than enthusiastic in the "Crusade" (as far as I know activities are still limited to the collection of dues, though there is a rumor we are to raise money for a monument to the dead. This presumably in answer to a recent newspaper report that "in all the provinces only San Basilio has not seen fit to honor its dead . . .") I had a sufficiently Sicilian answer: Caution. Ill-considered action could embarrass the Bishop. All aspects (of what? The Situation, naturally) must be examined to avoid this very possible inconvenience. He agreed vehemently; Evangelista will hardly thank me.

Boredom, not hot blood, makes some men desperate, drives them to pointless violence. Latin crimes of passion — those shootings and stabbings for which we are famous — are nothing more than Sunday amusements. Here, fortunately, energy is at a premium, so the Basilisks are content to stroll along the road for hours. After weeks of Sunday interruptions I have learned to close my gate. I do it against myself; I want friendship. They come, instead, to satisfy their curiosity. I can hear them. "Donna Giovanna has done well by the nephew. Wonder what he does up there all by himself." I read, I study, I write a bit and sometimes I just sit looking at the town — all heinous activities, I am sure. At first, when the men came, some with their wives, and stretched and yawned their way around the garden, interrupting me from time to time to ask very personal questions, I thought this must be the accepted

Basilisk preamble to acquaintance. Now I know I am nothing more than a "service area" which might offer amusement on the Sunday highway of their desperation. The medical officer and his arch young wife spent two hours one afternoon quizzing me about my "brother." They refused to believe I have no brother. Next morning Uncle advised me to be careful not to give the impression of "bad blood" among the members of the family. By now I should have acknowledged incredible wealth, a horde of nieces and nephews, and of course, even more important, connections in high places. Only about the last would they have allowed me to be less than explicit. So the gate is closed: Don Marco must be away. Instead he sits inside with all but the shutters on the town side closed – in peace.

St. Francis of Assisi
Patron Saint of Italy

The Bishop has decided to rule by bulletin-board edict. Several weeks ago he had a notice put up which, in this day of shorter skirts, has puzzled everyone.

DECORUM IN CHURCH

No woman may approach the confessional wearing a garment which hangs less than 15 cm. below her knees.

And now today, two more. One, headed "Films ABSOLUTELY forbidden to ALL CHRISTIANS of this Diocese," gave a list of the latest avant-garde efforts that no sensible distributor would waste on San Basilio. The other:

DECORUM IN CHURCH

The rental of garments or coveralls is strictly forbidden within the confines of the church proper.

Aunt tells me the last is to halt a burgeoning trade in smock rentals developed with unsuspected commercial acumen by the crone who lurks near the cathedral poor box with an armful of church magazines for sale.

She also scolded me for not paying attention at mass. I am never sure whether such remarks are the benign results of perception or trial balloons, but on principle I do not answer them directly. I said something about the Bishop looking unwell. Her answer was pure Aunt Giovanna: "No more liverish than usual. He *will* count the house and that makes him scowl." Her face had that bland, slightly addled expression that is her public mask. The truth of the matter is that I thought I heard my *fantasma*'s voice in one of the responses. It was very clear, not louder than the others, simply clearer because its range is well below the babble. I think I am haunted. I turned and craned my neck – rows of wooden puppet faces, not one of which could belong to my voice. I turned back and found the Bishop glaring at me. He held me skewered in place. He singed me with almighty wrath and quite rightly. I should not be so easily distracted. Later, however, he bored into the nape of Don Anselmo's neck with the same disgust and I was comforted.

Don Anselmo joined us for lunch. He is a deceptive man, which may just be a prerequisite for the archpriest of any diocese. When I am with him, I am completely under his sway. He is practical, an amusing storyteller, a flattering listener, devout without a trace of pomposity and always aware of the invisible web of events that makes life here so complex. But – when I see him in the street or across a room talking to someone else – it is as though my eyes were seeing two distinct images which they cannot pull together. One is Don Anselmo Lanfranchi, the fastidious dandy, whose expertly made cassock, always of the silkiest cloth, is a garment of studied secular grace and whose distant, almost supercilious manner suggests that only rigid self-control and a sense of the limits of courtesy keep him from raising an eyebrow and strolling off. He gossips. He is quietly sarcastic, always very busy.

He seldom smiles and then only with his lips. The gaze of those iridescent blue eyes chills. The other is the Don Anselmo the peasants know, whom they describe as they described Pope John – he is one of us. They know he is on their side. His long lean body bends toward them; the touch of his hand on a shoulder or an arm reassures. His young-old face with its high gaunt cheekbones and arched patrician nose softens into a smile and even the most harassed smile back. I am never sure which is the true image.

Today, of course, he was *in famiglia.* He lured Aunt Giovanna, whom he calls Zi' Gian, though no one else would dare, into talking about the first summer he spent in San Basilio; about his tutor, who thought Lucania would be a catastrophic experience for his liver and stipulated that the usual olive oil must be sent from the Lanfranchi estates, never guessing that the oil he had prized in the Roman household came from San Basilio; about the nursemaid who fell in love with one of Uncle's factors; and more seriously about Anselmo's long bout with typhoid, which in the end kept him here through the winter. Aunt was a bride then, a friend of Anselmo's much older sister. She had no children of her own yet and even as she talked you knew she had loved this little boy, "My Cricket" (impossible as it sounds). His mother had died the year before this first visit, and I see now that in his Zi' Gian he found the warmth and uncritical sympathy a little boy so desperately needs. He, in turn, supplies all the humor of which Uncle with his deliberate rectitude is incapable. Today he regaled us with the miraculous efficiency of the hospital. For three weeks the technicians have pondered over certain specimens Don Anselmo provided. Yesterday they reported the patient, A. Lanfranchi, to be clinically healthy and pregnant. Aunt actually giggled until the tears rolled down her cheeks.

I have just come in quite chilled from standing in the garden. I realize now I was half waiting for my *fantasma* to come. She did not. Would I have had something to say to her if she had? Not really, I suppose, but since each day her voice plays trickier obbligatos through my thoughts, I must find her soon or fall victim to the schizoid's imaginary friend. I can remember no particular accent, nor even exactly what she said. I must allay the monster. May she be quickly found — fat and moustachioed with a coarse sense of humor and disreputable friends — however she may be — but soon.

Each evening in the Piazza, Evangelista and I feint at each other with words. It stays within the bounds of rancid good humor, but the group of young men, hardly more than boys, who hang around him, snicker in confused appreciation. Last night he overreached and I will see he regrets it. It may take time.

He hailed me, drew me into his little knot and then leaned over to whisper in his best mock wonder and outrage that there was something I should know: with their infallible accuracy the Basilisks have found a new nickname for me — Re Sergianni. When I refused to understand, he looked sympathetic. He glanced around the group, catching an eye here, another there, but could not disguise a smirk of pleasure. Not so strange, I insisted, that the name of my house had been assigned to me. He had to explain. Re Sergianni, Queen Giovanna's lover, no? Queen Giovanna, Donna Giovanna! It is his own invention, of course. He will snort it out to any who will listen, and then they will watch and speculate. Here, where the owner of a large dog is accused of sexual abberation, no one is above suspicion. Logic, to them obvious logic, now that Evangelista has cued them, will confirm that I am my aunt's lover. So Aunt Giovanna's snubs are repaid. She, who understands so much, should have guessed Evangelista would be vicious. One needs to be less than clairvoyant to sense that life with Uncle has not been easy or exciting. Our evening promenade was enough to stimulate our friend's imagination one step further. I pretended indifference and wandered away as soon as he turned to another subject. Now I must consider what to do.

This morning, very early, I went to Don Anselmo's house and so impressed his housekeeper with the urgency of my problem that he rushed to the door with his razor in his hand and islands of shaving soap, like a clown's makeup, still on his face. He listened to my story of Re Sergianni, nodded gently, as though he was not surprised and then sent me into his library to wait while he dressed. Later we worked out a plan.

As head of the cathedral chapter he can propose that I be elected treasurer of the men's organization, which automatically takes the money out of Evangelista's hands and weakens his influence at the palace. Nothing is to be said to Aunt about "Queen Giovanna's Lover." I must find an excuse, maybe a cold, or better a sore leg, to avoid the promenade. Don Anselmo referred several times to "information" in his possession that would settle Evangelista, but would say no more. Disgrace is not enough; his aim is total exile. But, since the Bishop will overlook anything except the most flagrant turpitude in his favorites, our proof must be absolute before we move. Then, if necessary, the subject can be brought before the Curia, of which Don A. is also a member, and a review forced. I see now that Don Anselmo has taken upon himself the dangerous task of episcopal counterweight. His maneuverings are discreet and must keep the Bishop on an invisible seesaw, gently but perpetually in motion between proclamation and frustration. Until this morning my allegiance had not been clear to him. We are both relieved. He is not an enemy I would relish.

I caught Evangelista in the trap tonight, a minor one to be sure, but not unsatisfying. He was ambling through his favorite homily on the sanctity of the law as a profession. The nuances of responsibility. He would have it that through all history lawyers have been a special breed of human, the shepherds of the troubled, who judge dispassionately, advise the poor, protect society and close their eyes to human weaknesses while having none of their own. Few are chosen, fewer still are of the fiber. The acolytes crowded around murmuring approval. The other day I just happened to read, as I told him, that less than one hundred years ago in Naples one man in every ten was a lawyer — some twenty-six thousand of them. Not such an exclusive profession after all, nor immaculate enough to stand much analysis if so many found it profitable. There are no statistics to show the starvation rate among lawyers was high. The young men tittered; Evangelista was not amused. I will pay for it tomorrow, but the expression on his face will carry me through the Didactic Meeting scheduled for later this evening. "Attendance Required of ALL Teachers above Elementary Level" was the Delphic warning at the bottom of the notice.

The speaker did not bother to show up, but the time was not wasted: the ghost has been laid. When I arrived people were huddled in little groups, stamping their feet and grumbling about the cold. Nicola Benevento stood opposite the door talking earnestly to a woman whose back was to me. Without losing a word of his monologue he flicked an eyebrow at me in silent invitation. I hesitated. Something caught my eye, something familiar about his gestures, the frenzied, pop-eyed expression on his face, even the way he writhed, like a tweedy Laocoön, in an effort to control a tremendously long scarf that, wrapped around and around his throat, still trailed over his shoulders and down his back to tangle with his legs. Suddenly I knew. He was well into a quiet imitation of the Director of Schools and undoubtedly very sure of his audience's approval. As I joined them, he broke off to introduce me to "our colleague, another member of our unappreciated profession."

"I know Don Marco, but he does not know me. I think I said that the last time we met." And there was the melancholy caress of my ghost's voice.

She turned toward me and smiled very gently at my surprise, at my awkwardness too, I imagine. She is very beautiful — as her voice is beautiful — in a way totally her own. I should like to ask her sometime if she knows she is the antithesis of women her age. Of course I never will, if for no other reason than because the answer might disillusion. Her dark hair pulled back, the lack of makeup, her complete repose (Is "repose" the word?) are in such contrast they seem tricks in themselves. In the dark it was her voice that enchanted; in the light, her wide-set gray eyes with irises rimmed in black, her pale oval face.

I must have been staring at her; Nicola was very curt, asking if I had been struck dumb. I stuttered out some feeble excuse, and he slipped back into the imitation, his masterpiece as he put it, which I had interrupted. When he reached his climax of apoplectic silence, we laughed more than enough to satisfy him. He was very like the Director, who was at that moment trying to explain the delay of the lecture. Another hour passed before the official admission that our speaker had failed to appear. I, for one, did not mind. We had excluded the others with our incessant chatter: I even worked up courage enough to tell them I called her my *fantasma.* Nicola was gleeful. This was the perfect nickname; we would call her Fantasma. All lightly said, but with an undercurrent of seriousness. Apparently he too has found her elusive. In the end we walked home with our Fantasma. What we were talking about, I cannot remember; something very important for they decided to walk on with me. We stood at the gate. They would not come in; Nicola reminded me it would hardly do, which I should have remembered. Here no decent, unmarried woman enters a man's house alone. Even with me, she would be compromised. She must be chaperoned by another woman, whether she goes to a priest's house or to the dentist; there are no exceptions. Her position is doubly precarious because she lives in a rented room, "abandoned," as they say, by her parents. Her teaching appointment just saves her from being a loose woman — a very beautiful one!

Now it is past midnight and I am not sleepy. Discovery has not ruined my mystery; the face matches the voice. She is from a town near Vasto. Her father is the *medico condotto,* no more prosperous than most of his patients. He is Pugliese, the mother Venetian: as she says, a strange combination. They have done all they could for this only daughter, even sent her abroad for two years to live with relatives. Now I remember! We were talking about politics and graft. She was third in the national examinations for teachers of French, but a friend of her father's in the ministry had to "arrange" her appointment. Nicola claims his family is the Italian ideal — a Benevento relative in every ministry except the Ministry of Reform and no good southerner wants anything to do with reform. I told him not to overlook my category: Orphaned at Birth. Between subsidies and job preference, one can hardly do better. We are wrong to laugh, I suppose, but it is better than expecting change. For the first time I felt I had friends in San Basilio.

This morning Nicola was waiting for me in the Piazza. He was exuberant in his wry way. He almost chattered. What did I think of *her*? Does she like San Basilio? Teaching? Lucania? For once he seemed completely carefree and happy. Then suddenly his face changed, it melted. He sagged back to the skeptical, discouraged Nicola of other mornings. There was no point, he insisted, in talking about her. Speculation is a pastime reserved to the idle and to those who have a choice in what they do. He feels he is neither. I tried to talk to him, comfort him, but he waved me aside. Perhaps I was too insistent: in the end we almost quarreled. He was surly and bitter: What did I know about such things? How could *I* understand how *he* felt? No. *Basta!* It's futile and besides what difference did it make to me? I was to talk about something else, or leave him alone. For the first time we seemed to have nothing in common except teaching and schools, so I expounded on the relative merits of the Convitto as compared to the Liceo. (I suppose that was dangerous too — *she* teaches at the Liceo — but here every subject overlaps every other.) Nicola's enthusiasm for the debate (the Liceo offers greater teaching freedom! — the unknown always does) was an indirect apology, certainly as close as he will come to one. By the time we went to our separate classes, we had negotiated a peace of sorts.

He thinks I have forgotten something he told me, half-jokingly, a month or so ago. In this part of the world, he said, the Beneventos are very important. Land, background, houses – and influence. All on credit. Eventually even that comes to an end. It has. There is nothing left. Generations of Beneventos have not been extravagant, just improvident, until now the position and solvency of the family depend on Nicola, probably the first Benevento who cares little for either. He must choose a wife with a handsome dowry. How he feels is unimportant.

All Souls' – 1968

The boys are as though struck dumb by the cold. They cannot understand a question the first time. Huh? is the answer until I lose my patience with them. Then I see their hands, swollen, red with blue blotches and remember my own chilblains. The agony of being cold, the greater throbbing agony of those hands once they were warm. Perhaps it would be kind to leave them in this mute, semiconscious hibernation until spring. They would fail. It is an evil choice.

I am no longer flesh, just brittle bones that rattle in the wind or melt into fog to disappear like some black-wrapped Bedouin. I brood through the days in cystic isolation, careful to protect these vital humors for what? For whom? For God? For the eternal life hereafter which already I live on earth.

Here the first notebook ends. I was surprised to find, as I read the last entry, that it was already midnight. I decided that if I expected to be up and at work early, I should go to bed, leaving the second notebook for another peaceful evening, which, in fact, is exactly what I did and so the sequence of time and events remains as I lived it.

FOUR

I

But the next morning I did *not* go to work. Don Carlo Benevento died in the night and courtesy required what is so aptly called in Italian *un atto di presenza* – an act of presence – one of those brief, formal appearances without meaning if performed, an insult if omitted.

Everyone in town knew Don Carlo. He had spent the last thirty years rambling the streets, gossiping. The portly relic of a landed family fallen on hard times is equipped to do little else. He had no profession, of course. Employment in an office, assuming one so destitute could be found, would have been beneath his dignity. In his youth he was enrolled at the university for six or eight years, but his attendance, another *atto di presenza,* was too infrequent for a degree. Leisure was his life's work and eventually won him the reputation of being a True Gentleman simply because the ability to avoid exertion for such an extended period of time is worthy of respect. He certainly was not rich. His wardrobe was limited to one baggy, rather spotted gray suit which he had had turned and restitched every few years, a black cape and a hat for winter, and a wide-brimmed panama for summer. Bits of land, the odd lots of his inheritance, still provided food for the table, but he spent every morning in the market wandering around the fruit and vegetable stands with a leather-patch shopping bag over one arm. He was courtly to women, paternal to men, and if they smiled behind his back and joked about the herbs, a stalk of celery, a sprig of parsley and a wizened carrot that were his daily purchase, they never quite dared to be patronizing. He was, after all, a gentleman.

His wife, Donna Luisa, is a little brown mole of a woman, indistinguishable from a dozen others like her, who never leave their houses except to go to church. She is pious, too genteel ever to have carried a package, and does not approve of ready-made clothes, the cinema or smoking. The "new" covered market, which she has not seen, though it was built just after the last war, exemplifies the wanton extravagance of modern times. Actually it is a wall-less shed with a corrugated tin roof and a concrete floor. Don Carlo may have been wise to encourage her prejudices, for there is litttle cash money to spend and what there is comes from Nicola's salary at the Convitto.

I hardly know Nicola Benevento well, but occasionally on my afternoon walks I have met him striding along the road and he has joined me for half an hour, sometimes an hour, before leaving me abruptly for some rutted trail down a hillside. At times he has had nothing to say and so has been silent in an amiable, musing way that surprised, then delighted me. In San Basilio conversation is too often a compulsive formality. Other times he has babbled at me, like a breathless schoolboy, always about what interested him. He never pretends to draw me out; he purges his spleen and if I want to listen, fine – if not, presumably I will say so and we will part company.

I had not seen him since early summer when we met on a dirt track scraped out by the Forestry Department to serve what may, some day, be a forest. No one uses it now. It wanders along a ridge that slopes gently down toward the dry riverbed. In winter rain softens the clay to a gelatinous slick. But in summer parched reedy grass that can slash your legs like wheat stubble in a cut field whispers and moans in the wind. Bees drone as they circle about gentian thistle blossoms, and pale-yellow butterflies skip and flitter in their scatterbrained way. I know of few walks that offer such peace and freedom from the nervous civilization of steel pylons and squalid pastel boxes that man apparently needs for his mass security. The barricades of mountains, layer upon layer, blue, purple, misty, some pinked with jagged rocks, still hold, but not for long.

That day Nicola had suddenly appeared in front of me, marching uphill with his head lowered, obviously both in a hurry and irritable. I would have gone on, but he stopped, wedged his downhill foot against a rock and launched into a long, disjointed soliloquy about his "terrible mistake." He sounded like the victim of a good insurance salesman: sweet reason had forced him to agree to a useful program, but he resented the man who had caught him with his defenses down. Don Anselmo had convinced him to run for mayor. Nicola now knew all the reasons why he could not, why it was a "terrible mistake," why Don Anselmo had taken advantage of his good humor, why priests should not mix in politics. And besides, *he* was a Socialist. Don Anselmo said labels mean nothing. No, priests should not dabble in politics. Of course the Bishop does and that very fact had, in the end, tricked Nicola. He could not stand by and allow Evangelista, the Bishop's candidate, to be elected mayor without a fight. On the other hand – a Socialist mayor! Could I imagine a Socialist mayor conferring with the Bishop? Impeachment. That will be the first thing to come into his head. Christ never intended His bishops to suffer so! "Terrible mistake!" And with a nod of his head and still muttering "terrible mistake," Nicola had stomped off leaving me in the middle of the path.

Soon the idle seers of the Piazza had it that Nicola Benevento was to be a candidate for mayor – on the Socialist ticket! – but, sibylline as they were, they never mentioned any part, official or otherwise, played by Don Anselmo. Publication of the lists shocked both peasants and *padroni,* who, though they reasoned from totally opposite, negative suppositions, arrived miraculously at the same conclusion: that this was a contest between the Bishop and Don Carlo's son. Don

Carlo's unexpected death was credited to shame, which, in his gentle megalomania, was an emotion he probably never experienced. An entirely Anglo-Saxon sense of fair play nagged at me: to censure Nicola at this moment was unfair. His father's death could affect the elections. On the whole, peasants might believe Nicola was more his own man than before, but his father's friends, who vote almost without thought for the Christian Democratic candidate anyway, were sure to condemn him personally. So I decided to make a short, formal visit of condolence at Palazzo Benevento. I would be counted among those who sympathized with Nicola and, by implication at least, with his candidacy.

As the only woman in town who drives, I will admit I have a slight advantage over the average car owner: I terrify the police. The sight of my car in motion sends them leaping for cover and my gender is enough to absolve me of any legal comprehension. In San Basilio this is no mean convenience. All streets lead to the Piazza where vehicular traffic, and therefore parking, is forbidden by ordinance. Several hundred such decrees, imposed in the orderly thirties, still regulate every aspect of life without concern for postwar excesses. The town was rated a twelve-parking-place community and a twelve-parking-place community it remains. The overflow clogs the road just outside the Piazza and is a steady source of ticket income. My infractions the police ignore, presumably on the grounds of legal irresponsibility, and in so doing have encouraged me to disregard their ordinances with a nonchalance that borders on true Italian anarchy. I have an ideal parking place – in the spot reserved for buses. I know it is reserved for buses: it says so in enormous yellow letters. By self-declared feminine right, it is now mine. The other day I realized that the disease is in the acute stage: I heard myself state firmly that women in Latin countries deserve retribution for the dearth of ladies rooms; mine is willful illegal parking.

Each time I approach the Piazza through its rood screen of arches, I am surprised by a tunnel impression of a sanctuary of stone and shadow on view, like a single frame of film forever locked in a projector, for all to see and so judge San Basilio. By some alchemy of light, dust and mist the Bishop's palace looms imperious in the full glare of morning, ominous and black at sunset. The status quo, so carefully guarded, assumes the smug divinity of permanence. Intruders are not welcome; peddlers will be prosecuted. That morning, the men had already settled in for their daily wake. Because it was warm and sunny, they lounged in doorways. A peasant woman swayed by, carrying a plank loaded with bulbous round loaves of bread on her head. In front of a café, just under a droopy, tattered awning, Minguccio, the funeral coach driver, snored and bubbled to himself. He was already decked out in his official black suit with the frayed galloon. The stiff collar, white stock and shiny boots that complete the ensemble would come later. They give him "the sweats," he says; he can endure them for only the briefest period. Soon he would wake up, stretch, wiggle his toes in his open sandals, and then slouch off to the barber who would shave him, hitch up the torturous collar and coax him into his boots. Somewhere nearby in the shade, his four horses, their hooves blackened with shoe polish and their tails combed, waited patiently between the shafts of the funeral carriage, which, with its spindle spires and curlicues, looks like an ambulant, black-lacquer cathedral.

It is all so constant, so easy to chart! I find it hard to remember that repetition breeds repetition until inertia takes control; then only force can break the pattern. The Basilisks have neither the will nor the courage. As, a thousand years ago, they never thought of repairing the aqueduct which had supplied the Romans with water, canalized and ready to use, today they have done nothing to exploit the natural gas found in the subsoil of their own river valley. The water has slipped away to another vein, the gas has been piped to distant industries and the Basilisks remain in their Piazza, without water or work or the hope of either, complaining but loyal to the pattern of inertia which gives them the illusion of safety and makes their every movement predictable.

Twice a day the arrival of a bus mars the composition by

disgorging bundles, hoes, cardboard suitcases tied with rope, and bedraggled passengers, who, dazed by the finality of arrival, stand about like supers onstage in the wrong act. They blink, sort out their belongings and then stare dumbly about them. No one pays any attention. They shoulder their burdens and skulk away, not necessarily to their destinations, just away from that Piazza where already they sense they are out of place.

All Basilisks know without thinking when a bus has arrived: a flurry of people, a faint air of litter. I recognized it immediately and without interest until I noticed a mound of suitcases, soft, matching heavy plastic bags *not* tied with string. A prosperous traveler had arrived. Now who could it be? This right to an explanation is a mild psychosis which invades the mind of anyone who stays in San Basilio more than two weeks. I really wanted to know. I looked around. Men still lounged in the shade, watching through half-closed eyes the woman with her bread. The rather military voluptuousness of her walk could stimulate all manner of imaginary scenarios for use in a more private encounter. Multicolored plastic streamers, hung in café doorways to discourage flies, rippled in the breeze. Minguccio snoozed on: nothing had changed. I turned and almost collided with Marina Bova who had rushed out to meet me, apparently expecting me to move off in the opposite direction. The woman with the bread stopped to swivel around so that she could see us. The men straightened up. For Marina Bova to move precipitously was a novelty worthy of attention.

Few young women are grave: Marina is. Her composure may be natural. More often it seems deliberate, an acquired condition of mind she has forced her body to accept. She paces, she never ambles or charges. She listens, she answers exactly the question asked, she talks easily, but silence is equally comfortable and at times obviously her preferred defense. Seldom is she startled into nervous compensation. As though guided by her own personal interior radar, she glides through the mine fields of day-to-day problems with a stately detachment which is both admirable and irritating. I am not proud of it, but I felt a certain petty satisfaction in seeing her flustered.

"Scusi, Signora! Mi scusi. I wanted to ask you – Signora Cappella's son did not meet me, as he was supposed to. I did arrange it – but – I wondered if . . ." As I watched this tall, erect young woman in a shapeless gray flannel suit, the customary uniform of the schoolteacher, I was suddenly aware of how hard it must be for her to ask a favor. Her cheeks were feverish pink and her words came in spurts. "I know it is a dreadful imposition – so many bags." She waved toward the pile that had interested me. "I thought if you had your car . . ." Already she was less flushed and with the return of her normal pallor, her face relaxed into smooth, ceramic neutrality. She held her head so high that, looking down at me, her gray eyes were hooded and almost sinister. As you please, they seemed to say and for a moment I was tempted to refuse. I dislike my own ambivalence about Marina Bova, but I have never been able to overcome it, to accept that her arrogance is more shyness than challenge and that the gentleness of her husky voice, which colors the simplest words, is undoubtedly truer to her feelings. In spite of myself I react to the personality she presents, whichever, and am never completely at ease with her. She is very unlike the Basilisks. I respect her precision and her quiet, often amusing comments of the world around her. In our more congenial moments we enjoy each other; she can be extremely good company. Ours is a strange relationship. I am a sort of mentor-cum-lending library for her determined study of English. Her pursuit of this strange language and culture is, perhaps, as close to passion as I have ever seen in her and even then I sense challenge in her questions and immediately doubt my own knowledge.

"I thought you might give me a lift, that is, if you have your car." It was a statement, not a question. I was evasive.

"Don Carlo Benevento died yesterday. Perhaps you should call at the house first," I said.

"I never met Don Carlo," she said slowly, not sadly, but as though irritated by the intrusion of a flighty non sequitur. "Or Donna Luisa, for that matter."

"But you are a friend of Nicola's."

"We both teach, but not even at the same school," her voice was patient, detached. "A visit to his house would not be appropriate."

Defeated by the intricacies of Basilisk etiquette, I gave her my car keys, assured her I would be back in half an hour and went off by myself to find my way down the stairsteps into the Serraglio.

The sour effluvium of goat droppings and musty cellars, where pigs grunted in ferocious boredom, drove off visions of past splendors. Flies buzzed about my ankles. The alleys, their cobbles as jagged as the bed of a mountain stream, careened down. Occasional smooth, flat stones were greased by yellow-brown chameleon moss. Somewhere a hen squawked, a dog crawled by on his belly, a woman's voice wailed behind a closed door, but still I felt alone in a shaft that burrowed deeper without ever arriving anywhere. Suddenly sky and buildings vanished in a blaze of white light: the Piazza of the Old Fountain and Palazzo Benevento, as described – large, its walls a mosaic of stones and bricks and rubble held together with mortar riddled by centuries of torrential rains until it was porous as lava. Over the arched portal, an inscription carved in stone by some local artisan more willing than experienced: "Happy is the guest upon whom the host smiles" or, because the word for host and guest is the same in Italian, "Happy is the host upon whom the guest smiles."

Women swathed in sheer black veils passed me. Their lips moved in silence; beads chattered in their hands. A priest, blurred by a swarm of flies, held his cassock up high, like a ball gown, and picked his way through the debris. We nodded. One does not speak on such occasions. At the top of the stairs an old servant in a voluminous black coverall and felt slippers with cut-out corn holes intoned *"Poveri noi! Poveri noi!"* – the dirge the living chant for themselves. She stopped only long enough to point down a dark corridor. Loose tiles tinkled at each step. As black melted into brown, I made out shadowy figures ahead. One detached itself from the wall and came toward me.

"Let me lead the way," said a man's voice. I knew the reedy, insinuating tone, but could not immediately place it. Together, he with his clammy, but somehow caressing hand at my elbow, we went into the sepia world of an enormous drawing room stripped of all furniture except three brown plush love seats, which had been pushed into corners, as though for emergency use. A brass chandelier dangled over us like a monstrous prehistoric arachnid with tiny landing lights at the tips of frail, arched legs. When we drew up at the end of a long line of silent people, who exuded naphthalene, I had my first glimpse of my protector.

To some no occasion is without strategic possibilities. It was Pancrazio Evangelista who clung so solicitously to my arm and now began to grumble in my ear. I stepped away from him, freeing my arm, though no rebuff, however pointed, discourages him for long. He has always been conspicuously, doggedly affable to me, while I do my best to avoid him. An indefinable soft white larval quality about him repels me. He is an allover pale and medium man, impossible to describe if he is out of sight, which may of itself be a compliment to the success of his intentions. If no one feature stays in the memory, certain mannerisms do: incessant pattings at sparse, oily, mouse-brown curls; the jabs of a pudgy forefinger at the bridge of his glasses; a merry rolling and jingling of coins in his pocket. For a man so physically unimposing, his ability to create his own climate is remarkable. Few admit to liking him. Everyone is defensively aware of his intelligence and his sensitivity to the weaknesses of others, and still they never fail to tell him or to do exactly what he wants. No windfall is too unexpected to be exploited and my arrival was just that, for he knew he was not welcome at Palazzo Benevento. I could be his shield. He mumbled confidentially into my ear.

"Tragic! Really tragic, don't you agree?"

"What?" I asked, forgetting for the moment where we were.

"Don Carlo. If only Nicola . . ." he stopped and sighed. "Of course one never knows, but . . ." People in front of us were turning to see who dared talk at such a time.

"Indeed, one does not know," I agreed and moved a further step away, only to have him follow me. We were jigging like badly worked puppets. His hand shot out as though to catch me.

"Are you all right? You look suddenly pale."

"Yes, quite all right, but please, *do* be quiet. People are beginning to stare." I refused to look at him and instead concentrated on the floor, on the swirly patterns of grit left by the shuffling of so many feet on the dark tiles. From the corner of my eye I could see the bottoms of his trousers lying well down on the laces of scruffy black shoes. Prosperity is new to Evangelista and while he has mastered the general range of its subtleties, he has not yet overcome a few provincial frugalities which, were he to venture outside San Basilio, would identify him immediately for what he is. He has not discovered the economy of good shoes or the niceties of polish, and he will not wear a ready-made suit. Instead he persecutes a local tailor until his coats are molded to him like worsted corsets. He orders the trousers hemmed a shade too long so that, at the first sign of fraying, they can be shortened two centimeters and "present themselves" as new again. In case cuffs come back in fashion or patches are needed, caution dictates deep hems, which are inevitably narrower than the trouser leg and so pucker on the first damp day. I looked. Halfway to his knee were the telltale ripples.

Before he could notice, I glanced in the opposite direction and discovered the old, well-cared-for shoes and neat blue trouser legs of a man who was obviously sitting down with his legs crossed. Long, spatulate fingers were entwined around his knee, and ropy blue veins, those betrayers of exhaustion, stood out in high relief against the translucent skin of his hands. I looked up and was about to turn away when I recognized Nicola Benevento. Tradition is rigid: close male relatives do not shave between the death and the funeral. In extreme cases men do not shave for a month. Nicola's chin was black with stubble, but worse, the rest of his face was ashen and furrowed and his eyes, luminous red.

Without thought or design I went over to him. He stood up, introduced two men, who had been standing at either end of the love seat, as his uncles, and then listened with his head down to the few stumbling phrases of condolence I could offer. When I had finished, he smiled and though there was nothing more to say, seemed to want me to stay. If I would sit with him for just a few minutes. I perched on the edge of the sofa. The uncles settled into a screen, creating for me the kind of physical and mental blankness I experience in a voting booth. Alone with that harrowing choice of levers, I am tempted to vote the straight ticket, in this case generic sadness, rather than choose between clichés. I maundered on, surprised that Nicola nodded, evidently pleased by the stray memories outsiders had of his father.

"I should have been kinder, more understanding," he said quietly. "He was discouraged too." Before I could find the right lever, a head pushed between the uncles. Evangelista had come to chide me.

"Venga, Signora! Venga!" he ordered. "You will lose your place. Besides, *this* is scandalous." His was the emphasis of shock. I was startled at my apparent immorality, then puzzled. "Really a woman cannot . . ."

"Leave her alone," interrupted Nicola in a harsh voice. "I will see she goes in whenever she is ready."

Evangelista ignored him. "You have made a spectacle of yourself. I hardly like . . ."

"Then go away," Nicola interrupted again. "Don't compromise yourself. Above all, do not compromise yourself." His voice was heavy with sarcasm. Evangelista moved off with stiff, affronted dignity, and I finally realized what the whole exchange was about, what I had done that was so scandalous. A Canon of Mourning had been violated: I, a woman, had approached the men of the family. I glanced up at the uncles who had so instinctively blocked me from view, but their harsh, brindled exteriors of country cloth and their faces as blank as well-disciplined eunuchs betrayed no emotion. Their protection was entirely physical.

"I am sorry," I murmured to Nicola. "I know better. I simply forgot. Now, please, put me back into the line – as far from Evangelista as possible." I edged off the sofa.

"Stay a minute longer, at least until he goes inside." We sat in silence, he intent on an inspection of his fingernails, I cursing myself for a pointless gaffe. He sighed and then beckoned one of the uncles to lean down. "Don Anselmo is just inside the door. Would you call him?" He turned back to me. "Don Anselmo will enjoy taking you in. For a priest he is a bit of an iconoclast." He leaned closer. We were in a conspiracy together and it amused him. "You did the compassionate thing. Now we will establish you as a friend beyond the rules of San Basilio. Deferential treatment is a vaccine against criticism. You'll see. Ah, here is Don Anselmo." We both stood up, but he towered over us. Our handshake was not the perfunctory Italian gesture. Don Anselmo made it much more personal by keeping my hand and leaning over, as tall men do, to hear what we might be saying. I think he did it to hide a mischievous smile. For once his eyes were gentle with none of the cold silver glint that seems critical. In the end it was he who spoke first.

"I believe you have a small problem which I can solve very easily. Now, if you are ready," turning to me. "I think we might go in, slowly. Just pretend you cannot see them." The last was almost a whisper.

Don Anselmo and I caused quite a stir as he led me around the line, saying with the patient detachment of a man who assumes his commands will be obeyed, "If you would just move aside. Thank you. Signora . . ." and I preceded him. Before we reached the door, people had drawn back, leaving a wide aisle into another sepia chamber, this one smaller than the salon, and bare except for a black catafalque with Don Carlo's coffin and straight chairs ranged against all four walls.

Don Anselmo's hand on my arm signaled I must wait; mine was to be a private farewell. At each corner of the high platform enormously tall, fat candles in massive wrought-iron holders guttered in the draft, sizzled and then flared to gutter again, producing no light, only variations of shadow which revealed and then obscured the faces of the death-watchers who sat, unmoving as so many stuffed birds. High above them lay Don Carlo, paler than usual, in his coffin, but as placidly sure of himself as he had been in life. For one horrible moment the tableau seemed a macabre farce arranged by Don Carlo who delighted in such ceremonious attentions. I fancied he would rise and in his deep, rather quavery voice deliver a short sermon on the proper respect due the dead. Then the candles flared again, someone moaned and the large pale man, lying so neatly arranged in a dark suit and immaculate white bridal tie, was forever dead.

"Would you like to speak to Donna Luisa?" Don Anselmo asked quietly as we stood at the foot of the casket.

"I think not. She would not remember me."

"She knows no one at the moment, but it is not entirely grief. Carlo, somehow, has tricked her. This is his final bit of spite. He has gone off and left her. Come, then, shall we go?" And we heard the bell. The priest was coming for Don Carlo's soul. Donna Luisa wailed.

Slowly we paced back along that aisle of silent people. Curiosity had won over funereal self-effacement. They inspected me with the frankness of those who have little excitement in their day-to-day lives, and then speculated. For Don Anselmo they apparently did not exist. He led me through the salon, down the corridor with the loose tiles and out into the courtyard where the glare and shrill calls of children playing seemed unreal. And there, waiting in the shade of the archway, stood Evangelista.

"I must speak to you, Signora, quite seriously. A business matter." He eyed Don Anselmo pointedly, achieving an unpleasant mixture of insolence and fawning.

Don Anselmo only murmured, "*Business.* Hardly an appropriate time, Avvocato."

"Take my word for it, this would be to your advantage," Evangelista insisted.

"Then come to my house any afternoon," I said. "But not in the morning. I work then." It was a calculated risk. With the obligations of his day – office hours until two, an abundant lunch, a long nap (both a physical and social necessity) and finally the evening promenade where so much of the casual manipulation vital to his career took place – Evangelista might never be free to call in the afternoon. If he did, the urgency of his mysterious business would be established.

Don Anselmo thwarted further conversation by walking with me, handing me carefully up the treacherous stair lanes to the Piazza where, before he bowed and strolled off toward the cathedral, he said gently, apologetically:

"I too must come to talk to you – about a matter of business, very likely the same business. I am sorry, but you are apt to have many callers in these next few days. I hope you will not think me melodramatic, but be very careful what you say." And without further comment, he left me.

2

Marina Bova sat bolt upright in the car with all the windows closed. She was so absorbed by her own thoughts that she had ignored the torrid heat and the steam which had condensed and trickled in long runs down the windshield. As I opened the door a puff of sultry air, heavy with the odor of roast chicken and peaches, rushed out to enfold me. I eyed the luggage in the back seat. Somewhere, decorously concealed in those bags, was the Italian traveler's cache of "food from home," provided by mothers for children as a weapon against nostalgia.

"You should have opened the windows," I said without preamble.

"I'm sorry. I didn't think." Her voice was courteous, but vague. She shook her head as though she had forgotten something. "What was it? Oh yes, the *guardia* is in a rage. About the car and parking restrictions, I think he said, but I was not really listening. He went away finally."

We rode in silence to Signora Cappella's. After all, even the police were resigned if Marina withdrew from a conversation. She pointed silently to one house in a row of squat houses. Splodges of plaster and mildew gave it a piebald look which was only partially disguised by a snarled vine growing from a large red and gold tuna-fish can on a balcony over the front door. Marina was deliberate in extricating herself from the car. She sauntered to the door and leaned on a brass button that went off somewhere inside the house like a burglar alarm. The sun beat down on the car. No one answered the door, but Marina, in a daze, kept her finger on the bell.

"Marina! Marina!" I called. "There's no one home."

In San Basilio so many days are like this, I thought, watching her come back to the car. My mistake is to struggle against preordained defeat. No Basilisk would. With rather bad grace I invited Marina to come to the house. At noon, when Signora Cappella would surely be home, I would bring her back here with her luggage. She was brusque, almost rude, repeating with more insistence than just good manners required that she could not come. Finally I gave her a choice: either she could wait, surrounded by her possessions, in the dust and heat of the main road, or she could come to my house where I would leave her entirely alone, if she wished. She gave in, muttering something that sounded like "Sooner or later," but I already had the car in gear.

In the harsh light of an autumn morning the apricot house glitters on its lone promontory with prim self-importance. It would play castle to its fief, the town across the way, and like other fallen aristocrats, will not admit that the world no longer measures power in these terms. It preens in vain. I am its only serf, only I am subject to its powers, though I have not yet learned that. I watch people who come here, sure that finally someone will share the sense of peace and arrival that floods over me. No one ever does. As I got out of the car, I took a deep breath and turned toward Marina. Maybe she would be the one. Instead I saw her sway, as though her knees had buckled. She caught at the car door for support.

When I reached her, she was steadier, but pale. Beads of perspiration stood out on her forehead. "Lean on me. You will feel better inside, sitting down."

"Yes. If I could sit down," she said clearly enough, but she had begun to tremble. "It will pass. I have not been well." She hesitated. "An operation this summer." We had only taken a few steps when she stopped and sighed. "I know you have things to do. I am sorry to be such a bother."

"Nothing I cannot do another time. Are you sure you are all right? Did your doctor say you could come back?"

"Yes. Oh yes," she said. "Still a little weak maybe, but I had to come back early. I am assigned to the makeup examinations. The trip was long and tiring." A catch deep in her throat made her voice break. When she went on, the silken timbre was muted by some emotion close to controlled despair, if such is possible. "And I had hoped never to see San Basilio again. Never! Never again!"

Slowly we went into the house. She said nothing more; movement required all her attention. I pulled a chair around so that she would face out toward the town and found an old footstool which Teresa, who does not approve of anything worn, had hidden under my desk. Marina's color was already better, but she settled happily enough in the chair and put her feet up. As I started toward the kitchen, I asked if she would have a cup of coffee, but she was gazing out across the valley, smiling to herself as though the view reminded her of a happy dream. Without the scrim of composure she was startlingly beautiful – and defenseless. She glowed. Her thick brown hair, twisted in a chignon, gleamed. Her gray eyes were now wide and sparkling – no longer opaque, enigmatic one-way glass through which she could see without herself being seen. That long, smooth symmetric face softened. Tension was gone, washed away by that gentle surging flood of life and light and warmth which, unbidden and beyond control, always betrays a woman . . .

3

Diary on my usual yellow paper

September 27, 1969

Interruptions give me mental hiccoughs. If I were to finish that sentence now, I would not write, as I had planned, "a woman in love." The illusion may have been self-induced; it is shattered now. Women are moved by too many fleeting, contradictory perceptions. Male novelists to the contrary, we are not just sexual Geiger counters clicking away to one stimulus. Marina's softening could have been resignation – to what? San Basilio; the misdirection of her plans? Maybe her feet were swollen from the trip and it was a relief to sit down, or maybe she was thinking what she would tell me and pretasting sympathy. How can I know? Writing is a false business. I should make an absolute choice to explain that pensive gentleness of hers and present it as the answer, the explanation – but it is *my* answer, my explanation, not hers. The soft translucence made me grab for "woman in love." By accident I might be right, but that is instinct, not proof. Women never offer more than the externals of their love affairs to other women – again, male novelists to the contrary. We cannot talk about tenderness, yet without it we have no lasting sensation we would call love. Curiously enough, though, a flower, an including glance, a word can be tenderness, seldom any contact more physical. How often I have heard peasant women complain: "He was a good man, good enough anyway, but he never said a kind word, never even 'thank you' in all those years." They do not resent the work or the children or his taking "his rights," as they say, but never to have been thanked lingers in their memories. Sad commentary on female expectations. If I understood Marina as well – but then, I do not. Maybe someday I will.

My worst interruption was the other side of the coin: man's necessity to strut before women. Bruno Ferri. He lumbered in, without knocking, to demand Teresa's wages. It is, after all, the twenty-seventh of the month! Now I am a government duty-bound to pay on a certain date. Sarcasm did not shake him. He just stood, leaning on the desk with his hands splayed out on either side of the typewriter, and watched me with those huge, lackluster black eyes. Even here a father has no right to his daughter's money, but I almost paid to get rid of him. I felt very small; Ferri looked very large and intimidating. Suddenly I knew I was afraid of him and you only surrender once to a bully. I surprised myself; I barked – and it is so easy – "No man keeps his hat on in my house." He stammered and shuffled and excused himself. His hands were in front of him, behind him and at his sides, like a nervous recruit. The peasant-padrone relationship is never far below the surface and easy enough to revive. When I called Teresa, she came, but cowered in the doorway, afraid, I thought, of her father, though she never took her eyes off me. Yes, I was to pay him her *fifteen thousand lire!* And she watched me. Rebellion is still stronger than fear of whipping. *I* was the unknown quantity; *I* might give her away. She had held out five thousand lire for herself. Ferri was too busy with his own thoughts to notice my start or her relief. He began to puff up again and asked if he might sit down. Teresa was too weak to object to the upholstered chair he took. He motioned her out of the room, and she went, leaving me to listen to a masterpiece of self-deprecation, bombast, demands, pleas and even hinted threats that should really have been recorded.

First, I was cheating his daughter. He gave me three months to raise her pay. I assured him a hundred other girls would take her place and be glad of the work, the insurance and the food at the present wage.

He soothed me. He was just an honest man trying to get along on what he could make; not easy with a wife and five boys and a cripple for a daughter. Not easy to start from nothing after the war – and he fought the war too, years of it – fought hard in Vercelli,* been a prisoner of the Germans, then later worked with the partisans – *in somma,* he did his part.

Started from nothing, Bruno had. He skipped neatly over his black-market career. No money, no land, no job. Everything he has today, he has made. No one ever helped him, gave him a hand. He switched from bathos to boast quickly enough. He is master of implied injustice. No matter how unreasonable his demands, or how slight the opposition, he twists the situation until he is the victim of the unscrupulous rich . . . then he lists his assets just to prove you are not dealing with an ignorant *cafone* (a word he spits out as though it were a daring obscenity). As of today he admits to:

2 vineyards
3 building lots
an unspecified quantity of arable land
2 mules
1 donkey
30 pigs
100 sheep
1 icebox
1 gas stove (with electric oven)
1 television set – for his wife (he does not approve of women out after dark; not moral)
5 sons who are to be bookkeepers, or maybe even lawyers

* Vercelli is in northern Italy near Turin.

I know he has prospered in a bewildering series of trades, mortgage options, foreclosures and shady cooperatives, but they were not mentioned, and I did not ask. To peasants Bruno Ferri has the same appeal brigands had a hundred years ago: he has grabbed what he wanted and somehow, in the process, has done the rich in the eye. Watching his face as he talked, his forehead wrinkled, his eyes almost closed or at least invisible behind small rolls of tensed flesh, I had the feeling that he was less absorbed in his choice of words than in monitoring his own voice to be able to correct any phrase too humble or too obviously inflated. This was not just talk; he had a goal. His approach was a meticulous backing and filling maneuver, calculated to bring him into his chosen slip at a gentle glide. When he stopped talking and began to twirl the woolly green hat that had been hooked over one knee, I knew we had berthed.

To put it baldly, without his circumlocutions, he has bought the five hectares of scrub and fennel trees that slope from the road down to the bottom of my right-hand cliff. He says he intends to build *"villini,"* by which he means more four-room cubes of plaster with harlequin tile fronts and "modernistic" zigzag iron work. I did not ask with what.

The crux of the matter: Don Ferdinando is now cut off from *his* twenty hectares of land further on, below my orchard, *unless* I give him permission to come in through my garden, which is exactly what Ferri does not want. Between the stream full of boulders and the steep clay bank, approaches from below are cut off (assuming the costs of a road, a bridge, excavation of the cliff and massive buttresses to support the side walls to be totally disproportionate with the value of the land). Ferri thinks that if he can be sure I will refuse access through my drive, he can force Don Ferdinando to sell his good land. Ferri has already refused an easement. (Query: After a certain number of years would a passage across abandoned land become a public right of way? Don Ferdinando has always used it.) He was graphic about the disadvantages to my garden: farm equipment clanging through, peasants at all hours, animals. My first thought was that I am safe; Don Ferdinando does not want to sell. Then the real game was brought out in the open. Ferri has some way of blackmailing Donna Giovanna. "I know what I know," he said. "Donna Giovanna well beg Don Ferdinando to sell to me." He was careful to tell me he is doing it "the right way." Don Pancrazio has written the Sanseverinos presenting Ferri's offer. Evangelista must be very pleased to have *one* client who calls him "Don Pancrazio." I reverted to Madame La Duchesse and assured him I would guarantee Don Ferdinando's entry, even to letting him use my garden as a passage.

Ferri left grumbling, *"Voi siete tutti uguali!"* I am not sure which of us are alike.

Two days later*

After a good deal of thought the real puzzle is what could Donna Giovanna wish to hide that much? She seems an unlikely victim for any blackmailer, and Ferri is not the most subtle of the breed. I cannot imagine her, at least at this age, carrying on a secret love affair. It must then be some scandal within the Sanseverino family—one with which Ferri is *al corrente* and Don Ferdinando not? Improbable, but possible, I suppose.

* Note added in longhand.

4

Letter from Donna Giovanna Santoro in Sanseverino to A.C.

The physical appearance of this letter was exactly what I would have expected: heavy gray paper, matching envelope lined with white tissue, bold but extremely uniform writing in brilliant green ink.

Naples
28 September 1969

Gentile Signora,

This will be a difficult letter to write and an even more difficult one to understand. I must, as I know I can, trust your discretion and sympathy. Before we left, you remarked there remained a debt unpaid between us. There is no debt, but remembering your kindness, I am presuming to ask a small favor of you. The affairs of San Basilio are never simple. Distance only complicates them. Without going into a long and incomprehensible explanation, my present dilemma has to do with the disposal of land we own. I have reason to believe that a man named Bruno Ferri will approach you, asking you to support certain arrangements he will propose. Would you accept, whatever they are, as a favor to me? When my husband and I are in San Basilio for the Festa, I will explain, but it is most important that this Ferri not be irritated or frustrated in any way before I have a chance to make my own plans.

My little mystery is frail as vapor and no more important, so I would be grateful if you did not mention this letter to my husband, should you meet him before we have a chance to talk. He is irascible and has been unwell of late, not that he has ever approved of women mixing in business affairs.

It means much to both of us that you are living in the house and I hope, enjoying it. Until recently it was such a happy place for us – and now is again. My husband joins me in sending best wishes,*

Giovanna Santoro in Sanseverino

* An absentminded courtesy, which amused me under the circumstances. [A.C.]

5

Again my diary on yellow paper

Yesterday the new fence posts arrived and Sabato immediately developed lumbago, undoubtedly a natural progression. Today he and a "nephew" have been digging postholes — that is, the nephew has been digging to a basso continuo of Sabato's directions and admonitions. The nephew is a big, deliberate man of indeterminate age and probably humorless, but patient. I have watched him from the window. He surveys each site from all angles, then collects and lays out exactly the tools he will need. It had never occurred to me that terrain, and so the tools needed to cope with it, could change character in twelve feet. When he is through, he picks up his tools, one by one, accounting for them as a surgeon checks his scalpels and clamps after an operation.

Just now I found him in the kitchen having coffee with Teresa. His name is Rocco Di Luca. He is too large for a house, or this house is too small for him. He looked hedged round, intimidated by what might happen if he moved and the raucous complaints of the kitchen chair on which he sat did nothing to reassure him. The courtesy of peasants, in their own world, has an unconscious dignity about it that they themselves could never explain. What is proper where is a matter of intuition. Something tells them it is "meet and right so to do" and they act upon it. Di Luca had been sitting with his cap on, in a way accepted by all peasants, as a wise medical precaution against drafts. A man enters a house with his cap in his hand, but he is truly welcomed and at ease when invited to "cover himself." He knows exactly where he stands if he is not asked to: he should finish his business and leave. Years ago, in that period when my American mores were forever in my way and *every* human being needed a daily bath (according to me), I thought this hat business an uncouth custom. Now it seems companionable. I am no longer surprised to find three or four men sitting around a fireplace, drinking wine and eating walnuts with their hats on and usually their capes as well.

Nor was I surprised to find Di Luca wearing his cap. Having been licensed to put it back on, he need not have taken it off for anyone, would not have, except for someone he respected. For his uncle, for me, for Don Ferdinando probably, yes; for Bruno Ferri, Evangelista and so many others, no. It is in a way the peasant's only form of social comment, appropriately enough a silent one. As soon as I came in the kitchen, of course, he snatched it off, arranged it carefully on his knee and "combed" his thick brown hair with the palms of tremendous pawlike hands. This accomplished, he had nothing to do. He crossed his arms and began a detailed examination of the floor with desperate, almost virginal concentration. I offered a cigarette. He shook his head and pulled out a slender white clay pipe with a miniature white clay bowl which holds no more than a teaspoon of tobacco and which, after infinite care in filling, packing, loosening, and lighting, allows three stingy mouthfuls of smoke. Very economical and an excellent prop for a shy man.

Di Luca is one of the few truly handsome peasant men I have ever seen, with a fine aquiline nose, a large but delicately modeled mouth, which, though it is probably specious to construct qualities of mind from external features, suggests a balanced and at the same time stubborn personality. His heavy jaw and bristly blond eyebrows do nothing to destroy the impression. There is a quizzical expression in the brilliant, not large, but very clear blue eyes which may be accentuated by the deep white crow's-feet that seem almost a type of coquettish eye makeup. He enjoys working with his uncle, he says, and is free until the rains come and he must plow. And so the staff grows!

Teresa has just been in to say good night. We agreed that Di Luca is a "good man" and then were both surprised because we do not know why we think so. He is so calm and sure. Teresa really came to ask for an advance on her salary: the Festa is almost upon us, and I had forgotten. The market stalls will be set up in the Piazza, tempting her to buy – something she does not need, of course, and therefore the pleasure of buying will be great and the disillusionment afterward, as she realizes the tawdriness of what she has bought, will be greater. In this she is very like the other Basilisks.

I sat down at my desk to write some notes on the Festa itself and our patron saint, the Madonna delle Liberate; but after perhaps an hour, the curiosity which had been nagging close to my consciousness got the better of me. I opened the drawer and took out the second and last of Marco Santoro's notebooks.

FIVE

I

Marco Santoro Notebook #2

Epiphany 1969

Tomorrow school opens again. So much happened in November and December. Activity was my excuse for not writing, but now, thinking back over those weeks, I must admit, at least to myself, that not lack of time as much as fear of my own thoughts kept me from my journal.

During the holidays I have seen almost no one, except Aunt Giovanna and Uncle for the traditional feasts. Several times Nicola Benevento has come to brood in front of the fire. He talks little, and I am happier that he does not. Only once did his gloom break into words. His Fantasma has become all too real. He is puzzling over what is right. She means the end of his family's financial hopes, and he is bitter. A rich wife, or a poor wife – the choice should be his and is not. He cares nothing for money; as he says, he has never had any, only the pretense of it. Still his family insists. His salary would not keep them all. They will not receive her now, would not if they were married, and he would have to ask her to continue teaching to support two people who refuse to acknowledge her existence. He twirls round and round, snapping at solutions like a flea-maddened dog and in the end lapses back into silent depression.

Apparently he has said nothing to her. He is afraid, "a coward defeated before he tries," he calls himself, sure she will not have him. I see his point; it is very convenient. If he never asks, he can blame his family, can curse them for the destruction of his dream. Always better than the truth he fears: that he amuses her and nothing more. He has sensed, though he does not understand why; that she will never marry for the *sistemazione*. Her resignation maddens him. A spinster's life may be drab, but it is also free. I could not tell him what she said to me one day: that her dowry from a childhood of love is that she cannot settle for less than love herself. I prayed he would stop talking.

I ruin my health, he says, reading so much, studying, writing. And all for what? For peace, I tell myself, but not him. He imagines my days as he sees them. He cannot know that I wake at dawn and the faintest glimmer of clear sky sends me out across the hills in minutes. I have found a network of paths, twisting down the long, bare tentacles of land that anchor these mountains to the rocky valley below. I have explored one after the other, going where they go, almost always to the river and sometimes, if the rush of dung-colored liquid clay does not block my way, beyond to those even barer rock piles wrapped in a perpetual gray-pink mist. A few red-faced shepherds, bent against the wind, have nodded in my direction without curiosity. One squatted on the lee side of a boulder and watched me, but he had that most natural of all reasons for making sure he was alone. They, unlike the Basilisks, do not care who I am, or where I am going, or why. I am anonymous, free to wrestle in my own Armageddon of the soul. Each morning I set out to examine my sins in the light of what I know is my duty, what *I* choose to be my duty: "Sweet is the yoke and light, the weight"* but not in these last weeks. Each afternoon at sunset I admit to myself that I have been sidetracked again. The weakness is mine, only mine and so is

* I was puzzled at the wording which was not the usual Italian Biblical translation for Matthew 11:30. I believe it comes from *L'Ordinazione Sacerdotale* (The Ordination of Priests), Section III (*Vestizione dei Paramenti Sacerdotali*). [A.C.]

the guilt. The longing and the siren dreams that entice me from reason are also, probably, only mine. If I relive them, I harm no one but myself.

– The cold dazzling clear noon of the first time we went to Matera with Nicola. The Sassi, whose alleys, roofs and doorways vibrated with life that was new, not old and dissipated. Have they always been that way, or was there something different about that day? Something different in us that day? I still wonder. She talked about her family, about her future in a never-ending line of San Basilios, going from one teaching post to the next. She was depressed and lonely. I tried to encourage her; it was already too late for me. In the end I disappointed her with platitudes. "It is not wrong to want more: a better life, one that is more interesting, more constructive, happier. That is the nature of the human being, but he must recognize what he gives up in his search and be content, always, with less than his goal." Not entirely what I meant. Her somber eyes pleaded for reassurance, for sharing. I gave her sops. She must think me a placid goat, though she was kind. I have lost the habit, she says, of talking about myself. Maybe I never had it. But the moment was gone. We joined Nicola.

– Other days when I went with them in Nicola's rattling Topolino. Three-way conversations in which I felt her waiting for me to say what we both thought. We knew we would agree and spiderlike awareness spun strands of understanding back and forth between us until we did not have to talk. Nicola talked on, disconcerted at times by our silences, but always glad of an audience and particularly kind to me because, in agreeing to chaperone, I made the jaunt possible. Sundays and holidays we went off for a few hours, but we were always careful to be back by dark: to teachers' meetings in Matera, or the museum at Metaponto, the cathedral at Acerenza, once even to that most desolate of all Frederick's castles, Lagopesole. The gossips found nothing to criticize.

I brought those harmless outings to an end. I had to, but eventually she would have blocked them herself.

No! At least I can be honest with myself. The initiative was not mine. Poor Don Anselmo broke the pattern of those Sunday trips. The Bishop had ordered him to lead Advent retreats in every convent in the diocese and at the same time to organize "cultural lectures" for the women of San Basilio's parishes. Much as it distressed the Bishop, he was unable to provide a car, so like a drummer in pots and pans, Don Anselmo reorganized his life, if not his digestion, to fit the local bus schedules. Since they adhere to school and government hours and ignore the holiday traveler, Don Anselmo could never reach San Basilio on Sundays. He asked me to take the cathedral women on two consecutive Sunday afternoons. The subject: Past Glories of Lucania (which they received with all the enthusiasm of black-shawled mummies). I could not refuse him.

Nicola assumed the break was temporary and threw himself into a search for new places we were to explore when I was again free. I did not object. *She* must decide how much she wants to see of him. I have not discussed it. In fact I saw her alone only twice before Christmas.

– Once at the cemetery where I had gone, under orders from Aunt Giovanna, to see to the maintenance of the family mausoleum and she, to put flowers on the grave of a student killed in an accident. Her face was smooth and wide, glowing from fresh air and some inner contentment too. She said little enough. She twitted me, but gently, about Re Sergianni. Of course she would hear. Suddenly I was afraid she might believe the story and so was much on my dignity and full, too full of explanations. I should simply have said that with the coming of cold weather Aunt and I decided to stay by the fire. Before we parted at the road, she said one phrase, something like the wisdom of my decision about our Sundays, and thanked me. Her voice was gentle. I might have been standing, once more, enchanted in the dark at my own gate.

– The second time was the afternoon the schools closed for the holidays and then, if I had not seen her at the gate, she would have slipped off without a word. I rushed out in time. She had come to see her favorite view, but I lured her in to inspect my garden. It is a jungle. My excuses made her laugh. I am lazy, according to her, and she went on knowledgeably about flowers, showing me what I think is a Venetian aspect of her character. I insisted she come in for tea, then found that old Filomena had not only gone off without putting the water on, but had forgotten to buy tea altogether. We gnawed on some carob pods I had bought on my way home and talked of books, but there were awkward little silences. In a quarter of an hour she was gone.

And that is all of it.

I was right to write this. I have been a fool: there is *nothing* there. No reason to disturb my conscience. What I fear most, like Nicola, is the truth: that there *is* nothing, that I have imagined her feelings. My own are fluctuations of a pernicious fever. My attention wanders, though I have an endless ability to concentrate on every word of hers I can remember. And that madness of wanting to touch her, hold her, stroke her hair, cradle her head. It would be enough to be near her, to comfort her. Time and tramps over the mountains have only made my fever worse.

Tomorrow the term begins. Already I feel the gripes. Waves of anticipation leave me flushed and afraid. This is *pazzia*. I will overcome it, though I have not in three weeks of reasoning — no, not reasoning — three weeks of delirious reliving. Aunt says I look poorly and would administer a purge. I cannot tell her it is the mind, not the body, that is sick.

A week of snow and fog has dulled my obsession. I have not seen her, though once I thought I did. Who can reason with a runaway horse? Had it been she, I would have raced to meet her. As it is I have kept myself from searching her out and now am plagued by the thought she is avoiding me. And the Basilisks march up and down, blank as plastic soldiers, yet waiting, imagining, inventing.

Uncle has allowed himself a reluctant observation on my affairs to the effect that in San Basilio one cannot be too careful about one's friends. Even "appropriate" people can think "inappropriate" thoughts. At last I understood. Nicola Benevento has rebelled – a bit – and joined the Socialist party. Uncle will never understand. I did not try to explain.

Aunt Giovanna has me searching the diocesan records for mention of the family – Santoro deeds, legacies, transfers of land, acquisitions, benefits. They are all registered. It fits rather well with my own work of the moment: Minor Provincial Families, their relationship to the Church and the court of Naples. Odd the things one finds. An Evangelista family is referred to as the Counts of Serra. Sounds a made-up name, but real or invented, they managed to sell the title. Today's third cousin twice removed feigned boredom when I mentioned it in front of his little clique, but he has just come all the way out here to see me, to say in essence, keep track of any further references to my family and your diligence will not go unrewarded. Evangelista has a fly face. I only saw it tonight in the half-light – those global eyes, no chin.

Today at a certain point I realized it would be interesting to know how many parcels of land are still held by their pre-1870 owners, that is by the owner of record in the diocesan ledgers. The doyens of the registry offices were not pleased at the idea of opening up for me after hours, but eventually they were both civil enough. Rather than sit and watch me, the land office man helped in the search. He found it a game, sort of a treasure hunt; he said it was the first time he had ever felt his incessant scribbling might be of use to someone other than tax collectors. I can hardly blame him. They have exiled him to the loft of the ducal palace, supplied him with two chairs, a desk, a stove and great sagging towers of ledgers and told him to get on with his work. In the corner by the stove he has created a stork's nest for himself. The chill echo of the rest of the room is muted by a tanbark of cigarette butts, which are flipped over his shoulder to land where they may. He amuses himself arranging and rearranging a gallery of mildewed prints and portraits he found stacked against the walls. At the moment over his desk a buxom, slightly nauseated Salome, enveloped in a cocoon of veils that defy gravity, proffers the head and gory neck of John the Baptist. Across the way Garibaldi surveys the situation complacently. Kings, identifiable by Savoia moustaches, and bishops, by mitres, are scattered down the wall without relation to each other or the spaces they fill. Beauty spots, my friend calls them, to conceal the more glaring defects of what plaster remains. Over coffee he told me that for the tax deadline he plans to replace Salome with a frail St. Sebastian, so perforated by arrows that jets of blood arch away from his body like water from a public fountain.

I quite liked the little man. By the end of the afternoon we were friendly enough for him to confide in me. He thinks he has noticed something that has escaped general attention. Then a long explanation about how sales are registered, taxes assessed and reported to the Province in six copies, etc., until it was hard to be patient with him. But I was. As he explained, land does not change hands often. Most of it is not worth buying unless it abuts property already held by the buyer, and for that reason he particularly noticed the sale and resale of the parcels of land that stretch from the edge of town out to my house. In six months eight irregular plots, varying in size from two to thirty hectares, have had twenty-three different owners. At first I was disappointed. While I had to compliment his alertness, the information itself seemed less than stunning. To satisfy him I examined the bills of sale and the entries. The earliest sales showed no obvious similarities (probably men going off to find work in Germany who needed to sell what had never been of use to them). The later sales had a pattern. Three parcels now belong to a Bruno Ferri, two to women with different surnames, but whose maiden names were Ferri and whose father's name was Vincenzo, as was Bruno Ferri's. Of the other three parcels, one, the smallest, belongs to Evangelista and two belong – once again the same deception – to his married sisters, both having, of course, different surnames. My friend just thinks it is curious. I think it may be more than that. He let me copy out all the names and dates, which, under cover of my diocesan lists, I subsequently checked at the census office. Now I must correlate them, but it seems obvious that all the buyers in the progression were relations, distant at first, then with each sale closer to Bruno Ferri and Pancrazio Evangelista. Tomorrow I must show the list to Don Anselmo.

Not today. He is away on "church business" his housekeeper specified dourly, as though I would immediately suspect a private orgy. Whatever he is up to, she disapproves, but that tells me little as only prayer and contemplation have her *placet*. When pressed, she allowed that he might be back tonight, maybe not until tomorrow. I waited in the Piazza for the last bus, but he was not on it.

I have just walked home through a mist that blurs and glows too, promising a world one never quite reaches. Street lamps are pearly comets, their rays too weak to reach the ground. All sound was muffled except my footsteps that thumped in my ears like the beat of my own heart. A long blind trip nowhere.

Still Don Anselmo is not back. When I asked, his *umile ancella* [his humble handmaiden] twitched with irritation. She is jealous; and I always thought holy water, not blood, coursed through her veins. I recommended she rest. She looked liverish and wizened, like a fig after its first day drying in the sun.

Nicola is curt, absentminded. He too feels he is being avoided. He has a new complaint, closely connected with his political rebirth: evolution should be taught in the schools. Substitution of one discontent for another may be effective. I am tempted to try it myself.

Ash Wednesday
19 February 1969

The not-so-humble *ancella* took her revenge on us both. Without a word she ushered me into Don Anselmo's study where, collarless and in his slippers, he sat over his breakfast. My arrival coincided with the disappearance of a very large bite of roll which, combined with my first question, choked him. It is my fate to burst in on his toilette or his breakfast. We had to wait and start all over again with my question: Who is Bruno Ferri? He did not answer directly. In fact, now that I think of it, he never did explain who Ferri might be more than "So they are buying up land together. Interesting! Yes, very interesting." He inspected my list of land sales, checked each name against my birth certificate names and then sat, thinking, sometimes looking at my lists, at others staring off over my head. When he had worked out his own ideas, he sighed. All he would say was that it helped. When I pressed him, for I understood and still for that matter understand nothing, he began to talk of a totally different tack he had been following, based on information he discovered several weeks ago. (The old fox never tells all he knows, of this I am sure.)

Sometime early last spring a peasant filed a complaint against Evangelista, charging carnal attack on his daughter. Subsequently the father requested the Carabinieri drop the charge in view of the fact that he had received "just compensation" (which, as Don Anselmo commented, seems unlikely). Officially the file was closed, but Don A. just to make sure, has talked to the man who admits he is not entirely satisfied. He hints that if certain affairs (unexplained) do not work out as he expects, he would be inclined to file another complaint against Evangelista. Unfortunately for our cause, the father's prime interest seems not to be justice, nor is he particularly devoted to his daughter. Don A. curses himself for being a cynic, but thinks the girl is probably still granting "favors" to Evangelista – with or without instructions from her father – with an eye toward marriage-blackmail. And so *his* tack came to nothing and my information, instead, seems to have suggested yet another approach to him. How much one has to know before life in San Basilio can make any sense.

Next fall the Regional Planning Commission is to approve the definitive plan for the amplification of San Basilio's public services — new schools, a hospital, a new town hall, etc. The site would be the plateau extending along the road east, that is, away from the villa. It is convenient, near existing sewers and power lines, and perhaps most important of all is already communal property. But last winter there were three massive landslides and the commission engineers have mapped a land fault which makes the land on the east not merely unsuitable for such concentrated building, but dangerous. Evangelista is a member of the commission's review committee, which has not yet been informed, officially, of the land fault and the necessity of purchasing a new site. However, Evangelista is also the legal representative (in a civil suit) and close friend of one of the reporting engineers, ergo . . . (Ergo, how does Don Anselmo know about the land fault? He was so persuasive I never thought of it until I wrote "ergo.")

The pieces do fit. With this one bit of special knowledge a man less intelligent than Evangelista could pick out the only other logical site — near the existing center, close to transportation and utilities. The land purchases spread, as they are, among so many individuals would hardly attract comment, much less legal investigation, and the parcel in his own name is so small he can claim it is a house site — very apt too for a man who is known to be bargaining for a wife.

We agreed we have gone as far as we can. Don Anselmo will request an appointment with the Bishop, even though we know he may consider the manipulation merely legitimate shrewdness.

This afternoon a note in my box said the archpriest would like to see me at my earliest convenience. Since we were to have tea with Aunt Giovanna, I assumed Don Anselmo wanted to tell me of the Bishop's reaction. Instead he delivered a gentle, personal and entirely clear lecture re the "unwisdom of particular attentions to one student." At first I did not understand. Favoritism has never been a problem for me. There has been talk about the help I gave Petrucci last term — a slow, pimply boy who wants desperately to pass and whose family has already gone into debt to send him to the Convitto. I have irritated my fellow professors who plump up their salaries with tutoring fees. Their insinuations are easy to imagine; compassion would be branded the lamest excuse. Blackmailed at every turn to do what the town with its rigid schedule of acceptable graft would approve of: *this* is immorality.

At tea Aunt Giovanna's subject was politics and such is her dominance that we pursued it until she was satisfied. Conclusions: none. Points of view: perhaps, illuminating.

Aunt Giovanna: Democracy is a silly form of government, giving, as it does, the power (to vote) to the incompetent and leaving them prey to the maneuvers of the most patently dishonest but agile of politicians. She approves of absolute monarchy, or failing that, benign dictatorship. "Under a royal agent San Basilio would be vastly different."

Uncle: Italy has a new patron saint – Sant'Anarchia. Communists would divide the land. Socialists advocate revolution when they have not learned to tie their shoelaces. The Church party has a fine program – privilege and graft as usual with the added sanction of a majority vote* of approval. Sant' Anarchia and her minions! No one talks of government, just division of spoils.

Don Anselmo: A Socialist – even one who does not know how to tie his shoelaces – has a virtue others lack: idealism. Why not temper it with the *arte del possibile?* Convince a young dreamer to exchange The World, which he does not know, for The Town, then The Province. A wise mentor, a disinterested one, could harness that zeal. An intriguing idea, no? More practical today, at least, than monarchy or anarchy.

The old resent what they see and would retrogress. Don Anselmo is a pragmatic idealist, but his stratagem would require time and assumes a docile candidate, or at least one

* This is a misstatement often repeated in good faith. The Christian Democratic party does consistently poll the largest single block of votes, but has not in the last ten years controlled more than 40 percent of the *total* Italian vote. [A.C.]

not overburdened with initiative and a docile community, waiting for the Political Messiah. People are cynical. They could not accept Utopia if it were offered, or if they did, it would be to corrupt it for their own advantage. Or am I the cynic? No matter. There is no time.

Of fifty-two million am I the only apolitical Italian?

This afternoon Don Anselmo came straight from the Bishop to me in the Archives. Rumors of Evangelista's little love affair have reached episcopal ears. He dismisses it for "youthful exuberance" (the fraud of public money received less attention). He orders Don Anselmo to see that the girl's father is kept quiet. Evangelista is to run for mayor on the Christian Democratic ticket! Don Anselmo is black with rage and the Crusade marches on.

It is late, but the sky is clear and the moon tips the roofs of San Basilio with silver. I am going for a walk. Discretion, reason, eternal life . . . nothing seems of much value in a world where everyone, even one of Christ's stewards, plays at deception.

Two months later

Nights were never meant for work. Warmed by joy I have walked every night in the last months, through rain, blizzard and fog. My days are half-remembered dreams. I wake with a start to find myself standing before my class. My sentence is lost, my thought knotted in a skein of memories. Faces are smooth as alabaster and as lifeless. I see them in a distant glow. I hear voices not at all. This then is joy. She accepted our meeting as fated. She was glad I had come, but would never have come to me. The hand that touched my arm was steady, but her voice trembled and then slipped into a whisper. We talk of ourselves as we are in this moment of time. Each discovery is a diamond to cut and polish, whose facets, as they deepen, mirror our similarity. We have struggled through different hells to the same conclusion. The unholy future we push off into the black of the night. Only the moment is real.

Nobis cum semel occidit brevis lux
Nox est perpetua una dormienda.

The second notebook ends abruptly with that quotation from Catullus's "Carmina": For us, when our brief light has set / There's the sleep of one everlasting night.

2

Longhand note written on a page of lined paper torn from a spiral notebook

I had almost finished my translation when Marina came in, ostensibly to return a book, apologizing for the lateness of the hour – it was nine o'clock. I thought at the time that it was an excuse, that she was lonely. I believe she saw the handwriting; she showed some curiosity, unusual for her, about what I was doing. I prattled vaguely about my "writing" and suggested a cup of tea which she considers very civilized, very English. In the kitchen she was astounded by the number of dishes I have and the design, which is nothing more than modern Faenza ceramic. Rather like the man confronted by a gallery of pictures who says "I know nothing about art, but I do *know what I like," she explained she has no "gift" for houses; she simply recognizes when they are attractive. An unfortunate mutation in female genes, she said, and went on to ask a lot of questions about why I had made certain changes in the house – cupboards and shelves, simple, obvious things. In the end it was easy enough to ask her what Marco Santoro was like, not that I really expected an answer. Often a direct question trips her evader mechanism. It is, I grant, the conditioned reflex, now beyond conscious control, of a very private person. Especially if an evaluation rather than a factual answer is required of her, that moment of rejection which borders on panic, betrays her into puzzling, illogical solutions. Some are more revealing than she imagines. Once Nicola Benevento asked her if she did not think the local bus schedules were scandalously inconvenient: she denied* any *knowledge of them. To my entirely casual question, Would she like to have grown up in a large family with brothers and sisters? (some only children long for nothing so much) she flushed and seemed about to snub me with total silence. Then: "When my mother married my father, my grandparents disinherited her." So Marina's answers are never precharted. At best I expected a bland comment about Marco Santoro: she gave me, instead, double psychoanalysis.*

Marina says Marco Santoro was a good teacher because he was a hopeful man. Did not believe in the rigid human geometry of southern life. Resignation is not axiomatic; it survives in a climate of enforced ignorance. Apparently he argued that every caged animal, every imprisoned man is driven by a desire to escape. He will have at least one chance, and he must have the courage (and the knowledge) to take it.

She, on the other hand, sees the human being not as longing to get out, but as longing to get in — the old idea of a womb with a view — into a profession, a class to which he does not belong, an advantageous marriage. Her pessimism comes, perhaps, from too many civil service exams where she was one of sixteen thousand applicants competing for sixty posts.

I cannot reconcile "a hopeful man" with one who writes, "Only the moment is real" or, "For us, when our brief light has set, there's the sleep of one everlasting night."

3

My diary on yellow paper

Inspired by Marco Santoro's success with the registry offices, I decided to woo the land clerk. Nothing has changed there; the tanbark of cigarettes may be deeper, the air fustier, but the official scrivener is still kind and lonely and so, talkative. My concern for the deed transfer of my house he interpreted as an example of the "moral rectitude" for which "my world" is so well known. I was ashamed of myself, but pressed on with my historical double-talk: I must be the first new owner of that land in some two hundred years. Poor man! He blusters with his own importance, never expecting to be taken seriously. The flattery of acceptance at his own evaluation was too much for him. Two entries of interest resulted: one, dated 5 September 1969, shows Ferri's purchase of the land next to my cliff from the estate of a man who died in Buffalo; the other, dated 11 September 1969, shows that Ferdinando Sanseverino transferred the long fertile slope below my house to Carlo Benevento, Nicola's father.

Ferri's purchase was a week after the announcement of the Regional Planning Commission's findings – therefore an independent investment? It would seem that *l'appetito viene mangiando.*

Don Ferdinando's transfer suggests that he bothered to cultivate a source of information, but he would be more careful than Ferri. He does not share his secrets with his wife. Or does he?

SIX

I

The Festa

The Basilisks, perhaps all Lucanians, are pessimists in the dictionary sense: for them reality *is* evil. Slowly I have realized that the old saw "sufficient unto the day . . ." holds no comfort for them. Such evasion is folly. With the specter of confiscation of their worldly possessions always before them, they struggle through one day, dreading the trials which will, inevitably, haunt the next. Spring sees them praying for rain. If it comes, they pray all the gods to stop it before the hillsides wash away. How often I have seen tired, dejected men standing, looking out across their fields in a trance of frustration. Fall torrents washed the seed into swales where tender shoots now luxuriate; the high spots are sparse and ragged. Each square inch of dirt is so precious. They weed it as others weed floral borders, scratching the dirt free with a hoe, pulling up poppies that nod gaily amid wheat stalks and building a small protective mound around each plant. This year's yield will not even equal last year's. As the ears swell and turn yellow the Lucanians are deaf to the hiss of the wind through the reedy, black beards protecting the kernels, to the one wistful note like the dying tone of a pitchfork. Instead they watch the sky for hail. Finally they cut the wheat, stack it in sheaves to dry, and puzzle over last night's gossip. They will be too late for threshing. They need more help. But if the rumor is right, if the price of grain is due to fall, then they cannot pay an extra day's wage. Finally, for better or worse, the harvest is in and these people who would have no truck with the frivolous summer saints are now ready for their Festa. It would seem to be the joyous end to struggle, but somehow it is not.

The harvest is the annual disappointment; once again evil has won, the peasant has lost, and what should have been a celebration turns into a wrestling match between fiscal conscience and that human urge to be slightly improvident, but happy. The winter's debts must be paid first and they are. What is left could be swallowed a hundred times for essentials. Men who live with fear and women who yearn for a bit of the modern world have a hard time, together, defining vital expenses. The yeast of enthusiasm is short-lived. Squabbles become disagreements and gradually slip into sullen resentment. Still, the very presence of the Festa requires new clothes, sweets, shoes, always shoes, for every member of the family. The women hustle about with the stiff somber faces of wax statues; the men stand silent and disgruntled in the Piazza, each aware that there is no pristine right, only two evil realities. Each obstinately refuses to recognize the other's reality.

The sulky truce is broken by the arrival of market trucks with sawhorses and planks stored on their roofs and within a profusion of third-rate goods for first-rate prices. In the jumble and crash of setting up there is a certain order. These are peddlers on a regular circuit. They know the town, have their month-to-month arrangements with shopkeepers for a light line and, use of a toilet, and they even remember which boys of the crowd that gathers might appropriate wares left untended. And, of course, they know each other and watch each other with the gimlet eyes of comparison shoppers. They are helped by a semi-incestuous relationship: knife dealers come from Campobasso, shoe merchants from the Marche and old-clothes vendors from Naples. The members of each category compete constantly and exclusively with each other. A woman intent on buying a sharp knife may find herself in the cross fire of a feud carried on with scrupulous venom, but started so many years ago by fathers and uncles that the cause has been forever lost in a jungle of political differences, courtships gone wrong and imagined slanders. If she could hesitate and ponder with judicious uncertainty, she might arrange a real bargain. The chances are against it. The vendors may loathe each other, but are true anglers; they cannot bear to see a fish get away. One withdraws with the tacit understanding that the next "fish" is his. The woman, too suffocated by the trauma of investment to be aware of these silent machinations, is left to deal with one man. Only later, if at all, does she realize the advantage she had and did not use.

Noise stupefies, creating a sense of unbearable, almost hysterical urgency. From a food stand a man with a microphone at his throat rasps out a spiel about tuna fish and salami, salami and tuna fish, over and over again until a mystic connection between the two is established. The fat lady with the young face who carries a parrot in a cage screams, "Fortunes! Fortunes, ten lire! Let Franchino pick your fortune from the drawer!" Franchino looks fiercely intelligent and pecks at passersby. He frightens children. They scream and run away only to collide with a woman carrying a pile of aluminum pots. Crash. Down the way the antiharmonies of local songs, which must be Greek-Arab in origin, screech forth from a loudspeaker just visible on the top of a car. Gioachino, the record seller, is always around in his antique Lancia with dimpled fenders that flap as the vehicle crabs ponderously along the road. He tours nearby towns slowly – very slowly – hawking the little black disks everyone wants even if they have no player. Then each night he comes back to San Basilio so dazed from the clamor of his own product that he can hardly unfold himself from the front seat and limp home to bed. "Peanuts! Peanuts!" yowls the town drunk from behind his stand. His eyes are red and his moustache droops, fitting neatly into the deep grooves that run from his nose to his mouth. His is the face of a defeated man; his voice cracks under the strain of joy. "Peanuts! Everybody needs peanuts!" A child blows a plastic horn. The coppersmith draws attention to his wares by pounding on a cauldron with a wooden spoon, and a woman trailing five children of varying ages and sexes wanders up to a shoe counter a little too casually.

The vendor has watched her pass, has pretended not to see her, and now has just the right shoes ready for her to feel, smell, turn over and bargain for. He waits to be approached. She screams over the din; he pretends not to understand. Soon all five children are sitting in a row on a plank. Each is being fitted with white shoes, soft perforated summer shoes. Mother makes a sign she will be right back and goes off looking for her husband.

He comes with her reluctantly, his eyes veiled. He too pretends not to hear what she shouts in his ear, but finally grumbles, "Only Maria gets white ones!" Maria is the baby with the large brown eyes and the dirty nose – Father's favorite. But the sight of his brood, their faces flushed, their eyes fixed, disbelieving, on the white shoes, confuses him, makes him hang back and finally turn away to the neighbor stall where dozens of pairs of pants dangle from the awning rod. He fingers them idly to have something to do, an excuse not to be the one who says no to those five hopeful children. He is attracted by a black and white check: the material is light, too light for work pants, but there is something about the pattern. Probably not the right size. He speaks to a boy almost hidden behind the counter, who is very busy with a chunk of salami wedged into a roll as large as a loaf of bread. He goes on chewing, but motions the man to take down the trousers. They are the right size after all. He smiles at the checks, then holds the pants up to his waist. The legs trail away over his shoes and on out in front of him: extra material is always good for patches, he thinks. Want a pair like these someday, but . . . He turns to see his wife trying on shoes for herself. A pair of lace oxfords with thin rubber soles and low but spiky heels – a compromise between elegance and utility. The children, wearing the white perforated shoes that will not survive the first heavy rain, are playing tag among the stacks of boxes. Father is resigned. He buys the trousers and the dam is broken.

In the end everyone has clothes, Festa clothes. For the boys, flannel pants; for the girls, jumpers; for Mother, a skirt — all made of reworked wool, intended for cheap blankets, which with the first washing will become harsh and greasy-feeling and will somehow stay wrinkled no matter how long it is pressed. Father buys himself a white nylon shirt and nylon shirts for the boys, blouses for the girls. Nylon is the thing now. Everyone comes back from Germany with nylon shirts — no matter that it will seal them in as airlessly as Saran wrap. For his wife he buys a maroon lacework sweater labeled Dry Clean Only, but since she cannot read and there is no dry cleaner anyway, it is destined to shrink to child-size on its first trip to the washtub. Maria, who wants a green plastic saxophone and has been told no, sits down in the middle of the road and howls. A truck, loaded with sheep bound for the animal fair, almost runs over her. The driver trumpets on his horn and swears at the entire population of San Basilio until Father scoops Maria up in his arms and darts back into the crowd. She wails with fright. To comfort her he buys her the green plastic saxophone, which she blasts in his ear until he cannot resist the temptation of a pair of decent shoes. He had halfway promised himself new work boots this year. Instead he buys black, pointed shoes with highly polished cardboard uppers. They pinch almost immediately and later burn with a satanic fire that makes him eye the rich men who amble about the Piazza and wonder if this is a torture they suffer every day.

Before they start home they are exhausted. Packages slip and slide from under their arms. The children are whiny and smeared with dirt and candy. One is sick all over the back of a policeman's trousers. Too much money has been spent and tempers are short. Then suddenly in front of them looms an enormous buslike vehicle with glass sides that reveal a collection of glistening stoves, refrigerators, and strangely enough, motorcycles. "Step inside, step right inside," urges a hoarse northern voice through a loudspeaker. "Free admission to all the good citizens of . . ." Long pause. "To all the good citizens of San Basilio," the voice continues, but the citizens hang back. As they say of themselves they are diffident – not shy, but distrustful of a world that is not their own, and also, I suspect, of their own ability to resist the lure of that world. They gawk, their eyes wide open, unblinking as though the flick of a second would see the mirage disappear. They look very small and meek and ragged standing there, these Charlie Chaplins of the mountains. Then they turn away and with a quick impatient jerk of the hand signal the others in the family to follow them. They are going home.

That evening, after supper, Father goes to the Piazza dressed in his new finery – the shoes that pinch, the shirt that makes him sweat and the checked trousers that, hurriedly turned up and still a bit too long, lie crumpled on the tops of his shoes. His friends sport their new clothes with the same mute depression. They stand together, thinking their sour thoughts, but saying nothing. Eventually they drift off to a wine shop where they drink a carafe of sour black wine and grumble about the weather, the harvest, the cost of clothes, especially shoes, and even about their wives who are, at that very moment, busily swapping half-lies with the neighbors about how much they paid for their purchases. Strange that these men and women who are so uneasy with numbers and have no knowledge of printed words are each born with a mental abacus as efficient as a computer, that records quotients for veracity, probability, pride, rumor – all the variables of personality which time and proximity reveal – and tabulates the data of the given situation into a faultless estimate of the truth. Efforts to deceive inform, and by the end of the evening each, in his own way, has realized that he is neither better nor worse off than the others. The poor do not sympathize with each other; they stand alone, and alone and silent they go off to bed to awake next morning still depressed by the sour truths of the day before.

Small wonder the Festa is more a rite than a rollicking celebration.

2

Letter from Gabriella Brancati to A.C.

Strictly speaking this letter is not one of the pieces of my puzzle, but since Gabriella insists, against her own will, on becoming part of the story, I hated to leave out her snappish evaluations of Protestants and other European Catholics. She knows only too well that, if the subject were Italy, they would return them with double vitriol. I myself was both chastened and encouraged. In any case my notes on the Madonna delle Liberate, which I sent her and which follow, had to be included. Neither she nor anyone else would know who the Madonna delle Liberate is and the regular tourney of events which makes up the celebration of her feast day is bewildering to a non-Basilisk and yet vital to the reconstruction of what happened.

Santa Caterina in Val Gardena
15 September 1969

Ann –

Your Teresa, sweet and pathetic though she may be, hardly strikes me as the perfect servant. And all that squeaking! Would it strain your Principles of Social Development too much to buy her another pair of shoes?

I can hear the rumblings of your imagination all the way up

here, so you must be, once more, at work. What are you up to with all those Saints and *who* is the Madonna delle Liberate? (Of course I do not really mean *who*. Even in Lucania, She must be the Blessed Virgin.) The question is who (or maybe what?) was freed? No, I have no idea what a fourteen-year-old boy thinks the Madonna of the Seven Veils is (but fourteen-year-olds are remarkably silly, anyway) nor did I know that Sant'Antonio Abbate was both protector of animals *and* Patron Saint of Butchers, and I see no reason why San Giuseppe of Copertino should not be Patron Saint of Aviators. You might be less amused had it been you, rather than the Duchess of Something or other, he grabbed up for his flights over the altar. Long before Luther, the Waldensians decided they did not approve – and without strident Reformation trumpetings either. If *we* have too many saints, you suffer from the most appalling proliferation of sects. Once in Detroit or Denver (no, maybe Atlanta) I amused myself with the telephone book and counted forty-four different Christian denominations, some with macabre names. You have talked about chicken dinners at Father Divine's and those others, the Rolling Holies, were they?

I am no hagiographer, but it occurs to me there is a strong similarity between the national character of a country and the character of the saints it produces. If you like, our saints have a family or group quality about them. How many alliterative brothers and sisters cleaved unto each other! How many brothers unto brothers! And the foiled romances! Think about it. Quite different from those austere German saints, very blond and handsome they must have been, with their unpronounceable names straight from *Das Rheingold*. I would be the last to doubt that their lives were determined, joyless struggles against the evils of sin, heresy and climate. Have you ever heard of a Greek saint who did not sound like a close friend of Plato's? Years ago, when I was a houseguest in Spain, I remember a festa in honor of an exotic saint – St. Cucufatis, it was – entirely suitable to a nation of proud, silent men who dance or die with equal grace. And remember

St. Bridget, that determined Swedish widow, who turned herself into an international advisor. I am not sure I believe she always won her fight against the Devil (In my experience, Swedish ladies sometimes do not) but she did give the Popes wise counsel, which, being Italian, they did not follow, and ended her days working for the poor of a city not even her own. The French I do not pretend to understand, and so we are left with the English. Yes, the English. Well, let's take St. Ursula and her eleven thousand virgins* who journeyed all the way "out," as the English say, to Rome, only to drown on their way back, all eleven thousand and one, in the Cologne harbor. The English have been coming "out" ever since!

You see, my dear, it is easy enough to laugh, but in the final analysis saints have offered comfort and intercession, whereas your eternal schisms, divisions, quarrels, preachments and rearrangements of theology have led to just that — more divisions, uncertainty and anguish.

Guido sends his love and I will, undoubtedly, join him after a few short prayers for Christian Unity.

Gabriella

* Now sadly discredited. [A.C.]

3

A Note on the Madonna and Santa Liberata

The Madonna delle Liberate is an ambiguous name which some authorities, the less conscientious, have taken at face value – the Madonna of the Freed Women – and upon that frail foundation have built a touching myth of timid southern women, dragged by the hair of their heads to the harems of the East by those cruel, orgiastic conquerors the Turks. The date of the Festa, October 7, has added to the confusion, for, though it is now listed in church calendars as Our Lady of the Rosary, it was originally designated Our Lady of Victory after the Christian rout of the Turks in the Battle of Lepanto in 1571. Dramatic it might be to identify the Liberate as the Sabine women of the Christian world, but no Basilisk will ever believe it. The Madonna is, and will remain, the Blessed Virgin of the Liberate, the followers of Santa Liberata.

The disparity between what the learned scholar knows to be false and what human beings insist on believing has turned more than one sage a touch bilious. The Reverend Alban Butler, for instance, is frosty with scorn and disbelief, but his account of Santa Liberata will do much to explain the situation.

"Her story [that is, Santa Liberata's] is a curiosity of hagiology and is hardly worth including in a collection of lives of the saints but for the fact that it has the unenviable distinction of being one of the most obviously false and preposterous of the pseudo-pious romances by which simple Christians have been deceived or regaled."* Having made clear where he stands, he goes on to tell the story. Santa Liberata was one of seven (or eight or even nine, depending on the authority) children born in one single and unique birth to the wife of a pagan king of Portugal. From a different source I find that the royal father was so distressed by this plethora of princesses that their mother was forced to entrust them to wet nurses who promised to love and care for them and who were, incidentally, Christian. When Liberata was grown (and also Christian) her father decided to marry her off to the king of Sicily. A king who had managed to barter one of his seven (eight or nine) daughters for diplomatic advantage did not expect her to object: she had only to obey. Liberata would have none of it. She had made a vow of virginity. Such vows were the only weapons daughters had against ambitious fathers and so were much in vogue. Undoubtedly Liberata's father railed and ranted against Christianity, this pernicious religion, this new ethic which threatened to undermine all human society with its liberalistic ways. Self-determination, freedom to worship? What did they mean? They wanted to loaf without responsibility, to fritter their days away while the world crumbled around them, that was what they wanted. While he raged on, Liberata prayed for divine help and it came in a rather disconcerting form: a full beard and moustache bristled on her tender, childish face. The king of Sicily, gallant though he may have been, did not fancy a bearded wife and decided to marry elsewhere. Liberata's father could think of no better revenge than the crucifixion of his daughter.

Such is the story of Santa Liberata who, in spite of the skeptical Butlers, has established herself in the hearts of the women of Germany, England, France and Italy as the patron saint of women bedeviled by troublesome husbands. The few

* Rev. Alban Butler, *Butler's Lives of the Saints,* originally published in 1757–59. Modern edition edited and supplemented by Herbert Thurston, S.J., and Donald Attwater. London: Burns Oates, & Washbourne Ltd, 1956. Vol. III, p. 151.

saints who care for the frustrations of women are all but impervious to attack by hagiographers or bishops. Women will have their comfort and succor, and the women of San Basilio are no less determined than others. The Madonna is the Madonna of the followers of Santa Liberata. She offers them her special protection; they honor her on the seventh of October.

Saints, like mothers-in-law, are always around and the Basilisks treat them accordingly. Sometimes they curse them, sometimes they praise them, usually they leave them to their own devices in a dark corner, but should they suddenly become aware of them, their first instinct is to take them out for a breath of fresh air. Outsiders are confused by the sight of Christ, borne aloft on a platform, wobbling and jerking down a side alley on a not very particular Tuesday afternoon. He is "out for a walk," and the men accompanying Him will explain very matter of factly that He was tired of that dark, musty cathedral and needed a bit of air. Didn't you too, every so often? It has been a long time since He visited Santa Tecla dei Lombardi, so they just thought they would take Him along to see her.

They intend no sacrilege. Saints *should* have fresh air and since they were once human, they must also miss their friends. Sant'Anna calls on Sant'Antonio: as both are specialists at finding lost objects, they are assumed to have much in common. San Giovanni Battista is forever dropping in on San Pancrazio, and San Rocco with his dog has even wandered down the main road to call on the Madonna of the Swamps, although the logistics involved are too complex to make a spur-of-the-moment excursion feasible. The Madonna of the Liberate is not to be excluded from this round of visits. During the week before the Festa she spends one day of residence in each of the important parish churches of San Basilio. Each day toward sunset she leaves the church, accompanied by her host-saint and slowly proceeds to her next parish. Roughly halfway between the two, her new host comes to meet her and her former host retires with as good grace as he can muster.

Courtesy is the order of the day. No one wants to repeat the unholy incident of several years ago when, aroused by wine and an exchange of blasphemous insults, the various coteries abandoned their saints to bobble and bounce and had at each other. Two men ended up in the hospital and San Giovanni Battista lost his head – literally lost it. As a temporary first-aid measure it was replaced by a disused San Giorgio, which had been collecting dust in the cathedral sacristy for years, but, what with the helmet, earpieces and plumes, the effect was not quite the same.

Before she is allowed out for her peregrinations, the Madonna is carefully refurbished. Her crown is dusted and the minute lights of her halo checked and replaced along with any suspiciously ragged cord. Her gentle, flushed plaster face is dusted with a toothbrush. Her draperies of shimmering silk are taken away and laundered (I have often wondered where she is left to shiver in her chemise), and the gold filigree chain necklaces that drape lower and lower until they almost touch her slipper tops are polished. When she is finally ready to saunter into the world, the *Orchestrina* (for the real orchestra from Foggia does not arrive until the day before the Festa) tootles the procession down the tunnel streets where, in honor of her passage, rugs and bedspreads flap from every window.

The morning after her triumphant arrival mass is said and at each of the seven parishes a dwarf figure, dressed like the Madonna, with a miniature halo and holding a sheaf of grain tight under her chin, achieving the effect of a beard if not the actual fact, is placed in a socket at the Madonna's feet. The insertion of the parish handmaiden, the lighting of her halo, is the sign for the neighborhood celebrations to begin. No two are alike. At one a tall, greased pole is set up with a chicken, a haughty pigeon, a flask of wine and a faintly obscene, testiculate cheese tied at the top as prizes for the man who can shinny all the way up to claim them. It takes most of the day and demijohns of wine, but no matter who wins everyone will enjoy the suspense. Another parish, Santa Zita's, specializes in fireworks which are watched with ghoulish expectation by the whole town. The record is not uniform, but in the last twenty-five years three have been galvanic in quality. Perhaps the most remarkable thing about them is that they were all planned by the same man, a local peasant, who fancies himself a pyrotechnical expert. He is an artist: he designs; execution he leaves to a platoon of his own dim-witted children who work full-time in an old lambing shed, filling the canisters and preparing the fuses specified by the master. Occasional misinterpretations of the plan are violent.

The first incident occurred when a deposit of extra rockets and roman candles, hidden in the unfinished dormitory annex of the police station, ignited, scattering plaster and pale, terrified Carabinieri in all directions. Another year a defective fuse started a bush fire that raged for hours, destroying a gypsy encampment and frightening the aged cows in the slaughter-house pens to a matronly stampede. Not illogically the third disaster has given substance to the rumor that the world will come to an end some year during the Madonna's visit to Santa Zita. No one is sure exactly how it happened, but the most probable explanation is a powder drum that leaked as it was rolled from the fireworks shed down the hillside, across the valley and up to the clearing under the church. As the first small red, white and green rockets popped off in the sky, a sputtering trail of smoke puffed off down the hill. No one paid any attention. More rockets and then suddenly an explosion that was reported by the Bari seismograph service as a force-three earthquake. The fireworks "factory" had exploded and continued to do so for several hours to the delight of the entire population of San Basilio. There was talk of the Fire Department, but when, after forty minutes of static, the telephone operator got through to Matera, it was discovered that the provincial fire truck was in Valsinni, flushing out sewers, which was as well since there was no water in San Basilio that day.

The Madonna's itinerary is carefully planned to end on the seventh day at the church of San Giovanni Battista, the same San Giovanni who lost his head. It is several miles from town, too far for human bearers to haul her, so tottering but undaunted she returns to the Piazza by truck. The radiator and half of the windshield are obscured by a lace tablecloth and the sides, which are lowered, are draped with crepe paper and garlanded with lurid synthetic flowers, but in spite of this forest of adornments, her litter is still very much a royal blue, double-axle truck with a pair of identical stencils on the cab doors: a swivel-jointed hula girl and a leering tiger with the slogan "Put me in your tank!"

No one objects or senses any anachronism because the special feature of the Madonna's visit to San Giovanni is the blessing of all forms of transport that fall in the rough category of *vetture* – vehicles – donkeys, mules, horses, scooters, bicycles, motorcycles, buses, cars, homemade sledges of a plank with roller bearings for wheels and even dog-drawn bath chairs. After heated discussion tractors have been excluded. The *vetture* tangle in a monumental traffic jam close to the church and the babel of the drivers' most unchristian comments about each other's antecedents adds a touch of noisy gaiety that would warm the hearts of travel writers. To create the illusion of pilgrimage, the truck is parked down the road, behind the first curve, where it can be free of the melee. San Giovanni cannot be slighted. He must have his chance to escort the Madonna from the church and down the road just as all the other saints have done. Once she is settled for her ride, the vehicles jockey for position behind and slowly the procession rolls down the road with horns honking and bells ringing toward the Piazza and the final high mass that marks the real beginning of the Festa.

4

My diary on yellow paper

October 3, 1969

Lately my days have started with the tootling tarum-pum-pum of a religious tattoo played quite independently, but with great flourish by the *Orchestrina* – a clarinet, a piccolo and a snare drum. Teresa says so much attention means I made too large a contribution to the Festa committee. She may be right, but I maintain they come for the coffee she provides. Whatever the reason, I am sure this is not as the town fathers planned it. They must have imagined the piazzas, courtyards and streets echoing at twilight with the sweet tinkle of music and the resulting shower of coins, for that is the *Orchestrina*'s job – to raise money. Instead our three musicians perform on their own erratic schedule, which includes my house between 7:00 and 7:30 A.M. The drummer is the smallest, thinnest, most flap-eared member of a family which has, for centuries, passed on its right to sweep the streets as though it were a hereditary office. He makes up in verve what he lacks in experience – that is, in his music; he wastes neither on sweeping the streets. The piccolo is a policeman; the clarinet, a janitor at the grade school, where thousands of children have assumed that in all schools dictation is accompanied by the mournful squeaks and shrills of a state employee, sitting in a broom closet, teaching himself "The Triumphal March" from *Aïda.* They are not a trio. They are three stubborn soloists, each so intent on getting in all his notes that harmony is an accident, a very occasional one. Time and practice (or resignation) draw them each day closer together. Undoubtedly when the Madonna makes her parish debut in the Festa, they will finish in a respectable dead heat as they have in other years. In the meantime, every morning they warm up below my bedroom window and then settle down to coffee and biscuits in my kitchen.

The attentions of Don Mela, our sometime parish priest, are quite another matter and are more related to his own insecurity than to my contribution or Teresa's catering. He has called every day now for a week, first to remind me that I must come when the Madonna visits San Giovanni Battista. He emphasizes that I, as the most important member of the parish (there cannot be more than twelve of us in all), must set an example. The second visit was to prompt me: I must not forget to bring my car for the Bishop's blessing. The third, to remind me of my promise of flowers. Don Mela spends his life flitting from place to place, reminding people of duties they immediately forget. He is the perennial substitute in parishes without resident priests. He teaches catechism in the schools, is always the "other priest" on church outings, he visits the old and the ill, but still no one takes him seriously. There is something ludicrous about his personality in his body. He is very meek and earnest and has never been known to recognize the broadest witticism. He explains and explains in his high nasal voice, then re-explains to puzzled-looking people who have long since stopped listening. He is very small and thin and hunched with only a few tufts of wiry, blond-white hair that waver around his head like the fluff of a dandelion going to seed. When he is upset or confused, he flaps about and a lumpy protuberance of bone midway on his overlarge nose flushes bright red, so his nickname is, of course, Don Pulcinello, for Punch in *Punch and Judy.* He is so absorbed in remembering to remind others of those duties they are determined to forget that he has never actually identified who it is people call Don Punch.

He came again this morning to make sure I had not forgotten about the flowers for the altar. He is afraid there will be too few and I cannot tell him why I know there will be too many. He would think it sacrilegious. Sabato has challenged the cemetery keeper to produce as many and as beautiful flowers as are to come from my garden. For reasons I have not quite grasped, this is a question of *my* honor. Chiding Sabato is useless. He is hurt, or pretends to be, by my failure to understand his intentions, which were only to enhance my general reputation. His face is so doggedly blank that I cannot decide whether he is serious or secretly enjoying a tremendous joke.

Again this morning he has worked one of his solemn tricks on me. I sent Teresa off with Don Mela to clean the church (or anything else he might want done so long as she did not allow him to come back here), and to be doubly safe, I told Sabato to stay near the gate and ward off anyone who thought of coming in to chat. He did until Don Anselmo applied for admittance, but it seems he amused himself talking to passersby: Sad, sad day! He must leave his job. After all, it is hardly worth his time at only 160,000 lire a month (a neat sixteen times what he is paid). He hates to give it up. I am such a nice lady, but of course . . . Don Anselmo caught him at it. By tomorrow every man in town will be a self-declared gardener for that wage, and I will need a personnel officer to drive them off. Don Anselmo was amused. Recently he heard *voci* in town that my father is very rich and when I fell in love with a fortune hunter, he exiled me with the promise of a lavish monthly income for as long as I stayed out of America. Sabato has made me a remittance woman! When I scolded him, he gave me a little smile and drifted away. Now he has come to ask that I inspect his afternoon's work: he has cleared one patch of acanthus, *mirabile dictu*. Sabato's first concession-apology.

And this seemed such a peaceful place.

5

I can no more imagine Don Anselmo Lanfranchi in his bathrobe and slippers than I can imagine him speckled with *caffellatte* or blobs of spaghetti sauce, which, lightly dusted with talc and forgotten, convert the cassocks of many priests into almanacs of meals consumed. He, like the master actor who becomes the character he plays, has forfeited the offstage existence of a private man. Every situation in which he allows himself to be involved, he controls, or so it seems. His visit to me that morning was a singular honor; its purpose, for of course there was one, was handsomely landscaped with gossip, admiration of the house, and random excursions into the apparently unrelated byways of human experience. He understands the elliptic wiles of monologue and slips with easy humor from one subject to another, until I felt, as I am sure I was supposed to, that he and I are amused and touched by the same things. All the while those silver eyes that are so haunted with the melancholy of the brown eye, watched me. We both knew he had come about the land, but he is by instinct cautious and I, unhelpful, so the afternoon threatened to slip away in charming circumambulations through his youth, Rome of another day, and finally, gently, to San Basilio.

He was born in Rome early in this century when, as he put

it, that city had its last great period – after the sheep were driven from the very steps of Santa Maria Maggiore and before the thunderous invasion of the automobile. He grew up in a family house with the comforts and casual affection a large staff of servants could provide. He hardly remembers his mother. Contessa Lanfranchi was gentle, absentminded and could always be counted on for a marrons glacés. After her death the house seemed cold and gloomy to him. Everyone was too busy for children. As Don Anselmo said, it might have been a lonely childhood for him, had he not come to San Basilio one summer so many, many years ago. Could I imagine what it had meant for a boy to find someone who was enchanted by his adventures and who comforted him in his moments of heartbreak, who loved him, as a mother loves a son? If I could, then I would understand his devotion to Giovanna Sanseverino and would forgive his interference in an affair which, on the surface of it, was not his concern.

At last he had reached the point. I robbed him of the pleasure of further exposition, which for the Basilisks is in itself a baroque art form, by showing him my notes on the land transfers. I must have been brusque, or at least less *dolce;* he stiffened visibly and pursed his lips more at me than at the notes, but he listened to my questions.

1. If Don Ferdinando is unwilling to sell, why not lease the land, as usual, or even let it lie fallow?

2. Whoever owns the land now, what does he/they expect to do with it?

3. What plans could be made without my permission for an easement, and why had no one asked me directly?

The answers were simple enough. The transfer to Don Carlo Benevento had been exactly what I thought – a non-financial evasion to frustrate Ferri, one which, except for Don Carlo's sudden death, would have worked very well. The proper price for the land could have been extracted from Ferri and the money passed on to Don Ferdinando without the complication of blackmail. Now, technically, the land belongs to Nicola Benevento, who, I was told, would join us later to add his more extensive explanations.

My first question Don Anselmo treated as a prime example of absurd feminine innocence. The land can neither be leased nor lie fallow. The first whispers of Ferri's blackmail campaign will be warning enough that *aria di vendetta* is circulating. No peasant would lease the land for fear of reprisals, burned crops and worse. To leave it fallow is to transfer it to Ferri. He would annex it without a by-your-leave.

The easement remains embarrassing. They cannot say it, but they assumed I would do whatever they asked and only now realize they have been less than courteous.

It is a matter of principle . . . it seems. The Sanseverinos are adamant: they will not be threatened or blackmailed, so they temporize, asking me to lie to Ferri! Uffa! My exasperation made Don Anselmo laugh. We both laughed. The idiotic complications of the whole situation. Surely it makes sense to no one, not even to Don Anselmo who will not comment beyond a wry statement that intrigue at one remove is most uncomfortable. And nothing would he say about the blackmail issue, though I conclude that he does take it seriously and must know what the threat is.

In retrospect I am glad we had so long together in peace, because the rest of the afternoon was tragicomedy no scriptwriter could invent.

Nicola Benevento arrived full of brio and not-so-amusing remarks about the miracles rich Americans work on decayed Italian property. The witticism of an unreconstructed Fascist, I told him. Then we both apologized. He had brought Marina with him "to read in the garden" while we talked. She, in a spasm of pseudogentility, refused to come in for fear of intruding. She stood just inside the door, very tall and stiff in the ubiquitous gray suit (made less drab, for once, by a turquoise chiffon scarf tied in a band around her head). She was ready to bolt. Don Anselmo said very quietly that they had never met and introduced himself. Only a slight change in her eyes, the fractional lowering of the lids, convinced me she had heard him. For what seemed fully two minutes she said nothing while she inspected him with leisurely detachment that bordered on insult. Her acknowledgment, when it came, was terse. "We both know *of* each other, however." "San Basilio sees to that," was his calm reply. Threat countered by shrug? Challenge by retreat? I hardly know, but I felt, somehow, a crisis had been averted and now cannot imagine why. Neither offered to shake hands: most un-Italian.

Don Anselmo resigned from further land discussions, leaving Nicola to pick his way through my nods and silences. If Don Anselmo tried to make the simple complex, Nicola reversed the process. Nothing could shake his air of guileless consultation. He was sure I would understand, would agree that he had a moral duty to carry out his father's obligations, which included the acceptance of the title to the land below my house. He had found, and once more he was sure I would agree, the Ideal Tenant-Purchaser. A man of good reputation who had worked for Don Carlo, whose father had in turn worked for Don Carlo's father. An unusual man, solid, dependable, no debts, unmarried – no children to bother me. When this paean of generalities seemed destined for a second verse, I asked the man's name, and it was none other than Rocco Di Luca, who was even then stringing wire on my new fence posts.

Since he was already a vital part of this arrangement, I insisted we bring Di Luca in to join the discussion. Had Nicola realized how irritable, how condescending he sounded with Di Luca, he would have been shocked. I was. He spoke as his father and grandfather must have spoken to peasants, intending no insult, but implying, all the same, that the man before him had better state his case, his defense, quickly and without the usual number of lies and excuses. At first Di Luca stood hunched over and oddly subservient with his head down and his knotty hands closed tightly on his cap, but he could not in the end accept Nicola's tone. He fixed him with a stare of such violent yet strangely impersonal contempt that he swept aside not only his immediate target, but the entire class he represented. He took matters step by step, very deftly separating Nicola's jurisdiction from mine. He would discuss the sale contract with Nicola, the easement with me. A good lesson for a budding Socialist. Don Anselmo smiled absently at the ceiling and asked me for a cigarette. He had decided to ruin his liver, and incidentally hide his amusement.

Di Luca and I have struck a bargain. He may come through my garden in exchange for caretaker service when I am away. It seems advantageous to us both. His tone with me was so amiable that I was surprised to hear him snipe at Nicola with a remark about lowering the sale price in view of the fact that he was paying me for the easement.

Whatever it might have led to was interrupted by heavy thuddings in the garden and a banshee wail worthy of bloodthirsty cinema Indians. A wave of gravel splattered against the windowpanes and swirled in through the open door to bounce and careen around on the tiles. Slowly the outline of a horse, a gray horse, took shape in the doorway. He stretched his neck until his head was well inside the door, inspected us with wonderously mournful brown eyes and then sneezed full in our faces. Not illogically we backed away from the door, an abrupt gesture he seemed to resent. Seeing that we would not join him in the garden, he began to grope tentatively with a hoof on the stone threshold in preparation for joining us in the sitting room. We flew into action. This particular gray horse, Otello by name, is known to everyone: he is the faithful steed and devoted companion of the town eccentric, Don Serafino La Vista.

Every town has an eccentric. If fortune smiles, he is a recluse; if not, then he will be some form of Don Serafino — omnipresent, garrulous, a fey obstacle to the course of every normal day. Tall and gaunt with the face of an aged Byzantine Christus whose features have drooped with the passing years and whose hair has been reduced to a limp white moustache and a feathery ruching around a bald dome, Don Serafino patrols the streets with his horse, looking for excitement. And something always happens, though whether he simply arrives in time for the event or whether his presence creates it has never been established. He cannot tolerate boredom. When desperate he has been known to whip the placid

Otello into a frenzy and then carom down the narrowest alleys at a full gallop, spraying mothers, children, stools and chickens in all directions. This was, in fact, how he made the first of his many television appearances. He crashed around a corner upsetting a tripod, a cameraman, a correspondent and a deaf, toothless lady who had been asked to evaluate television as a moral and social force. When the equipment had been reassembled and the old lady pacified with five hundred lire, Don Serafino condescended to express his views on the magic eye, which he had never seen, but about which, naturally, he knew all. He is so willing to talk that newsmen rush to him whenever they need a "southern reaction" to balance their reports. With their encouragement, he has become the resident authority on any and all subjects.

Time and outstanding talent have made him the dean of the regional *corps d'aberration*. His wife disappeared immediately after their marriage and has never been seen again. Ever since he has devoted his monstrous energies to all sorts of *bizzarrie* with remarkable success. Twice his younger brothers have retired him to the local mental asylum, only to be frustrated by their aged mother, who manages his release with the excuse that she needs someone to look after her. For some reason a double commitment would be unthinkable, so they bivouac, surrounded by years of their own mess, in a tall narrow house which, half a century ago, was part of her dowry. A scrawny creature with the naked bulging eyes and beak of a newborn sparrow, she only appears in public when Don Serafino has forgotten to lock the front door. Then she reels about the streets, flapping her black draperies and mouthing to herself until her son captures her and leads her back home where she can tipple in comfort and recite to herself the conquests of the past.

Don Serafino and Otello are, on the other hand, always in sight. If they are not jousting with streetlights or terrorizing pedestrians, they are in the fields seeing to the family land. Don Serafino's dementia, if that is not too strong a term, is aggravated by the approach of St. Martin's Day, the traditional wine-making season and also the deadline for the accounts he must render to his brothers. Theoretically each enjoys a fixed share of the profits, but under Serafino's stewardship there have been none and the meetings end in acrimony only slightly blunted by his peace offering of a barrel of wine for each. He has never understood that they do not care how he squanders the harvest as long as their mother is comfortable. Does she eat well?

"Can you ask a man of honor such a question?" We have all heard him reel off his answer so many times that we know it by heart. "I am insulted. Yes, insulted! We dine on caviar and whale steaks; on doves and fried poppies and essence of malva. Fresh salmon in season, river trout and lobster. Nothing is too fine for our beloved mother and with all due modesty I pride myself on setting the finest table in the region." The brothers interpret the statement accurately as meaning sufficient quantities of bread soup and pizza with garlic and so retreat for another year to their careers in Rome.

There is no harm in him. In winter he is quiescent; from September through the first snow he is the victim of an implacable hysteria that drives him to excesses, particularly where women are concerned. His passions are short-lived, virulent and always carried on in his own private concoction of French-Basilisk. We are nearing the dangerous period. I heard last week that he was discovered in the upper halls of the Convent at six in the morning, rapping on every door, even those of the toilet cubicles, looking for "my little jewel, the pearl of my heart," whom he did not know by name, but would be sure to recognize. The girls and nuns alike were struck dumb at the sight of him, and he might have completed his survey had the Mother Superior not thought the kitchen pantry an odd place for Otello and given the alarm. The Carabinieri were very gentle with him, though they did not believe his dignified explanation that he had come in his capacity as veterinary to inspect the cows.

This afternoon he came to invite us to a bal masqué, as he called it, to be given at his house (that should be an experience) on his name day, the day after the Festa. Once we understood what he wanted, we all accepted with as much enthusiasm as we could summon. Nicola says Serafino may even forget the invitation, but if not, it is still better than his last project – a discothèque. Don Serafino was wildly declaiming Dante *alla francese* to Marina when Evangelista appeared and the fiasco was complete. Such a bacchanalia was shocking, I am sure, but Evangelista seemed relieved by my quiet assurance that we need not discuss the "business matter" he had mentioned on another occasion: I was determined to protect my land and the peace of my garden. Eventually they all went off. Nicola apologized profusely for bringing Marina. He is worried about her. She spends all of her free time haunting the post office. She still hopes for a transfer to the North. He says she is obsessed. He was very tense and nervous, I thought, and said something *sotto voce* about wanting her to stay in San Basilio. I wonder . . . Don Anselmo insists that he will be my chaperon at the bal masqué. Don Serafino had a terrible struggle mounting Otello. He reminded me of Will Rogers, immured in his armor, being hoisted onto his charger in the only scene from *The Connecticut Yankee* that lingers in my memory. As they left, Otello, who had been snacking in the flower beds, dribbled a long string of slime and rose leaves down the back of Evangelista's jacket, a sight which did much to restore my good humor.

6

The Festa (*continued*)

To Anglo-Saxons punctuality is a demivirtue, an unofficial second cousin to cleanliness and courage. It follows easily, too easily, that a person who is casual about time is shiftless and an entire nation afflicted with temporal elasticity is slothful and in all probability treacherous. Italy is the land of Cockaigne to us, and Italians are handsome, pleasant souls with the black hearts of Neapolitan stevedores. Like lovers enamored in spite of their better judgment, we insist on reforming it and them in an image we consider more respectable. Italians, bless them, will not be reformed. They were very proud of Mussolini's trains that ran on time to the minute, or maybe not so much of the trains themselves as the international approval they earned. With what appears to be stunning bravura Democracy also runs Italian trains on time, or a bit ahead. The technique is elementary and realistic. Tourists are entrusted to nonstop flyers between historic cities. Others who must travel have at their disposal a network of national commuter locals, euphoniously called *direttissimi* and *accelerati,* that allow so much time between stations that, if a team of mules were substituted for the locomotive, the schedule would be undisturbed. Having made this graceful concession to international approval, Italians conduct their private business as they please and so are not susceptible to ulcers and youthful heart attacks. Everything that should be done is in due time and the Anglo-Saxon will simply have to learn that it is pleasanter to sit reading his newspaper and sipping a cup of coffee at a sidewalk café than it is to pace around a stuffy anteroom, stumbling over rubber plants and cursing the official who does not keep his appointments with military precision.

It is all a matter of what I call a dalliance quotient. Naturally, in the case of a public event which involves more than one power, the quotient must be multiplied by the correct number of units if the spectator wishes to arrive at exactly the right moment. For example, allowing half an hour's delay for each element, if a Bishop and a Government Minister are to perform in a ceremony, the formula goes something like this: Bishop plus Minister plus Crowd (no ceremony is worthy of the name without a crowd) to give a good working estimate of the delay one can expect, that is, one hour and a half. The Bishop must recover from the rigors of the journey, perhaps with a coffee; then he is affable with the local clergy, and finally there are vestments to be donned. The Minister, always harried by too many appointments, leaves his office late, cannot find his police escort, must meet with the local politicians, and when all should be ready, he and the Bishop are closeted together, perhaps for another resuscitating coffee, but certainly for their own mutual, public benefit. The crowd, kept under close surveillance by an army of assistants and local small-wigs of the Carabinieri officer corps, can collect and wait as it expected to anyway.

On the whole the formula works. I used it again for the Festa. In this case there was the crowd plus Bishop, so I arrived at the little church of San Giovanni Battista half an hour after the mass was to have begun, expecting to wait and so carry out my duty of public appearance for half an hour. Already dozens of cars were parked along the road and people and animals milled around in front of the church, like characters out of Aesop's fables. Under a tree the young boys and the very old men who make up the confraternity sat with their vestments scattered around them, guzzling wine. Couples strolled along the road oblivious of the waspish drone of scooters, motorcycles and motor bikes that zoomed about in an impatient gymkhana. Most of the people just stood, waiting. Basilisks enjoy waiting. At the first sign of delay they retreat into an Elysian reverie that removes them from the scene as effectively as actual levitation. A raucous noise or an abrupt, mass movement will usually call them back to the moment at hand, but Don Mela fluttering about in his cassock, trying to divide them into two crowds with a wide, neat aisle between, was not forceful enough to attract their attention. That they neither saw nor heard him was so disconcerting, such a sign of displeasure, that his face was beaded with sweat and his nose glowed vermilion. He clung to me as to a life preserver.

In a fit of pique the Bishop had announced he would *not* bless the *vetture*. Some new and gross immorality had imperiled the entire Festa.* Evangelista had been dispatched to negotiate a temporary armistice and Don Mela was beside himself: how was he to pacify the crowd while Evangelista pacified the Bishop? As far as I could tell everyone was quite content. The members of the confraternity passed their wine around, the animals were happily eating grass, the strollers strolled, and all the others were enraptured by their own visions. I tried to reassure him and then escaped to see what wonders he and Teresa had wrought inside the church.

I threaded my way across the grass and through a shady grove of poplars which protects the little building from every disorder. It is very small, no larger than a two-room farmhouse, and very simple with whitewashed walls and a roof whose tiles are so precisely ranked one on the other they might be new except that only aged terra-cotta is flashed with moss and mellowed by shade and damp until it looks like soft apricot velvet. The windows, too, are small and guarded by wrought-iron grilles that curve out gracefully at the bottom

* Later I discovered that the daughter of the cathedral's new sacristan had run off with an itinerant vendor of black-market sausages.

and cast lacework shadows on the wall. There is no bell, no tower, no priest's quarters. A simple cross at the peak of the roof is all that identifies it as a church.

The interior, as spare as the exterior, is the antithesis of the local bedaubment school of churchly décor. There are no Victorian oils of saintly ladies in vaporish transport, no fake marble, no pink and blue plaster martyrs, not even the garish, visceral ceramic Stations of the Cross of this postwar period. The walls have the dry look of fresh whitewash. The altar is a plain slab of stone supported by columns. From his pedestal a strong polychrome St. John, whose bearded face is both melancholy and compassionate, gazes directly at the penitent. His eye is not to be avoided. He is no gentle imbecile, but a saint who accuses and would forgive. The Basilisks are not comfortable here. They avoid confrontation and do not like to be alone with their consciences. They complain that this is no house of God, this cold, uncompromising church, and so they come only once a year, on the day of the Madonna's visit to St. John.

Through the steamy miasma of sweat, candle wax and garlic, I could just make out the lumpy figures of women muffled in black shawls. They sagged in their chairs, haunch to haunch, like blobs of dough that had settled slowly, spreading their weight sideways. These were the lucky ones. They were content to wait, to rest, to click their beads occasionally and enjoy these few moments when no one expected them to be doing something more useful. The retreat has little to do with religious ardor. If they doze in solemn rapture, it is understood that they are marshaling their energies for the celebration to come. Their devotion will be measured by their ferocity.

All but forgotten at the altar, the Madonna delle Liberate and San Giovanni were shipwrecks, floundering in a raging sea of flowers. Her face, the only visible part of her in a swirling foam of daisies, had a look of gentle dismay. He, mired chest high in a flotsam of zinnias and ivy, was prey to killer-gladioli trained on him from every direction. Only the

Bishop's arrival could rescue them now from Sabato's competitive excesses.

Outside people bustled about in a confused but purposeful way. Don Mela brayed at the men of the confraternity who were giggling drunkenly at some unknown joke. Don Anselmo arrived, carrying his vestments over one arm, and patiently worked his way toward the church. Word had come that the Bishop had relented. Already the crowd, in the first stages of awakening, had closed in around the church and stood, murmuring in good-natured anticipation. The mass could begin.

Against the current my progress was slow, but I did finally escape to the road which I found narrowed to little more than a scooter lane by cars and trucks. The owners and the couples out for a stroll stood watching the melee below with the amused detachment of superior beings. Their comments irritated me. They scoffed. They shrugged off the ritual as a magic show put on for the peasants – yet they too had come, many with their *vetture* to be blessed. Were they so different? Every human being needs comfort and reassurance. To me there is no source that is not valid; certainly there is none that deserves sneers. My blood pressure was unresponsive to soothing reason, but before I could destroy my reputation for courtesy, which I would surely have done, Nicola wandered by and urged me to join him for coffee. If we were to wait until the end of the mass, we might as well try an improvised bar he had noticed along the road.

My fulminations about arrogance did not impress him. He lifted his shoulders as much as to say "Women are tiresome" and plodded on in morose silence which he broke only when we met people drifting back and forth in the soft glow of late afternoon. Then he stopped to talk pleasantly, casually. Conversation was the most effective campaign style he could have found. Without effort and with just the right touch of modesty and humor he reminded people that they knew him, all about him, and could not suspect him of political treachery. It must have been an effort, for as soon as we were alone, he was again silent and taciturn.

Around the curve we came upon the Madonna's truck bedizened with limp, slightly dusty tablecloths. The driver was intent on fixing a crest of blue plastic tulips onto the cab and never looked up. Just beyond was the roadside café Nicola had seen. Battered trestle tables and folding chairs had been spotted around a clearing graced by one lone olive tree and a peasant's squat shed where, on a counter set up in the doorway, a pyramid of soda bottles glittered green, red, orange and yellow like a stained-glass window pricked by those last most fleeting rays of sun. Eight or ten men stood silently around one table watching a card game. On other tables greasy papers and glasses with dregs of wine indicated that the service was haphazard. A man with a pointed face and a hairline moustache looked away from the cardplayers long enough to nod to us. A long dish towel, looped in his belt, identified him as our host. Nicola whispered that he was Giorgio Cappella, the shiftless husband of the peripatetic Signora Cappella, Marina Bova's landlady. We settled down at a table some distance from the card game, collected its debris in a pile and waited. Our host apparently felt he had lavished enough attention on us, for he turned back to the players and with his eyes half-closed continued his private assessment of their hands. Nicola tried to get his attention; he waved repeatedly. Nothing. Undecided what to do, he fidgeted with a cigarette, rolling it between his thumb and forefinger. When its tobacco began to dribble out onto the table, he sighed and lit it. To be ignored is difficult for any man, but for a Basilisk, there is the added torture of decision: How can he attract attention without risking loss of face? He may overreact in passion, but in cold blood he is caution itself, pondering, weighing, considering, usually until the situation resolves itself. Nicola sighed again and slowly got to his feet. At that very moment, as though the two men's bodies were connected by invisible strings, Cappella turned.

"Wine?" he called.

"No. Coffee, please." Nicola eased back into his chair.

Cappella shook his head.

"No coffee?"

Another shake of the head. "Beer, if you like. Cold beer."

Nicola started to object, then thought better of it and nodded his head. Cappella might have been blind. He turned back to the game where play had been suspended. The men, who, as far as I could tell, had never looked directly at us, leaned over the table, talking with great animation. Finally Cappella straightened up and ambled toward the hut. The cards were dealt again, and the watchers stepped back to peer over the players' shoulders and then murmur behind their hands to each other.

For the first time I could see the four players. Three were men I did not know, wearing clean shirts and billed caps pushed back on their heads so that a ghostly stripe of untanned skin showed above leathery faces. Their eyes were clouded and watery from so much wine on a hot day, but figuring their cards seemed to cost only one a particular effort of concentration. He had a square, jowly face that registered varying degrees of dull irritation as he moved his cards first close, then further away, then back up close. Apparently they stayed out of focus, but he forgot them to slap and grab at an elusive insect. The fourth member of the game and the controller of the carafe of wine, which he sheltered in the crook of one arm, was Bruno Ferri. He was the only one who wore a tie, pulled down to ease a tight collar. A jacket hung on one corner of his chair, his hat on the other. With his clean white shirt, his smooth chin and the large golden horn against the evil eye that dangled from his watch, he might almost have been a visitor from the city. His face was very flushed and his eyes flickered restlessly from face to face.

Cappella reappeared with two bottles of beer and two glasses, dripping wet, on a wet tray which he banged down on our table. As he opened the bottles, Nicola asked, "Had much business?"

"No complaints," was the sullen answer.

"How much do I owe you?"

"Nothing," he jerked his head toward the card game.

"Bruno has already paid. He's celebrating. Today is his name day – San Bruno." We both looked up, surprised. Ferri had been listening. He stood up and bringing the carafe and his glass with him, he headed, none too steadily, for our table.

"We should offer *you* a drink, not . . ."

"Drop the compliments, Don Nico'. We know where we stand, you and me. I did it for the Signora." He leaned on the edge of the table and grinned at me. "Guess I know a real lady when I see one. We understand each other." He leered at me. His unfortunate choice of words suggested a "relationship" which in San Basilio could only be sexual. Cappella edged closer. Nicola stiffened, but relaxed again when my answer was bland.

"Neighbors should," I said. Before Ferri could lumber into more equivocal specifics, I went on with the conventional toast to his good health. We raised our glasses. He downed his wine and with the flood a totally different subject drifted into his mind. He turned to Nicola.

"Don Nico', tell me just one thing. You know you can't win, don't you?"

"Bruno, another time – *va bene?* Politics and celebrations do not mix."

"Sure, sure. Now, let's pretend you've said all that crap. *Scusate,* Signora – no offense meant. Tell me the truth, Don Nico'! Admit they tricked you. You don't see the regulars volunteering to get beat. They knew nobody had a chance against Evangelista." Nicola said nothing, but smiled slightly, pleasantly as though amused. Ferri glared at him, then flushed. He expected his victims to react to goading. "Oh, so it's like that. Well, if you're so sure, maybe you'd like to make a little bet – a friendly bet – say three-to-one odds. How about it, Professor? Not afraid you might lose your money, are you – Professor? *Su!* Three-to-one odds." He erupted into mirthless shouts of laughter. We watched him dance about in front of us until he was short of breath and his laughter dwindled away to bursts of giggles. Our silence finally sobered him enough to listen.

"Not a bad idea. Three-to-one odds, you're offering," said Nicola. "But I am not your man Evangelista, you know. *My* conscience is clear and my pockets empty. I will bet anything I have in them right this minute and that is all I have in this world." Very seriously he started taking change out of his pockets, searching through bits of paper for ten-lire coins; then remembering his billfold in his hip pocket, he pulled it out dramatically, inspected a wad of dog-eared calling cards and receipts, found a thousand lire and another, then five thousand. In all the crumpled bills and coins came to 8,720 lire,* which he counted twice before he looked up. Ferri's face was mottled purple and red. "There it is – my wealth – all of it: 8,720 lire. At three to one it will cost you – um, let me see – yes, it will cost you 26,160 lire. Not such a bad dowry for an impoverished mayor." Ferri started to curse him, but Nicola turned away to call the men from the card game to be official witnesses to the bet. "He says Evangelista. What do you think of that? Good old Bruno has joined the *padroni* – and the Bishop! He never was one to pass up a good thing. Makes you wonder though. Evangelista! *Beh* . . ." He did not finish his rumination, but left it hanging, inviting the others to speculate.

The men shifted their feet and looked uncomfortably from Nicola to Ferri. Sarcasm, particularly the sarcasm of the educated, makes them uneasy. They are not sure they really understand; the joke may turn out to be on them. The players looked down at the smudged cardboards in their hands.

"Figlio di puttana!" snarled Ferri with grim, drunken venom. *"Che non sei* . . ."

"Shut up!" yelled the square-faced man who had been unable to focus on his cards. *"Figlio di puttana?* Son of a whore, that's you! Pig! A father who'd use his daughter as bait, then go partners with the man who took her – he's no better than a pimp. He's the *figlio di puttana!* He's . . ."

But he never finished the phrase. Ferri had him by the throat, shaking him, twisting his collar until the veins stood

* Approximately $14.50.

out like rubber hoses. The sudden collapse of the chair dumped the man on the ground with Ferri sprawled on top of him. It also woke up the men standing around the table. They pulled Ferri off and walked him toward the road, while Cappella and the two cardplayers were left to brush off and soothe his victim.

Nicola and I got up and slowly walked away. It strikes me now that we exchanged not a word or even a glance; it was just obviously the moment to escape, leaving the two gladiators to rant and grumble and wave their arms until they calmed down. Cappella came running down the road after us.

"Don Nico', I don't want any trouble. You know how it is — temporary license and all? Bruno had soaked up a couple of liters before he came, and everybody knows two glasses is one too many for Tommaso. I — I don't want any trouble. You know how it is."

"Yes, yes, I know how it is," Nicola said sadly. "I know."

And we walked back to the church in silence.

7

The End of the Festa

The road, the clearing and the grove swarmed with people, many of them leading donkeys and even mules as though they were pet dachshunds. At the church door two old men, over-anxious and tremulous as the old are inclined to be when performing in public, pumped up their bagpipes and then understanding it was still "too soon," let the air wheeze out with the shrill moans of dying calves. Nearby members of the confraternity winced in exaggerated pain. They had finally slipped their ragged and no longer very clean surplices over their heads, but the loose-jointed vagueness of their movements hardly suggested they were on the *qui vive*. One wore a soft felt hat pulled rakishly over one eye; another, though there was no hint of rain, flourished an open umbrella whose spokes had torn away from the cloth to become deadly antennae about his head. Adults and children milled around, and the animals worked their necks back and forth to ease the ropes that kept them from nibbling grass. They knew, intuitively, that the Madonna would tarry yet a while and so they waited, enjoying, without knowing quite what had changed, the damp purple chill of the shadows and the calm of sunset that stilled the trees.

I left Nicola talking to two Carabinieri who carried rifles

and so were on duty, posted to keep order at this most orderly of festas, and looked for a comfortable place to wait. Marina Bova sat on the low wall of a bridge over a ditch, eating *fusaie,* those large orange-yellow beans like giant limas, with tough outer skins that have to be pierced before the tart, crunchy pulp can be squirted into the mouth. She was alone, completely detached from the crowd, but apparently fascinated by it. She ate her beans with absentminded precision, never glancing at the coarse brown paper cone from which she took them. When she discovered she had a fistful of puckered skins, she laughed entirely to herself, but gaily, and then looked around to see if anyone had noticed. I waved and she pointed at the wall beside her in invitation.

"I don't know when I have had such a good time," she said as I hoisted myself up. "San Basilio has one advantage – I can do all the things I was never allowed to do at home, like eat these. Here, have one." When I shook my head, she looked disappointed. "I love them, or at least the idea of eating them this way, out in public. Oh what my father would say, if he saw me! That it is undignified, that *we* have to be examples to the town and who knows *what* hands have touched them! Only a *cafona* eats in the road! Uffa! This is so much nicer." I tried to imagine her as a little girl, solemn and obedient, with wide eyes that missed nothing and somewhere down inside her a tidy card catalogue of experiences missed.

"Have you heard anything?" I asked after a moment's silence. She turned to look at me as though she had not understood, as though perhaps I meant something about the Festa, then the muscles around her eyes tightened.

"Oh yes, I am confirmed here," she said, her voice very low and even. "School opens day after tomorrow, so that is that for this year." She hesitated, frowning slightly. She drew herself up very straight and looked at the few beans left in the cone before she went on. "It's odd. I am almost glad. I cannot run away now."

A horn sounded short arrogant blasts. The policeman, *pro forma,* pushed the people closest at hand, those causing the least trouble, back into the ditch. The crowd in the grove bunched together, leaving the merest suggestion of an aisle. The horn came closer, one continuous blare and the bagpipes let out piercing bleats of excitement. Marina poked me. Giggles had reduced her to tearful silence. She could only point — at the Madonna, on her back in midair without visible means of support or locomotion, gliding feet first back into the church. Almost immediately her head and shoulders popped out again. For one brief second, while her halo lights lashed about her like enraged serpents, that broad innocent face seemed to beseech the crowd for help, then she gave a sickening lurch and vanished once more not to return. We were left to imagine for ourselves the confusion inside the church.

A long black car swept around the curve and pulled up beside the Carabinieri. Two priests and a driver rushed around to open the back door, but no one got out.

"See Evangelista run?" Marina whispered in my ear. "It must be the Bishop." A white hand protruded from the car; Evangelista kissed it, said something and straightened up to look around with the high head and wrinkled nose of a man offended by some noxious odor. He leaned back inside the car and stayed there, half in, half out, presenting his bulbous rear for our inspection.

The next few minutes were such a blur of people and animals surging between two poles of attraction, the Madonna and the Bishop, that I can only guess at exactly what happened. Just as it began, I noticed a donkey, all by himself and on his best behavior, saunter up to the Bishop's car and stand, looking in the window. No one paid any attention. The Madonna, finally right side up, danced above the heads of the crowd. A cheer went up. She did a little jig, then almost a pirouette before she acquired some equilibrium and slowly made her way toward the Bishop's car. Flashes of white surplices and a general bubbling and jostling movement told of a tussle. The bagpipes were silent, the pipers lost in the crush.

Just as some sort of order might have been possible, a solid column of women in black, still haunch to haunch, lunged from the church like a well-propelled battering ram and the procession turned into a human stampede. They ran, staggering and tumbling across the grove toward the Bishop, who had emerged from his car with weary dignity and now stood his ground. The Madonna loped in midair, her draperies and chains twisting round her like a harem dancer's. She hesitated briefly in front of the Bishop, which must have been his only chance to bless anything, and then jogged up the bank and out onto the road.

Finally we could see the cause of the commotion. The village idiot, known only as Buccio, had seized the cross and appointed himself crucifer for the day. Neither the pipers, the confraternity nor presumably Don Mela had been able to stop him. Our first glimpse of him was striding off down the road, decked out in a woman's long muslin nightgown and on his head the leather helmet, from which he refuses to be parted no matter what the occasion, with its ear flaps tightly fastened down under his chin. The Madonna's bearers had no choice; they followed the cross. The confraternity with tipsy determination closed ranks behind. Don Mela was driven in their wake by the women and somewhere in the rear guard of animals and cripples, the pipers must have been gasping for breath, though they produced no sound.

Buccio, beyond the reach or control of anyone, marched with blatant majesty through all the largest, most slippery piles of manure, and there were a great many, in the road. It was a mad, zigzag course, but the men and women behind him, who could see nothing, pursued their neighbors' backs and so skidded and squelched along, more inclined to curse than sing as they should. Eventually San Giovanni appeared and trailed some fifty feet behind, as though ashamed to be identified with such rabble. Slowly the procession snaked its way along the road and disappeared round the curve.

"Now there will be trouble," said Marina. "I think the Bishop has just realized that he too is caught behind Buccio." The Bishop, still attended by Evangelista and the two priests, stood in the middle of the road, waving his arms and shouting at his bewildered driver. Soon all five men were gesticulating in what, from our vantage point on the bridge, was a ridiculous pantomime. Finally, their faces red with rage, they got stiffly into the car. Marina and I bowed as it passed and bowed again on its return, but no one inside paid the slightest attention. The car swept on, straight into San Giovanni returning with his bearers and his weary escort, who scattered like sheep into the ditch at the side of the road. Don Anselmo, watching the debacle from the relative safety of the sacristy door, hid his face in his hands. But there was to be no final disaster. The men regrouped slowly and San Giovanni proceeded down the embankment, across the clearing and so back into the custody of the archpriest. Nicola, who had been one of the unfortunates in the ditch, brushed himself off and joined us, leaving the rearrangement of San Giovanni's bower of zinnias to the experts.

"The Bishop will never get by. My God, what a mess Buccio has made of us!" He inspected his shoes, then began scraping them on the culvert. "Whoever let him get the lead anyway?"

"No one," Marina said. "He fought for it – and won." She had jumped off the bridge and was brushing her dress.

"He slipped around in front of the truck too. It will be an hour before they reach the Piazza." Nicola glanced up from his shoe-gouging and said to me, "Why not leave your car here? My clutch is already ruined, so come with me. Whenever you want to come back, I'll bring you."

I had not planned to go to the festivities in the Piazza, had no real reason to and have often wondered what would have happened had I spent the evening at home. Speculation is futile. My character is weak, or at least very subject to the flattery of being included. Marina's enthusiasm was more than I could resist, though it was all directed toward the flying chairs and "rocket ships that twirl," which, like *fusaie,* had undoubtedly been on her father's list of indecorous activities for a young lady of good family. The fact that carnival rides frighten me almost as much as that most devilish of all machines, the airplane, went completely out of my mind. Two separate and distinct personalities seem to exist in my body, for I heard my own voice saying, not those prearranged excuses, but "And if we win one of those monster dolls with real hair, Marina, *you* can put it in the middle of *your* bed." So it was decided.

We had only to wait for Don Anselmo, who, when he joined us, moaned at our plan. "Ah, youth! Enjoy it. I assure you it is over soon enough." I know he felt his own was over. He looked tired; his skin was dry and crinkled like used tissue paper and his shoulders sagged. We crowded into Nicola's car, the two men in front, Marina and I folded on the back ledge, and started along the road. Just beyond the curve we came up behind the last draggers in the procession. Without warning a deep blue pall had settled softly, gently around a world where only a moment before ghostly silhouettes, each with its own shimmering nimbus, had moved mysteriously about on a golden twilight ground. The streetlights of the town were switched on, but they are dim, more symbols of civilization than sources of light. A stiff breeze, funneled down through the narrow streets, set them winking and dipping like particles of phosphorus in a sea swell and still we crept along, easing forward, stopping, easing forward again. Finally Nicola turned off the engine.

"We might as well wait here. The motor is heating up." He slumped down to peer through the windshield where, already, the black outline of the procession had melted into the dark. Suddenly, as though on cue, four naked bulbs flared up just to our right, lighting the tables, the small counter and the card-players of our café. "I wonder if they went on playing," Nicola muttered.

"It's eerie," Marina whispered in my ear. "Almost a play. We're the audience out here and over there is the stage."

I cannot explain why, but more than a play I saw arrested violence that made the back of my neck cold and numb. Instinctively I wanted to escape from the car, to get out in the open, to run. I remember feeling the same flood of panic on my only visit to a wax museum. There the spectators were in total darkness when spotlights glared onto a scene, freezing it at the peak of its horror. The guillotining of Marie Antoinette was patently funny, but one or two of the murderers had vibrated with such evil they made me shiver. Here, the lights startled the men around the table and for an instant paralyzed them in strangely tortured positions. One man hung over a table with his arms outstretched, grasping for a prey who may have been flesh and blood in the dark, but who evaporated with light. Another stood crouched, holding a chair in front of his body, ready to tame lions. Several strained forward with their hands high in the air, like wrestlers maneuvering for a hold. Then the moment of shock was over. Men lunged at each other, tumbling away from the table, stumbling, crawling on their hands and knees to the protection of the dark. Dust billowed up around them. In the door of the hut Cappella stood, squinting into the light. He reached down, grabbed a man's arm and pulled him up, then separated two others. The dust began to settle and we could make out figures standing well back in among the tables, intent upon something we could not yet see. Several of them heaved and gasped for air; a few brushed themselves off, but none took their eyes away from the one last cloud of fine, silting dust that slowly settled on the ground.

"Be right back," Nicola announced, halfway out of the car.

"Don't interfere. Stay where you are," came a curt order from Don Anselmo. "Let them settle it." Nicola sank back into his seat.

Legs wheeled through the air and crashed into a chair, splintering it. A table teetered and fell. A lump rolled over and then heavily, lazily over again, like a bale of old clothes dropped off a moving truck. With each thud puffs of dust rose. Suddenly a clear figure reared up, staggered after the lump and fell on it. A howl of agony roared through the valley, the horrible, searing howl of a wounded animal who, finally trapped and defeated, is terrified. The man unfolded the lump, dragging it up until it had legs and a body and arms wrapped around its head. For a second the two men stood directly under a light and a face twisted with pain flashed upward as he screeched once more: Tommaso, the man with the jowls who had already lost one fight. His legs began to melt under him. He was jerked up and held in a brutal hug by Bruno Ferri, who bared his teeth deliberately and then clamped onto his victim's ear and tugged and gnawed and wrenched at it until blood streamed down the man's neck, into his eyes and over Ferri's face. The blood only recharged Ferri's rage. He tore at the man's ear with his teeth, as a starved beast devours his kill.

"For the love of God, do something!" moaned Marina, shattering the spell that held us all.

The sight of the two men rushing from the car set the spectators in motion. Seconds later Ferri was pulled off his victim. Cappella propped Tommaso against a table trestle and poured brandy down his throat, then over his ear. One last hollow grunt, a feeble effort to twist away, and he fainted. Nicola and four men still wrestled with Ferri, always on the verge of losing him. Drunk as he was and crazed, he fought like a cunning octopus. Somehow his arms hooked around the necks of the men who held him. While he choked them, he thrashed out with his feet, sometimes meeting his mark, sometimes not, but always a moving target no one could immobilize.

"Get him down, Nicola! Down!" shouted Don Anselmo. "His legs! Two on each leg. Watch out! The arms!" Slowly the sheer weight of men hanging onto him brought Ferri to the ground. Two held his legs, another straddled his chest, pinning his shoulders with his knees. His arms were useless. He heaved for breath, but even he was exhausted and willing to concede it.

"Here, you two women," Don Anselmo called us sharply back to usefulness. "Take this handkerchief. Get some rags, cold water, there at the hut – from the ice tub will do – and brandy. Clean the ear as best you can, then wrap his head tightly so the ear won't tear more. Nicola!" he called. "Nicola, where in the devil are you? Oh, sorry. Didn't see you. Move your car up. No. Better yet, get hers," pointing at me. "It's bigger. We have to get him to the hospital right now."

Neither Marina nor I seemed able to move very fast. Cappella handed me a bucket of water, and I wobbled off down the slope until I came to Ferri. Then quite irrationally, but with great accuracy, I threw the water square in his face. He roared. Completely without thought, an automaton, I turned back for more water. Cappella stuck a bottle of brandy in my hand, refilled the bucket and once more I headed down toward Marina, who had dragged Tommaso upright again and had him braced against the trestle of the table. Cold cloths on his forehead brought him to. He sat up abruptly, retched, then vomited with such shuddering spasms it seemed next his stomach must turn inside out.

But it is pointless to go through the whole struggle again. We did get him cleaned up and bandaged enough to make the trip to the hospital. I remember it all, but at several removes, as though it were a scene dimly viewed through one of those incidental windows in Renaissance paintings. The human mind protects itself against revulsion. It turns in upon itself to hide, to deceive itself with trivia: He bites his fingernails, I commented to myself; those stitches on the shirt patch prove his wife cannot sew! Why his wife? His daughter? Then a round of words, silent ones, I thought. The ear! Why the ear? Why?

"Because, under our laws, a bite does not constitute assault. Hitting, yes. Biting no. Have you never seen men here fight?" Don Anselmo with several others was lifting Tommaso. "Forgive me, my dear, for ordering you around, but use some of that ice water on yourself and then follow us in Nicola's car. Here are the keys."

Of the next few hours only soundless flashes remain in my memory. The Piazza, tatty with its Festa ornaments of white cardboard arches and naked light bulbs—yes, the Piazza where the Bishop on his throne looks bored and the Madonna twinkles while priests mouth the mass into microphones for the benefit of an apathetic crowd that stands shelling peanuts.

Then the examination room in the hospital, lighted by one hooded gooseneck lamp that casts giant shadows of bottles and instruments on a mottled wall; and Tommaso, with the handkerchief, showing blurred spots of red, still wrapped around his head, lies on a table covered in black oilcloth which has a rip long enough for nubbins of grimy cotton to squeeze through. Still the examination room, now like a pharmaceutical illustration of primitive dentistry, the patient is held down while a man in a blood-smeared smock sews the ear back in place with a curved upholstery needle. The search for Tommaso's wife. Faces of the old, the defeated young, the bemused, the curious, the dumb – hundreds of faces without expression, covering minds too lethargic to connect a question with some reasonable answer. And finally a woman in black tearing her hair, her mouth open, but emitting no sound, her eyes fixed on me. The Ferris wheel twirls sedately in a cosmos of colored lights. Spectral neon lightning flickers on and off the spacemobiles. Passe-partouts of black scallops, human heads without bodies, neaten the foregrounds, even at the candymaker's high counter where, in the glowing shade of a canvas awning, his cleaver gleams softly, menacingly as it snips back and forth at nose level. A hunchback in a pink paper hat beckons from his garish shooting range: green cans set against a bloodred curtain. In the Piazza the bandstand, a collapsible gazebo fringed and furbelowed with cardboard passementerie, is deserted except for two musician-guards who lean on the fragile balustrade, picking their teeth. My woman in black claws her hair. On each cheek one enormous tear glitters. She cannot get through the crowd. Then finally the ward – two rows of cots, four rows of shadowy iron bedsteads and a dim light near our patient, who is now swathed in bandages and almost asleep. His wife leans on the foot of his bed and weeps. Her shawl has fallen to the floor, her hair sprays in all directions, and the man on the bed smiles comfortably.

I saw Nicola's lips move before I heard his voice. He touched my arm and repeated, "We can go now. He will be all right. His wife will look after him."

Out in the street we stood for a moment, listening to the cacophonous grumble and screech of the Festa, surprised to find it still going on. My watch said ten o'clock. Two hours before the "first night" fireworks would go off and peace would settle again, briefly. A breeze ruffled my hair and cooled my face and some semblance of the present took over in my mind. I was tired. I looked at Marina. She was ashen and a little stooped. She gazed at the pavement vacantly. Nicola watched her. I felt my chest tighten against a twinge, uninvited and for a moment uncontrolled, of the envy known to every woman who, for whatever reason, is unmarried: how nice it would be to have a man concerned for my shock, my weariness – or was it my fear? He reached out his hand, drew it back tentatively, then let it drop, but still he watched her and still she was unaware of him, her eyes lowered. I put my arm around her shoulders.

"No rides tonight for me. I hope you don't mind. I'm tired."

She shook her head.

"Can I give you a lift home?"

She straightened up, almost shook herself. "Yes, as far as your gate. Then I can walk back." She sounded far away in her own thoughts.

"I'll lead the way through the crowd." Nicola was no longer hesitant; he took command. "You'll never get through alone. I have to see what happened to Ferri, anyway."

Nicola's car butted and honked a narrow path through the hordes who churned about dazed and half-asleep. A policeman gaped at us, apparently shocked that anyone should attempt normal movement at such a moment. When asked for help, he shrugged and turned away, saying "There's no hope in this confusion." But we did get through to the edge of town where all was black and silent and the breeze sent greasy papers and ice-cream wrappers skipping across the road. A candle flickering inside a rickety showcase on wheels revealed the purveyor of roast pork dozing on his stool. Only bits of crackling and fat were left; for him the Festa was over.

Nicola's headlights picked out a tall man strolling toward town and gave me an extra second to recognize Di Luca. I pulled up beside him.

"Is everything all right at the house?" I had no reason to ask.

"Oh yes. I left the gate unlocked. I thought you might not have the key with you." How sensible of Di Luca. I had, indeed, failed to pick it up; when I left I had only planned to be away for an hour or two. After an exchange of good-nights we drove on to catch up with Nicola at the little clearing where the café had been. He stood talking to Cappella and two men who leaned against stacks of folded tables and chairs. They were waiting for a truck to come and take them away; the Carabinieri had already withdrawn the temporary license. Ferri, it seemed, had become quite reasonable, or at least tired of a man sitting on his chest, and had promised to make no further trouble if allowed up. He had stayed around for a while, sitting morosely on a chair. Occasionally he muttered to himself, as though trying to work out a problem, but had said nothing until he asked for a beer. He was thirsty. They had given it to him; he drank it, cheered up some and said he would walk toward the church and maybe on to my house to meet Teresa. They were not to worry about him. They had watched him only long enough to be sure he turned away from town. Neither Ferri nor Teresa had been seen since, and we all agreed that Ferri, at least, was asleep either at home or in some comfortable ditch.

As I pulled up to the gate, Marina spoke for the first time. Her voice sounded very far away. "Do you really feel safe here? With Ferri on the loose, shouldn't we look around the garden and make sure no one is in the house?"

I dismissed this as farfetched and wished her an extremely curt good-night. I was physically too tired and mentally too exasperated by intrigues, plots and conundrums to be frightened of the idea of Ferri, drunk or sober.

As I unlocked the door, the wind sucked around the corner of the house and hissed through the cypresses. Towns glittered like beaded skullcaps on distant mossy-black hills; closer, San Basilio stretched in front of me in its deceptive nocturnal finery of lights and shadows. But I was blind. I went to bed and slept so soundly that not even the fireworks disturbed me.

SEVEN

I

THE UNDERSIGNED . . . DECLARES THE FOLLOWING: THAT ON THE SEVENTH DAY OF OCTOBER 1969, HAVING AWAKENED AT 8 A.M. AND HEARING NO SOUNDS THAT WOULD INDICATE THE ARRIVAL OF HER DOMESTIC SERVANT *Ferri, Teresa,* BORN SAN BASILIO SARACENO, PROVINCE OF ——— ON 14/8/51 OF THE DECEASED *Ferri, Bruno* AND OF THE DECEASED *Barone, Maria in Ferri,* RESIDENT IN VICO DEI TURCHI 8, APARTMENT NUMBER 7 OF SAID TOWNSHIP, SHE [the undersigned] DID DRESS, MAKE AND EAT BREAKFAST WITHOUT NOTICING ANY SIGNS OF AN INTRUDER OR OTHER ILLICIT PRESENCE. FURTHER SHE STATES THAT UPON UNLOCKING THE FRONT DOOR AND ENTERING THE GARDEN, THE SCOPE OF WHICH [i.e., entrance] WAS TO TAKE A WALK, SHE WAS NOT AWARE OF ANY UNTOWARD FOOTPRINTS OR OTHER MARKS ON THE GROUND THEREOF; THAT SHE DID WANDER IN THE BEFOREMENTIONED GARDEN FOR AS LONG AS A QUARTER OF AN HOUR CIRCA AND DID PROCEED, ALWAYS FOR THE SCOPE OF DIVERSION, THROUGH THE ARBOR TO THE POINT OF LAND WHICH OVERLOOKS THE STREAM BELOW, KNOWN AS THE BILIOSO, AND THE VALLEY THEREOF. THAT SHE DID, UPON

GLANCING TO HER RIGHT, ESPY THE FIGURE OF A MAN LYING IN A POSITION ANYTHING BUT NORMAL ON THE LEDGE EQUIDISTANT BETWEEN THE POINT OF LAND AND THE VALLEY FLOOR BELOW, THAT IS ON A LEDGE SOME FIFTY METERS BELOW THE POINT ON WHICH SHE STOOD AND SOME FIFTY METERS ABOVE THE VALLEY FLOOR. IT WAS NOT POSSIBLE, AT THAT TIME, SHE FURTHER DECLARES, TO ASCERTAIN THE IDENTITY OF THE PERSON, THE EXACT EXTENT OF HIS INJURIES, IF ANY, OR TO COMMUNICATE WITH HIM BY VOICE OR ACTUAL DESCENT IN SITU. THIS BEING THE CASE SHE DID CONSIDER IT HER FIRST DUTY TO INFORM THE PROPER AUTHORITIES AND TO THAT END DID TAKE HER CAR, THE HOUSE BEING UNFURNISHED WITH A TELEPHONE, AND PROCEED WITH HASTE TO THE LOCAL COMMAND OF CARABINIERI.

THE IMMEDIATE INTERVENTION OF THE AFOREMENTIONED CARABINIERI UNDER THE COMMAND OF BRIGADIER MINETTI BORE FRUIT IN THE FORM OF AN INANIMATE BODY, SUBSEQUENTLY IDENTIFIED AS THAT OF *Ferri, Bruno . . .* see FILE # 56342 SB/O IN CONFORMATION WITH LAW 65729 (A and B) IN ITS INTEGRAL VERSION PASSED 8/5/62.

THE UNDERSIGNED FURTHER DECLARES THAT SHE IS IGNORANT OF THE CAUSES WHICH BROUGHT SAID *Ferri, Bruno* TO ARRIVE ON THE LEDGE BELOW HER GARDEN. NOR IS SHE ABLE TO STATE WHETHER HE ARRIVED THERE THROUGH HIS OWN INITIATIVE OR THROUGH THAT OF ANOTHER PERSON AS YET UNKNOWN. *Ferri, Bruno,* BEING THE FATHER OF HER DOMESTIC SERVANT, *Ferri, Teresa,* SHE FURTHER DECLARES THAT SHE KNEW HIM TO THE EXTENT CONSONANT WITH SUCH A RELATIONSHIP AND THAT SHE DID FURTHER WITNESS THE EVENING BEFORE THE MORNING HE WAS FOUND — THAT IS PRECISELY THE EVENING OF 6/10 — AN ALTERCATION BETWEEN HIM AND ANOTHER REPORTED TO BE *Marrone, Tommaso,* BORN IN . . . RESIDENT IN . . . , ACTU-

ALLY LYING IN THE SAN BASILIO HOSPITAL (see FILE # 56323 SB/O) . . .

THE UNDERSIGNED FURTHER DECLARES THIS TO BE A TRUE STATEMENT IN ALL PARTICULARS AND STATES THAT SHE WILL HOLD HERSELF AVAILABLE TO THE PROPERLY AUTHORIZED OFFICIALS OF THE COURT FOR ANY FURTHER INFORMATION THEY MAY REQUIRE OF HER.

(signed) A—— C——

2

Disaster exudes a musk of its own, one to which the idle are morbidly susceptible. The Carabinieri's battered khaki panel truck picked its way slowly, in reverse, around the hedges of my garden. Of its load only three long poles waving a red-and-white-striped caution flag were in sight, but still peasants on their way to the fields stopped to cluster around the gate and watch. Soon others joined them. Cars slowed down; some negotiated frantic U-turns and rushed back toward town, others stopped. People got out to line the road. A few ventured down the slope, but, whatever their hopes, they were foiled by a rusty barbed-wire fence disguised in luxuriant blackberry brambles. The more brash drove in through the gates and if Di Luca and a young Carabiniere had not blocked their way, would have driven right up to the house or even through the orchard. Six Carabinieri who had ridden in the back of the truck ignored the confusion and settled down to their task of unloading the equipment – first the timbers, then enough rope to rig an entire fishing fleet, six of the largest pulleys I have ever seen, an assortment of wheels and handles, walkie-talkie radios, tool kits, posthole diggers, shovels, picks and finally a stretcher. By the time the gear was laid out ready for inventory, for military procedure remains military procedure even in mid-crisis, the Brigadier had arrived bringing with him Don Ferdinando and Nicola. He announced with evident relief that they had come to protect my interests. Freed of this awesome responsibility, he turned to the deployment of his troops, which included Di Luca and Sabato. He inspected them doubtfully, as though there were something sinister about their willingness to help, and in an audible aside instructed his driver to watch them every minute. Sabato's face stiffened, but Di Luca said something and they both laughed. Whatever resentment they felt was put in mental cold storage until that sometime-never day of reckoning when such men expect to be avenged. In silence they brought up the rear of the little company that marched off to the cliff.

A sentry on the gate did his best to sort the legitimate visitors from the curious, but it was a losing battle. Officials, semiofficials and acquaintances came in bewildering numbers. Any man in possession of a uniform had not only the right, but a duty to be present. And they came, the forestry guards, the sanitary police, the highway maintenance men, even the postmen, to supervise. They strewed the garden with their jackets and caps, their midmorning snacks and their cigarette butts. They lined the cliff, they shouted directions, they argued with each other, but were careful not to be drafted into the work crew. They had come to *represent* the government and there is a pronounced difference between representation and toil.

Our civil magistrate, the Pretore, was the first to arrive. He is a pudgy little man with a high, nasal voice that tends to flute and warble under the pressure of an emergency. He trundled around, getting in everyone's way. He discussed "the particulars" first with Don Ferdinando, then with the Brigadier, who is after all only a sergeant, then with me, becoming more and more agitated with each examination of the details. His experience — well, this was unusual, not an everyday — yes, well, the only thing to do was to notify the Procuratore della Repubblica, the state prosecutor in Matera. They must send someone immediately, before the body was brought up. Yes, that was it. They could notify Potenza and Rome and arrange for the autopsy in Bari – or was it Naples? The best solution. No question later that he had failed . . . and still reciting all the details to himself, he commandeered a car to take him back into town and a telephone.

He was closely followed by the current Mayor and his brother, the medical officer, who came out of a sense of duty. They are swarthy Neanderthal men who look forever glum because, though bent on pleasing, they disappoint everyone and are universally blamed for all calamities. This too would be their fault, but they were sure they should "inform" their own, separate ministries. Evangelista slipped by the guard. Marina came in from her morning walk. Don Ferdinando took me in hand and settled me on a ledge by the front door in the shade. This was not, he said, anything that should be witnessed by a woman. He ordered Marina to make a pot of coffee, which she did, except that something distracted her as she stood waiting for the thick brown foam to gurgle into the top of the pot and she went off, leaving it to wreak its own havoc. Once they have warned you, like pressure cookers and almost-toilet-trained children, espresso pots will not wait. They spew. Coffee stippled the kitchen wall, while I mused in the garden.

Each minute it looked more like a public campground toward the end of the annual staff outing of the Ministry of the Interior. People streamed back and forth enjoying the sights. At various times four carpenters appeared, carrying coffins on their heads. While the crowd speculated on mass murder, we argued them and their wares off the premises. By far the most persistent was one who had understood that *I* was the victim and had proportioned his box accordingly. The sight of me alive and attended by Don Ferdinando depressed him, but only long enough for his mind to reverse its commercial gears. Just the thing! I must buy the coffin and keep it by me. For one fleeting moment I imagined myself a latter-day Sarah Bernhardt, traveling with it, hopping into it whenever I needed a quiet spot to cogitate. Then he too was ushered out the gate to be replaced by the Captain of Carabinieri *and* Don Serafino on his faithful Otello.

The captain with a solemn face and more humor than I had thought him capable of entrusted "communications" to Don Serafino and ordered him to stand by at the police station for emergency action. As Otello thundered off down the road, the captain smiled rather sadly and turned to apologize to me. He is the classic product of his heritage and his career: one, the Spanish, of which his long pendulous nose and liquid eyes circled in black are evidence; the other, the officer's code of rigid perfection. His gallantry is florid, but it never interferes with performance of his duty. As soon as he had delivered himself of the *convenevoli,* he sketched a salute with his swagger stick and hurried off to the cliff where he stayed except for a brief conference with Don Ferdinando about Di Luca's ability to replace the young Carabiniere down on the ledge.

A tree had been buttressed with the three timbers, thereby converting a fork in the trunk to a fulcrum. Ropes had been passed through it and rigged to the pulleys to form a two-line hoist. We had watched Di Luca at the top of the cliff manipulate an improvised winch. Slowly, patiently he lowered first the two men down the steep, crumbling bank until they reached the ledge which had broken Ferri's fall and now held his body. When they signaled that they had a safe foothold, he reeled in the ropes, attached the stretcher, extra rope and tools and once more, slowly, patiently let the ropes slip over the edge out of sight. For long minutes nothing happened, at least nothing that Don Ferdinando and I could see. Finally Di Luca strained at the winch. Two Carabinieri put all their weight into the ropes, trying to get slack for him to wind, but progress was measured by the inch, by the half inch, then by a frantic effort to hold. The tree swayed. Men rushed to lean against the timber props, others to drag on the ropes. Slowly, carefully the ropes were eased down the side, the winch turned slowly backward and the load came to rest once more on the ledge out of sight. We watched the Captain and the Brigadier lean out over the cliff to talk to the men below. They turned to Di Luca who nodded. The Brigadier hurried back to the truck and sent the driver off to the station for a net. The ropes were not enough to hold the body on the stretcher. It was then that the Captain came to confer with Don Ferdinando. His men were young, inexperienced; one was already green from the height, or fear, or a combination of the two. Di Luca had volunteered to go down onto the ledge. Don Ferdinando assured him that if Di Luca were willing, he could be trusted and added, almost to himself, "He and Ferri were in the *Alpini* together."*

Through it all I sat numb, a spectator, a participant and oddly neither. I could see and hear and think, but I was vaguely aware that certain circuits were closed: the three processes remained tantalizingly uncoordinated. People I knew well were suddenly strangers, while the interference of strangers seemed logical. And always that bizarre, suppressed amusement that people, including myself, are so irrevocably themselves even in an emergency. Marina would not quite manage the practical demands of the coffeepot; Evangelista would buttonhole officials to bluster. Nicola would wander back and forth searching for something he could do. Don Ferdinando would protect the one person who, perhaps, did not need it, while Don Serafino charged around on Otello and Di Luca methodically went about the rescue. In the midst of this *ballet fantastique* I deluded myself that once Ferri's body – for we assumed he was dead – was retrieved, the show would be over, the crowd would disappear and life would slip back into its old pattern. The duplicity of shock: my mind would have nothing to do with the world in which my body was functioning.

"The Vice-Procuratore, followed, naturally at two paces, by his dogged clerk," said Don Ferdinando at my side. "Amusing that they all look the same." As I turned to watch the Captain join two men, I remember thinking that Don Ferdinando did

* The *Alpini* are the Italian Alpine troops trained for mountain warfare.

not sound amused and suddenly with the physical embodiment of law and bureaucracy there before my eyes, I was neither amused nor detached. I was frightened. The official mill grinds fine, and we were all grist, nothing more.

Probably they did not look like anyone else, but the impression of having seen them a hundred times was inescapable. They epitomized the middle-rank government employee who has neither failed totally nor succeeded and who must consider exile to such a minor province a temporary state of affairs. Efficiency will win their release, they hope, and so they are laconic, a shade arrogant and not above an implied threat when they deal with the lower orders who are unlikely to have champions in high places. Their suits are always of sturdy, medium-gray worsted – darker being reserved for higher rank, lighter too vulnerable to spots – and their trousers are always worn shiny from thousands of days spent sitting on wooden chairs at battered desks crammed into malodorous little rooms at the end of some labyrinthine corridor of the Questura or the Tribunale. No matter how drab his surroundings or how dull his days, an assistant prosecutor knows he is a man of power. Dr. Emilio Dante is no exception. A medium-gray cashmere cardigan and a white shirt with a modish, high, wide-spread collar are his blazons of superiority, for superior he is. Every movement of his long, thin body, every carefully controlled expression of doubt that crosses his angular face or makes his very-black eyebrows twitch declares it.

He listened gravely to the Captain's account, frowning slightly, occasionally nodding his head, but never so vehemently that one single well-combed silver hair was displaced. His manner was an infinitely subtle combination of attention, deference and impatience which confused the Captain and eventually threw him off his pace into testy silence. Dante shrugged.

"Mancini, did you get all that down?" he called over his shoulder, expecting his clerk to be, as he was, several paces behind. The answer was a mumble. "What possible use can you be, Mancini, if you *never* hear anything?" This was apparently such a usual complaint that Mancini just stood looking at a large paper pad he had braced on the armload of manila folders he carried. For Dante, Mancini does not have a first name. This is a courtesy not due the lowly rank of scribe, so it is "Mancini, a pen." "Mancini, did you get that right?" "Read it back to me, Mancini." For himself Mancini is undisturbed by his superior's evaluation of his ability. As though he were too tired to object, he accepts it without resentment. He must be totally without ambition, content to plod through each medium-gray day avoiding trouble. His shirt is frayed; an inch of ginger-mustard wool undershirt shows under his cuffs, one of which is held more or less together by a rubber band. His fingernails are ragged and not too clean. He does not mind. He is too dogged to forget the point of his life – the pension that awaits at the end of his rainbow. He plods. If governments need the pedantic Dr. Dantes who worship the statute books and in so doing nourish their own power, then governments also need an army of Mancinis, for an inexorable law of bureaucracy decrees that, during his career, every Dante has a right to innumerable Mancinis – at least one for each post. When you get right down to it, the Dantes know how to bludgeon the best out of the Mancinis, and the victims are not the victims at all, but men resigned to their own mediocrity.

Dr. Dante went off with the Captain to inspect the field of action: the cliff, the body, the winches and pulleys. Dr. Dante led the way. Everything he touched, Mancini touched after him and nodded his head knowingly. When they were satisfied, they turned their attention to us, the bystanders. Several people tried to stop Dr. Dante as he strode back through the orchard, but he waved them aside impatiently. He was not to be distracted from his leisurely inspection of the grounds and the people who now cluttered it. They, in turn, felt the disapproval of his glance and retreated before him, heading as nonchalantly as they could toward the gate. One municipal policeman hesitated too long and found himself dispatched to direct traffic on the road. Don Ferdinando and I were the next subjects of Dr. Dante's scrutiny. He prides himself, I am sure, on his detachment and neutrality, but to me his detachment smacks of skepticism, his neutrality, of contempt he does not bother to conceal. He lounged over to within a few feet of where we sat, focused on us briefly and then before he spoke, checked the condition of the house, its plaster, its shutters, its downspouts. Nothing he saw earned his approval.

"The house is, I believe, yours," he said, bending ever so slightly toward me. I nodded. Don Ferdinando stood up. "And your relationship with the deceased?"

"Quite improper," broke in Don Ferdinando testily. Any pretext, I realized, would serve. He found Dante's manner offensive.

"And *your* name?" Dr. Dante asked in the same even, condescending tone. Italian lends itself to courteous insults. Verb voice is a barometer of social standing. Don Ferdinando had been demoted to *Voi,* and since Dr. Dante had used the more formal *Lei* with me, the slip was obviously intentional.

"Sanseverino," he informed him with the dignity of a man who seldom needs to give his name, but is sure of the respect it will command. "And *yours?*" (*Voi* again!)

"Ah, *mi scusi, mi scusi,* Don Ferdinando!" (Back to *Lei.*) "We met several years ago in Matera. My name is Emilio Dante. I am, perhaps you remember, the Vice-Procuratore and was able on that occasion to offer my slight . . ."

"Indeed?" Don Ferdinando gazed at him with eyes as pale and unseeing as boiled potatoes. He pursed his thin lips, as though trying to remember, then waved the subject aside, dismissing it to the realms of the inconsequential. "If you need information about this lady, I believe I can be of help, but let me repeat – your question was quite out of order." He turned to smile at me and patted my arm, a gesture so alien to his personality that I jumped. The two men tripped through the measures of the verbal andantino that followed with great agility. Apology and clarification, reprise, clarification and more intricate apology – they enjoyed it all. I had never heard Don Ferdinando speak at such length and though his voice was high and fretful, he lingered over his words, caressed them with leisurely self-appreciation and admired their humbling effect on his prey. He stuck his long neck even further out of his starched collar and peered down at us like an amiable giraffe pleased at the sight of tiny creatures gamboling about his knees.

"Come, my dear, Dr. Dante will, I am afraid, have to use your sitting room as a temporary office."

"Mancini, the door," came Dante's order and we went inside.

In the next hour and a half Dante listened to our – mine, Don Ferdinando's, Nicola's and Evangelista's – statements while in laborious copperplate Mancini homogenized our speech to bureaucratic acceptability. After hours of patient stylistic honing he would produce for each of us to sign an incomprehensible, typewritten account which was his amalgamation of our, by then, three separate statements.* Nicola and Don Ferdinando played a cruel game with him. They noticed that he was ill at ease with complicated words, especially those which required a choice between double *b*'s, *t*'s and *d*'s. Like so many southerners, he found the sounds indistinguishable. The two men interrupted the dictation, from time to time, with hyperbolic interpolations which Mancini dutifully inserted into his version, erratic spelling and all. Dr. Dante, who thought they were amusing themselves at Mancini's expense, joined the conspiracy by default. He sat with a smile of patient amusement on his face to show that he understood the fun, but must maintain his neutrality. He could tolerate this little comedy out of deep respect for Don Ferdinando and appreciation of his wit. Power could bow to greater power: let the old gentleman have his joke. Dr. Dante underestimated his man. Don Ferdinando is not fatuous and understands better than most the privileges of power, if it has been established. His target was Evangelista; the question, one of advantage: a dead client-partner versus the indebtedness of a powerful man. Given time to consider, Evangelista chose to

* See pages 155–157.

limit his remarks to generalities about Ferri's affairs. He cast his lot with Don Ferdinando; the field below the house was never mentioned. Mancini was just finishing his copperplate gibberish when the Brigadier knocked on the door and said quietly, "Dr. Dante, we're bringing him up now."

Outside, the garden was desolate. People had been cleared out, but crunched cigarette wrappers and *aranciata* bottles caked with dust rolled about the paths. Sections of newspapers wrapped themselves around the trunks of trees and even the filigree leaves of daisy bushes were shot with butts. Across from the house, under a small pine tree, two women enveloped in black shawls stood immobile, almost leaning on each other as they peered out toward the cliff. They clung together in bleak sympathy. The fringes of their shawls rippled, the corners slapped at their legs, but they paid no attention. Their eyes never left the procession of men who bore the loaded stretcher, slowly, cautiously, at a pace more funereal than any approach to the cemetery. Each step was a commitment. Before they dared put their full weight down, the men tested the ground. They hesitated, sought balance by swinging their load slightly to one side and then began to scan the crusty dirt with their boots in search of their next foothold. With each pause and sway the women stiffened and it seemed they must flail out in some violent motion – toward the stretcher, away from it, or perhaps just sag like broken springs. But they did not.

They stood carved of stone while the stretcher was put down in front of Dr. Dante and the blanket pulled back to show the face of the man who lay beneath. He gave it a casual, sidelong glance and nodded to the Brigadier, who walked over to the two women. When he was still some distance away, he spoke to them, but too softly for us to hear. The women drew away from him. He held out his hand; they shrank further back until they could grasp the trunk of the pine tree. At a sharp order from Dante, the stretcher bearers stumbled off through the shubbery, grabbed the women and started to drag them toward the house. One, the taller, more slender of the two, made no objection, but she would not suffer the Carabiniere to touch her. As quickly as she twisted one arm from his grasp, his hand clamped down on the other. In the scuffle the voluminous black shawl, which had masked everything but her eyes, slipped down onto her shoulders, revealing Teresa's set, half-mad face. She kicked the Carabiniere and caught him in the shins. He released her and hopped away in pain. She smiled a thin, toothy little smile after him, then turned to inspect us with almost the same vicious disgust. One by one she stared us down. She did not want our sympathy; she would not accept our help. She was alone. The bitterness that had grown slowly, like a parasite in her bowels, had finally taken over. She no longer dreamed of being like others. She wanted nothing to do with them. She would slough them off, ignore them as they ignored her. When she finally decided to move, her rough step-and-slide gait was almost stately. She never looked at us again and hardly glanced at the stretcher where her father lay dead. She stood dry-eyed, her fingers linked loosely together in front of her, waiting for the formalities to be over and the long inquisition to begin.

Her stepmother fought, but in the end was hauled up, half-fainting, in front of the stretcher. Her shawl was dusty, one corner dragged in the dirt and tripped her. A long braid of black hair had come unpinned and was slowly freeing itself into three coils down her back, but she made no effort to put it in order. She stared at the lumpy form covered by the blanket with eyes so wide that white showed all the way around the irises. Whether it was terror or shock or a sudden stroke was hard to tell; she seemed to be paralyzed. Dr. Dante pulled back the blanket.

"Is this your husband?" he asked in his cold, disinterested voice.

A wail, a hollow, dissonant wail, more like the screech of an untuned stringed instrument than any human sound, soared out to pluck at our spines. Still her eyes bulged, unseeing. Before anyone realized what she intended, she threw herself on the stretcher, rocking and wailing and tearing her hair which now was completely free and fanned out over the head and shoulders of her dead husband. Suddenly she stopped, looked around, her eyes wild, almost detached from their sockets, and screamed.

"You killed him! You killed my husband! You'll pay. God will see that you pay!"

Muttering to herself, she began to claw at her face, leaving great welts that instantly turned red, then welled up with blood that trickled slowly down under her chin and onto her neck. Teresa made no move to stop or comfort her, nor did she look again at the stretcher, but stood there, all her weight on her good foot, waiting patiently like a horse. The Carabinieri took her stepmother by the arms, gently this time, pulled her hands away from her face and led her, drooping, still screaming curses, to the police truck where they held her until the stretcher had been slipped into the back compartment. Then she was half pushed, half lifted onto a side bench. Teresa climbed in beside her and the doors were closed on a muffled shout. "You killed him. You'll pay! God will . . ." As the truck pulled out of the gate, I saw Teresa's face at the small oval window in one of the truck's doors. She gave us that same thin, toothy smile again. I still am not sure whether that smile was a smile of scorn or triumph.

EIGHT

I

An Exchange of Telegrams

The original texts of all three telegrams were in English, or as close to it as the local post office could manage. For more years than anyone can remember Gabriella's fiend-friend has been her faithful Cavalier Servente. *In his free time he has some obscure duties at the Ministry of Foreign Affairs. Several days later I discovered how effective my wire had been. An uncle of Teresa's came to see me, asking that I help the family arrange the release of the body for burial. I went to Matera and applied for an audience with Dr. Dante, which he granted. We exchanged elaborate courtesies and expressions of fictional respect and, of course, Mancini was sent out to get coffee for us. When the preliminaries were over, I explained the family's anguish and requested any help he might be able to give. He smiled at me and shifted some papers around on his desk.*

"Since you find me so unsatisfactory – so 'inept' I believe the word was – I suggest you apply to your influential Roman friends. Not to the Ministry of Foreign Affairs; better the Interior, I would say." He smirked at my embarrassment.

Before I left he had me sign the statement *(see pages 155–157)* *in which I promised to "hold myself available to the properly authorized officials of the court." I was confined to Lucania to await Dr. Emilio Dante's pleasure.*

ASSUME PEWSNAPERS RETORT YOUR INVOLVEMENT IN MYSTERIOUS DEATH GROSS AGGERATION STOP COME HOME AT ONCE STOP INSTRUCTING OUR FIEND AT FOREIGN MINISTRY TO INTERVEN STOP PLEASE CALL ME LOVE GABRIELLA

TELEPHONES NONFUNCTIONING STOP PERFECTLY SAFE AND WELL STOP PLEASE DONOT REPEAT DONOT HAVE FRIEND INTERVENE LOVE ANN

HEADSTRUNG AS USUAL STOP HIGHPLACED HELP ESSENTIAL FRIEND ARTING GABRIELLA

2

My diary on yellow paper

October 16, 1969

All the notables and a surprising number of peasant men were at the funeral today. Ferri would have been proud, though their watchfulness gave me a feeling they had come because they were afraid not to. Dr. Dante was there to observe from a distance. Evangelista, as chief mourner, supported Teresa on one arm and the widow on the other. Both wore such heavy layers of black veiling that their faces were moiré enigmas. Up to the very last moment Marina debated whether she should or should not appear. Would it be unseemly if she did? If she did not? What would the town think? Should she send flowers? That was easy enough to answer: flowers had to be ordered two days ago from Potenza. I tried to be patient, but the concentration on self only, vis-à-vis what "people" will think, must cripple her life. It is not unfair to wonder if she ever feels anything, or feels it deeply enough to act without a complex social assay. In the final analysis ego and lack of confidence are locked in a tournament of falls. Her Position means that everyone should be interested in what she does. Tradition and the superiority of the teacher guarantee it. Innate good sense warns her that somehow no one cares and she worries: is it her failure, or an unnoticed truth? She is too intelligent to be a teacher. She cannot measure her own worth by the respect of frightened, illiterate mothers, by how many links of sausage they bring her at Epiphany or how deep the olive oil around her portion of chicken may be. Her tragedy is that she tries. Until she decides which person she believes in – the public Marina or the private Marina – she will be *antipatica*. She should be included among the women of my book, but she remains a two-dimensional person, a paper doll without blood.

Of course, in the end she went with me and then evaporated when Don Ferdinando came over to invite me to tea. Teresa evaporated too, between the cemetery and the house. No one knows where she went or seems to care, though I hardly blame her for escaping all that black crepe and shiny Formica "period" furniture. I wanted to tell her again that she could come back whenever she chooses. I said it the other morning, but she looked at me as though she had never seen me before, as though she could not even understand the words I was saying. That laconic *"Non basta!"* is true. A job is *not* enough, but for her it is still an escape. Now tradition controls Teresa's life, at least for a while, and no matter what she thinks or feels, her stepmother, her relatives and her neighbors will see to it that she abides by the rules. Except to go to the police station, she has not left the house since before the funeral. There is no fire there. All food is brought in by relatives and will be for another month at least. For six months she cannot work, cannot show herself in public places. The black of death – her dress, her stockings, her earrings, her shawl – will be the ensign of her state, of her physical state. We may never know what she feels. I must find someone to take her place. Di Luca has suggested a woman he knows.

The Donna Giovanna of tea was very much the Donna Giovanna of Marco's diaries. Had I *enjoyed* the funeral? Oh yes, quite. Enjoy may not be the word, but one *can* enjoy watching people. They mime so well when they understand what is expected. Now your expression of total blankness (it seems I succeeded) – very suitable, I must say – but you did rather start at the violins. You did not know, perhaps, that every funeral done *in stile* must have the violins *and* the tenor. They are recent adjuncts of grief. It is over at last . . . God works in mysterious ways – for the best – and her serious brown eyes searched my face for understanding. I will hear no more about her "little mystery": God has taken care of that too. Don Ferdinando mentioned, casually, that Di Luca would rent the land until the temper of the heirs is known, which means the Sanseverinos want to avoid the sale if they can.

The Festa lighting is still up in the Corso. Garlands of naked bulbs, strung from buildings on both sides of the street, meet at the center and twist themselves into shields around the sweeping curly initials M.V. (Maria Vergine). For a township with a deficit of 120 million lire and an electric bill unpaid for six months, it is an extravagance, but no matter. The members of the Festa committee were unanimous in their approval and most of them are merchants with shops, naturally, on the Corso.

These same gentlemen stood in their shop doorways, one step above the level of the street, waiting with aloof optimism for customers and admiring the daylight effect so cunningly, so cheaply achieved. Under their chins solemn, portly couples bobbled like free-floating buoys in a calm sea. This evening pavane invigorates both – shopkeepers and the self-important professional men, the *borghesia* – with new confidence. In some undefined way each is proof to the other of his own gentility. For the women it is *the* public appearance of the day and so the only matrimonial obligation Basilisk husbands cannot escape.

Castiglione himself would admire the rigid etiquette of the performance. The women, plump and excruciatingly corseted, cling to their husbands. They smile coquettishly; they talk with the tense animation of brides facing the outside world for the first time since the ceremony. The husbands contribute nothing but their right arms and a bland puffy dignity usually associated with the recently embalmed. They are props for the respectable display of their wives, their most precious possessions. Again tonight I wondered if the husbands exert any control over their wives, maybe a sharp pressure on the arm or ventriloquistic asides. And do they dictate their lady's toilette? I decided not. This seems to be a feminine battle enjoined by women of the same class who believe in just two schools of fashion. While one confuses drabness with morality, the other, in garish prints and annealed makeup, pursues that elusive quality, chic.

The couples pass and repass. The first meeting requires a full-dress investigation of the day's events and meals, the second, a grimace and a nod; the third, a nod. If particular notice is to be paid one couple, a repeat conversation, this time with a pinch of purpose, can be attempted, but often the courted do not wish to be courted and drift on with determined blindness. This patient stalking for an extra word, the plotting to be seen in courteous exchange with an important, or at least more important person, is the protein of Basilisk social life. Night after night these couples sink fragile piles of respectability on which they plan to build future marriages, business deals, lawsuits and even further acquaintance with the influential. It is a lonely process. One cannot be too careful. Close friends are dangerous; loyalty is for the sentimental. So, ever watchful, the couples avoid the questionable, bow courteously to the unstained, a bit lower to the important and when in doubt cling to each other in public devotion. From the balconies ranks of giggling, toothless old women wrapped in black shawls watch and study with the eagerness of race touts. They know the past records and the track. Every day they adjust the odds on future change.

Ferri's death has brought on cautious social rigor. Too many people are involved. Too many are, probably, relieved. Tonight they strolled in silent determination as though their physical presence on the Corso were a guarantee against guilt. Off in the Piazza, loudspeakers amplified the swoops and sneers of political rhetoric, but try as they would Evangelista and Nicola could not distract the strollers. They paced on, unwilling to give up until their neighbors did. Release came with a late evening mist that greased the cobblestones and eeled its way into our throats. Autumn is here and the Basilisks know it. Hunched and shivering they scurried for cover. Soon rain will sting us with its icy needles, then drill slowly, patiently into our flesh, into our bones until the very marrow is one long icicle. They dread it. I dread it.

NINE

I

Notes on Giulia, and on Rocco Di Luca

I have tried any number of times to write about Giulia and have never succeeded, at least to my satisfaction. In an attempt to organize myself I lifted the paragraphs from my diary that had to do with her. These are here combined with the transcription of a long taped conversation which, at first, was a monologue and only a conversation in that she was talking to *someone and was not aware the recorder was running. Together they may come closer than I imagined to explaining something of this typical yet atypical woman whom I have learned to respect and trust. She still surprises me. I find myself wondering if this* now *is all of the person, or is there yet more that may someday be revealed. She has made fact her reality and has been so severe in pruning imagination and emotion that she no longer feels. This may be the escape she sought.*

A cold, blowy morning brought Giulia into my life. She arrived sometime after dawn, chaperoned by Di Luca. He put her on a straight chair just inside the front door where I found her hours later, sitting with her head down and cocked on one side, her eyes fixed on the doorframe. She sat with her feet flat on the floor and only a few inches apart; each knee was capped by a burled, arthritic-looking hand. She might have been there, that way, for several hours, or several days. Like so many women of her caste, and it is a caste, once she is in the right place, her responsibility ends. She wastes no energy on random activity. Her body is there awaiting command; her mind, all that she holds private, is deep within its fleshy armor. She seldom has time to do more than protect it. When these odd minutes or hours, she neither knows nor needs to know which, offer themselves, her withdrawal into thought is a careful tracking of words and events. The traces she finds, the order she gives them, will never be explained. They are private. Words, spoken, would commit her to the prejudices and understanding of others, who require proof. She cares nothing for *their* proofs, she wants only to arrange and rearrange her own until she is at peace. This is a good man, that is a bad man. Her visions do not have to match anyone else's. Once she has sorted the strands of her own thoughts, she can begin to reweave them. She can forgive and plan and dream, and her surrender to time has brought the miracle of tranquillity. If, as has been said, every woman needs time to herself, few have achieved this portable isolation so natural to Lucanian women.

She wore a bottle-green dress of indefinite shape and a dark-gray sweater, both very neat. I have never seen her wear anything else, except an old, matted shawl to protect her from rain and cold. Her shiny black hair was pulled back in the traditional and very practical seven-day arrangement of slender braids coiled around and around each other to form two perfectly symmetrical, hooked mats, one behind each ear. In the mornings a few swift drags of a comb smoothed it for the day; Sundays the pins would be taken out, the braids forced apart and the brush applied. Chased gold loop-earrings dangled from her ears; one cast a shadow on her cheek. As I stood above her, I could see a long, surprisingly rectangular face with heavy black eyebrows and a strong blunt nose. When she stood up, slowly, without haste or guilt, I realized how tall and spare she is and met, for the first time, those huge glowing brown eyes of a type too often described as "velvety." There is nothing of soft wonder in hers. The world is what it is, and she neither panders nor pretends. Those eyes gleam with mild skepticism which is never critical, but never more than an instant away from total appraisal.

At the moment I was the person before her and she inspected me carefully, impersonally, being sure no detail was overlooked, until I felt like a laboratory frog, stretched, pinned and expertly dissected on a tray of rubbery gelatin. If she came to any conclusions, her expression did not give them away.

As we toured the house I heard my own voice drone on and on in a one-sided battle against her silence. She nodded; she understood what I wanted; she made no comment. When we had seen it all and were again in the front hall, I knew hers was a Presence which, even in silence and without thought of invasion, would fill the house, making it each day less my own. But I was curious about her; anyone writing a book about southern women would have been.

I told her what I had paid Teresa, the hours she could expect, and then hesitated, seeing a new glitter in her eyes – amusement or disapproval, I could not tell which.

"Is anything wrong?" I asked.

"Nothing," she answered in a softer, more gentle voice than I had expected. It had none of the straightforward determination of her manner. When I did not go on, she added, to placate me, "I never turn down a regular job, if I think I'll be paid. Here people take your work and then forget to pay. Rocco says you're not like that." I nodded. She arched back her shoulders and stood very straight, a mannerism which I have since come to recognize as the forerunner of a pronouncement. "If I take a job, I keep it." A warning?

"When can you start?"

"Right away. Today, if you like. I've got my bread in my *sacco*." And she tugged at a pocket in her dress, finally extricating a large chunk of bread. Their pockets are their "sacks" and always placed just below the waist where no inquisitive hand can wiggle its way into what is precious enough to hoard – money, keys, food. When I said she would not need her bread, that she would share my lunch, she searched my face with those large somber eyes and then said very quietly, "Yes? *Beh* – one never knows."

And that, I think, is her entire philosophy.

Giulia has attacked the house as though months of dirt had silted up in the corners. If she sees me watching, she mutters "That Teresa!" but it is more a strategy to attract attention to her own industry than to discredit her predecessor. To my surprise she talks little. Not that she is sullen; she has her work and I, mine. She does not interfere with my affairs and prefers that I not interfere too much with hers. Her schedule is entirely her own. To her a day's work means bodily presence from dawn to dusk; that is the contract. These first ten days she has concentrated on organizing my possessions to her satisfaction. This morning she arrived with what I am sure was a preestablished plan to bring Sabato to heel. Had I known beforehand I would have discouraged the project as impossible and likely to inspire his peculiar brand of rebellion: And I would have been wrong. As it happened the battleground was right under my window just after daylight. Sabato must have been carrying a load of wood, because Giulia objected to the amount of kindling he thought sufficient for a fire. Sabato was silent. He *never* brought enough, she declared. Still he was silent. Well, if he was going to be like that, where did he keep it? She would get it herself. That was too much; no one could root around in *his* shed. They bellowed and howled at each other – about who had authority to do what, about how he cleaned out a fireplace, and where she dumped the garbage, about sweeping the stone walk, the driveway, about a vegetable garden and a drying yard where that sloppy jungle of acanthus was allowed to flourish. Sabato had a tantrum. He jumped and danced and stomped around grunting until it occurred to him to throw down the wood. Nothing impressed Giulia. She bellowed on in a loud, flat, hard voice that would have terrified a team of mules. As far as I could tell, they switched complaints too fast for either to claim ascendancy in any category, much less a clear victory.

When, an hour later, I dared to face the demon in my kitchen, I was torn between irritation and a cowardly desire to ignore the scene. I found a smiling Giulia, polishing a cupboardful of unused copper with her own home brew of wine and salt. No substitute for muscles, she told me. Later I would see. My copper would shine like the Holy Ghost. While I tried to straighten that out in my mind (she meant, I think, the symbolic dove with its golden rays that hovers over the cathedral altar) she made coffee and talked about all the things she had to show me. Giulia likes to be admired. This time, at least, she had every right. Sabato had laid the fire properly, the walks and drive had been swept, by whom I do not know, and both Sabato and Di Luca were chopping out acanthus. She did not gloat, but watched them with almost maternal satisfaction. When I dared to hope there was no ill feeling, she looked at me as though I had said something very foolish and then included me in her maternal patience: Men are like children; they know from your tone of voice whether you are enjoying a friendly grumble, or mean to be obeyed. The first rule: Men must never be allowed to think they can get away with anything. To judge from the amount of work that has been done today, she made herself entirely clear and, more remarkable, I can hear them joking in the kitchen right now.

As he was leaving tonight Sabato delivered his judgment on Giulia. "Good strong woman. She works, knows just what should be done. She'll do nicely." They, at least, understand each other.

Giulia has just exited with "You learn to get along any way you can." It was a statement without rancor and without even pride in cunning. Her directness disarms me. Already I have accepted the idea that she is what she seems and of course she is too shrewd for that. Expediency dictates. Not that she is sly; she is not, but she says only what is necessary and that with great candor. As a result I find myself slipping into a convenient assumption: If Giulia speaks, she speaks the Truth.

Every day for the last week I have asked her to bring her

insurance book so that I can do whatever it is I have to do—declare she works for me and pay. Each day she has said, yes, she would try to find it. Today finally she stood her ground. Would I give her the money, rather than pay it to the government? When I balked, she explained that she is covered under her husband's insurance book: "That's the only thing I get from him." I asked where he worked: In Germany! I have assumed he existed without knowing or asking anything about him. I never imagined him anywhere except in San Basilio. She claims she does not know what sort of work he does, which is odd. I thought she was going to say more. She hesitated for a moment and then repeated her question: Would I pay her the insurance money? I have agreed.

"You learn to get along any way you can" was an apologetic explanation and the truth.

Every day Giulia washes the windows and rubs them with newspapers to make them sparkle. Printer's ink has some unknown ingredient that cuts grease, she tells me. It will rain again tonight and again tomorrow she will wash them. She considers the weather her enemy; she will not be defeated. We have established a pattern. After lunch we have our one formal conversation of the day. She presents herself before my desk and waits patiently while I run through what I think we might eat the next day and what supplies we need. She is like cooks all over the world; she is long-suffering and intractable, leaving me each day with the impression that it takes all her self-control to deal with the mentally infirm.

"If that's what you want, but I saw some nice celery and it won't last long, you know." Of course she called it *l'ace,* not *il sedano;* humoring me does not include speaking Italian. She expects me to understand dialect. She wants to string some "apple" tomatoes so that we can have "fresh sauce" anytime I am here in the winter, and she plans to cure a special quality of olive, for which she will need *la medicina;* after some probing that was more clearly defined as potassium. It goes in the "first water," a statement that intrigues me. Apparently I do not know how olives are cured. I intend to follow the process very carefully – if allowed. Giulia reads quite easily, but does not care to write, and she trusts her own memory, but not mine. She has me write out a shopping list, which has little relation to the menu I have proposed, then she takes it with her and shops in the afternoon. Next morning the list is back on my desk with a figure beside each item. She will have it no other way; she offers daily proof of her honesty. I am to figure the total and repay her.

To find out what she has concocted from our purchases, I have to wait until lunch. She is an extremely good cook, so I eat in grateful silence. She is determined to make *"aurrichitid"** and has been surprised, I think, by my grim lack of enthusiasm. If the simple life does not amuse Gabriella, homemade pasta amuses me and my stomach even less, which reminds me – I wish I could see Gabriella and Miss Emily "training" Giulia to cook and serve those elegant little dinners they imagine to be part of my life. They might learn, instead, some domestic chemistry that would astound them. If they were kind, she might even teach Cook to make pig's blood pudding with chocolate and raisins! One thing she certainly does not need is Miss Emily's special course in scouring porcelain! I wonder how long the glaze can resist her attacks.

Giulia has brought me two presents. They were just here, on my desk, this morning. One is an oil lamp with a tall chimney and a collar of mustard and pink enamel swirls that slopes down and outward slightly to hide the bottom reservoir. It has its own wrought-iron hanging bracket whose broad loop of metal fits right under the decorative collar and masks all the lower, business end of the lamp. This, she says, in case "the light goes out." We have put it up in my bedroom, reasoning that storms and power failures haunt the night hours. The

* *Aurrichitid* are small shells, "earlike" shells as the dialect word suggests, made by taking a pellet of dough, rolling it back and forth with your thumb and then pressing down and pulling back (with the thumb) so that a thin layer of dough curls over the fingernail. The part remaining under the finger forms the trumpet of the shell.

other present Giulia calls a *galletta*. It is a mug, maybe ten inches high, wider at the bottom than at the top, made of softwood staves tapered and shaped by hand to fit tightly side by side. One, slightly larger than the others, incorporates a rough finger-hole grip. The bottom is a wooden disk, beveled around the edge, which seats itself in a grooved channel formed by a notch cut in each stave. Three rounds of twisted rush – top, middle and bottom – force the pieces together and hold them. It is both simple and complex. I thought it was a grain measure, which brought a smile from Giulia. It is a drinking cup, the kind every field worker used to carry, and some, she says, still do. The staves swell with water and jam together so that virtually nothing escapes. Giulia tells me that when she was a little girl her mother always kept a *galletta* with wheat sheaves below the picture of the Madonna and since I have some sheaves from the harvest – the fullest ears with long serrated black whiskers I have ever seen – she thought . . . and then she would go no further. She was suddenly shy and afraid she had presumed. Together we have put the sheaves in the *galletta* and decided that it looks very well on top of the bookcase beside my desk. I think she is pleased. I took a picture of her, holding the arrangement, but it will be a leering death's-head by Daguerre. She goes rigid, opens her mouth to display a fine array of teeth in a facsimile of a smile and "holds it" the way the photographer "in the Piazza" taught her when she was a child. I cannot convince her that such immobile joy is no longer necessary.

I have tried to send Giulia home in the afternoon. There is nothing for her to do here; it is too cold and damp to work in the garden as she would like; the housework has been done and I have had lunch. She prefers to stay; that is her "contract," though we have none. Today she told me for the first time that she is a knitter, that is, she knits on commission. Her customers buy the wool, tell her what they want – a shawl, a sweater, a scarf – and which pattern they prefer and she knits it for a small fee. It is the only way to earn a bit of money in the winter. If there is nothing for her to do, she will sit and knit either on her commissions or, if I would like one, on a sweater for me. I have told her to come in here and sit by the fire, so this afternoon she did, bringing a low nursing chair* she found in the shed. She says it "bunches" her up just right, so that she is both comfortable and warm. She sat by the fire in complete silence for two hours. Only her hands moved, hooking the yarn through her stitches in a motion more like crocheting than knitting. Twice she did a rapid count of her rows, picking them off with her blunt calloused thumb and forefinger as though they were nubbins to be plucked off a rug. She looked so defiantly intellectual in a pair of large horn-rimmed glasses that it was hard not to laugh. She does not hold with doctors. Obviously she chose her own lens from a vendor's cart, for she squints at her needles and finally admitted that one side is good for near and the other for far — exactly the combination she would consider a bargain, even if she has to close one eye to knit or sew.

There was something comforting about that strong, solid figure by the fire. No barriers, no contact. We were just two women working at our separate tasks. Our tolerance of each other may be all we have in common, but I think I like having her here.

* A nursing chair is a normal rush-bottomed chair with very short legs which allow it to be tipped back and forth easily and so lull a baby to sleep with its gentle motion and even ta-tata-tum, ta-tata-tum drumming on the floor.

2

During one of these afternoon bees, I played a tape of Marina speaking English. She had asked me to record her voice so that she could hear her own accent and I could criticize it. I was really checking to see that I had the right tape before winding it back ready to reuse, but the sound of a familiar voice and several Italian words caught Giulia's attention. She had always ignored my machines, as she calls them, because they do not "do" anything. Suddenly they were magic. Would that "hold" her voice too? She is not superstitious about photographs, that is, she does not believe that in taking the image part of the soul is stolen from the subject and placed under the control of the photographer, but I could guess that this machine that held voices might threaten to rob her of her own voice. I talked to the machine, then stopped it and repeated what I had said to Giulia, before I played back the tape. I still had a voice and the tape had my voice. I let it run on: Marina deplored the English word *love* as harsh and cold, a word we could spit out and then run from in our embarrassment. *Amore, amore,* she repeated, was soft and could change implication with the slightest shift in tone. *Amore!* I asked Giulia if she would like to talk and without waiting for her answer, pressed the "record" switch. She shook her head. "I haven't anything to say about *amore*. She sounds just like a schoolteacher, full of ideas and nicey-nice little reasons why it don't suit her. *Amore!* What does she know about it?"

Like most women who seldom express an opinion and would not expect to be listened to if they did, once she started and was over her original belligerence, she murmured on, talking as much to herself as to me. Occasionally she looked up from her knitting. I nodded or asked a question if she seemed inclined to stop, and she went on quietly, cataloguing facts, eliminating emotion. At best the translation of any dialect is awkward. The strengths are lost in the vernacular of another language; what is vapid and commonplace resists and persists. I have tried, without going to the extreme of *Uncle Remus,* to put what Giulia said to the fire, and indirectly to me, into English in such a way that her language is not insulted and yet ours is not fractured.

The Tape

I haven't anything to say about *amore.* She sounds just like a schoolteacher, full of ideas and nicey-nice little reasons why it don't suit her. *Amore!* What does she know about it? You can waste a lot of words on it, but there's still only one kind: Love of God and you can leave that to the priests. If you're a woman, all the rest is what someone else wants from you. Your body, your milk, your work, your dowry. It's all called *love* — they take it, they don't give it.

They who, Giulia?

Men. All men and don't ask me why. *Sacciyee?* [How should I know?] They're just made that way and the sooner you learn it, the better off you are.

You learned it? [Long pause while, judging from the sounds on the tape, she poked at the fire.]

Oh, I learned all right [she started slowly]. I learned and only God knows what I've lived through with men. Only God knows, and He doesn't care. [Another long pause.]

I was covered at eighteen, just like a mare taken to stud. "It's a good deal, Giulia," they said. To their way of thinking it was. I had six hectares of land for my dowry; he had a house and ten sheep – that makes a "good deal," a *sistemazione* for them to brag on and for me to live with the rest of my days. There'd been others wanted me, even one I wanted, but they said I was too young to know. I loved him. That was when I believed in love. I loved him and maybe I still do, but they wouldn't give me to him. We had an agreement between us. It didn't mean a thing; I always knew they wouldn't have him. He was worse off than me, they said. It was always *they* said, *they* thought, *they* arranged and I had to do what *they* decided. People like you can sit and talk about "love." I wish you luck, more at least than I had, but don't expect too much – or maybe for you it's different, maybe happiness just comes. Not for my kind. No, not for us.

They say the family is a good thing. *Ah si, la famiglia è sempre una cosa bona!* Why? I never understood why. Mine never did anything for me. I had three brothers – they're all dead now. One was older than me: Carlo, born in '19. He meant to be somebody and not with land, like *Tanname.** He'd figured out that wouldn't get him anything but a broken back and tax collectors. Not for him. Before the army took him, he was the dentist's assistant: he carried the tools – what he called "the instruments," looked like pliers to me – and he held the patients down and he watched what the professor did. The professor said he'd never seen a boy so strong, could do anything, like Carlo. He was an apprentice, only instead of helping a carpenter or a barrelmaker, he learned the dentist trade. If it hadn't been for the war, he'd be a big dentist right now. But there was the war! No use talking as though there wasn't. My other two brothers never paid any attention to me. They were too busy with their own problems. One died of a fever, typhoid they said, after I was married. The other got drunk and fell off his motor scooter here a few years back. His widow's still trying to get a pension, the kind that pays more for a workman being killed on the job! I told you once, we get along any way we can.

* *Tanname* is the dialect form for "my father."

Carlo might have helped me. At least Jowan* was scared of him – no, not exactly scared. Jowan's not scared of anybody. He respected him and because of that he halfway respected me till Carlo didn't come back. Carlo said it was a good deal, my marrying Jowan, but maybe that was because of the house. It had two rooms, one on the street where we ate and a separate bedroom – on the back, so it had a window, a real one. There was a dark sort of passage between the two where I put the chickens at night – and anything else we had, a pig in good years. No water, of course. No toilet either, but it had a good fireplace with iron shutters so you could control how fast the wood burned. Good as central heat, not like this fire where the wood burns and burns and spits out smoke instead of heat. That house was damp in the winter, all right. Came from the house on the street above. Their stall was over our kitchen. *Figurati* what came through – still we got along. You might not have thought much of the place, but I was proud of it. I kept the brick floors clean and the bed spotless with its white cover and the pillow runner, all embroidered – I did it myself. To listen to Jowan, I didn't do nothing but sit there in the dark and play the *signora* – that's what he said – with five kids to take care of and six hectares of land to farm by myself. That's love! "It's yours, you farm it," he said and I did. I plowed it and turned it and planted it and harvested it. Then he took the money and called me a lazy slut to boot. But the house was good. I'd be glad to have it now.

Oh yes, I'd be glad to have it still. My brother-in-law and the others, they took it away when Jowan ran off to Germany. Said it belonged to them, always had been in the family and if Jowan wasn't going to live in it, one of their sons would. That's who's got it now, a nephew of Jowan's, and I sleep in the kitchen at my brother-in-law's. There's another example of love! The partition goes halfway to the ceiling between me and them. I might as well be in the bed with them, but, *grazie*

* Jowan is the closest I can come to a phonetic version of her pronunciation of Giovanni. She never calls him anything else, so I have adopted the elision.

a Dio, I'm not. He's a real sticker, that one. Never has enough, never gives her any peace.

I guess it all comes out even. I don't help my children; they don't help me either. They've gone about their business. Two girls are married. Their husbands —*beh,* what can I say? Any husband you can put up with is a good one, I guess. One thing, those two have moved up north. That much they've done. I could lie down in the street. They'd never help me. And the little one, Antonio, he doesn't know what helping anybody is. He's only fifteen. I sent him off to the institute to be an electrician. He wants to stay here. A few weeks back he jumped out the window when the bus slowed down at the crossroads. Said he wouldn't go back, he was staying with me. I put him on the next bus. Now they call me cruel. What would you do? I already share my bed with Maria and she's not even mine . . .

[There is a break here. I asked how many children she had and we immediately became tangled in the names and ages. She went on to explain more clearly, so I have excluded the questions and answers as unnecessarily confusing.]

Is it straight now? Five children, I had, not from love — from rape. Jowan's Right, that's what he called it. Two girls. I told you, they're both married and up north. Two boys died. One starved to death with a "crooked intestine," the other from what they call *fevre maligna* [a malignant fever]. They didn't tell me any better than that. Then there's Antonio. That's five. It was — let me see — it was four years ago Jowan decamped, went to Germany to find work, he said, but he took *una femmina* with him — I call her a gypsy, but let's just say *una femmina.* "I'll send you money. You'll see," were the last words he said before he got on the bus. I didn't know about the *femmina* then. Never saw the money, never saw Jowan except once when he came back with Maria. She wasn't even a year old then. Oh that *femmina*'ll give him others. She's most twenty years younger than me. I know her, or I did before she went off with Jowan. Well, here he was. The *femmina* couldn't work 'cause she had to keep Maria, so he dumped her on me. What would you have done? Left her on a hillside? No. I kept her. She's a sweet little thing, poor *piccinin.* Not her fault. They call her Jowan's bastard! So that's love. I'm forty-six years old, had five children, three living. I farm six hectares and give the crops to my brother-in-law, so he'll keep me – for love! I share my bed with my husband's bastard and I work where I can, when I can. Sometimes I think of Carlo and imagine things might have been different. He loved me, then – but he was a man too and men change. Poor Carlo.

Was he killed in the war? [I remember the way she stared at me, as though surprised to see me, still sitting at my desk, still listening. I think she was not aware she was talking out loud until I asked about Carlo.]

Carlo? Yes, he was killed in the war. I guess you'd call it that. All I know is what Rocco told us. That's all we ever heard. Rocco could tell you – he knows.

[Here the tape is interrupted by several minutes of squawks and bangs and muffled voices. The last sound is the chalk-on-a-blackboard sound of a chair being drawn up. Rocco Di Luca had come in to say it was almost dark, shouldn't Giulia be on her way home. Her brother-in-law might think . . .]

– my brother-in-law! He won't lock me out again, not after the night I spent at the police station. Couldn't call me a whore that time. I sat right in front of the Brigadier's desk – all night. And if the Signora keeps me an hour extra, what can he say. Never mind him. Tell her about Carlo. She asked just now. Tell how he got killed. Tell her.

[Giulia never said another word until they left together. She picked up her knitting again and bent over it, but did not take the first stitch. I do not know whether she listened or not. She sat in the same mute, huddled isolation I have seen at the cemetery when women stand hours on end before the graves of their men.

Di Luca talked slowly, telegraphically at first, unsure perhaps that he should tell me and that I was really interested. As he remembered, he forgot me, and the story told itself in his emotionless voice. He did not look at me; he watched his own rough fingers twisting a piece of string. When he was through, he stopped for a moment, then said "Come on, Giulia. There isn't any more to tell. It's time to go home." Neither conversation has ever been mentioned since; they might never have taken place.]

The Tape: Rocco Di Luca

Not a long story. There's the stink of a coward in it. Had to tell her and her family. Hardest part – well – that's not the point.

The war came – not here. Never saw any of it here 'cept hunger and that's not new. Anyway, it came and Carlo and me, we didn't have to go just then – we would've gone later, not then – but Carlo was what you might call patriotic. Said if Italy had to fight, then he had to fight – stuff like that. [He stopped and looked over at Giulia for a long time before he went on.] We were young then. Giulia and me had sort of a pact, just between ourselves, you understand. Nobody else knew. Her father couldn't see me. I thought – we were young, remember – I thought if I volunteered with Carlo maybe they'd think better of me. I don' know. Let's just leave it, we were young. So the three of us – Carlo and me and [here there is a long pause] and a *friend* of ours – we called him Mammone – we signed up. Put us in the *Alpini* and sent us to Vercelli. Spent the whole war there – in and out. Fought some, sat around a lot. Just war. Three of us always in the same company. We were around in town long enough so we knew everybody in the cafés. It was all right with Carlo and me, but this friend, Mammone, got the itch. Wanted to do something. Pretty soon he found himself a big mule of a female who didn't have much of a husband. He got so he'd pay her a call almost every day, whenever he could sneak off.

Then he'd come back and tell us all about it — everything. Better than a show!

Pretty soon she hooked him up with the Partisans. Turned out her husband was captain of one of their squads. They kept talking at Mammone until they sold him the idea we were losing the war and the Germans hated us anyway. They did a good job of it. He came back telling us we were just peanuts to the Germans, that they'd squash us like bedbugs. This went on for a while till they softened him up, then they put it to him that if he'd let them know when something was brewing — like a patrol going out, or guards changing, things like that — then they'd be able to set traps. They weren't going for anything big, but they needed the kind of information all of us had. Well, it didn't take him long to make up his mind. The female helped him. He did it. Every night he'd argue with Carlo. Carlo said we had to fight with the Germans for Italy and the Duce, that Mammone was wrong to sell out just to have his afternoons with that big whore. Besides he had a wife; how would she feel? Mammone made us swear not to tell her, but the fights went on and on about the war, the Germans and the woman. Once or twice they really tore into each other and we had to separate them. Next night they'd be back at it, till finally one day Mammone came in scared, shaking. It's funny when I think of it now. That bitch's husband had heard from the neighbors about a big soldier who came every day and stayed a couple of hours with the shutters closed and the door locked. Scared the shit out of Mammone. He *knew* the husband was looking for him. Carlo kept saying "Relax! Relax, can't you? Could be anyone for all *he* knows. Any big buck in a uniform!" That's what he said — *any big buck in a uniform* and that's what gave Mammone the idea; I still say it gave him the idea.

It was the next day the Germans slapped the company in prison — we were disloyal, they said, something like that. Didn't make any difference; it was an excuse. They were going to ship us to a camp, a work camp somewhere in Germany, maybe even Russia some said. We just sat waiting for weeks in that hole, and Mammone and Carlo kept right at it – arguing about the female and the war.

All of a sudden one day the guard called Mammone out and that's the last we saw of him. He sent word back the Partisans had "fixed everything up right," just to wait. It was maybe a week or ten days later, before dawn one morning, they rushed the guards. Weren't but a few left; the armored stuff had already run for Germany. They rushed them and got us out. They lined us up. We had to call off who we were and where we came from. When it came Carlo's turn, he got out his name and San Basilio and then one of them said, "*That*'s the one. *That*'s the one put horns on the Captain!" and they pulled him out of line and marched him around the corner into another courtyard. All we heard – all we heard was some shots. And – and Carlo didn't come back, that's all. He just didn't come back. They shot him.

[Here there is a very long pause.]

We didn't wait for military orders, we all scattered. When I got down here – finally – God what a trip! – I found my old *friend,* Mammone, had already been here, talked to the family and everybody else in town. *He'd* arranged for us to get out, Carlo'd be along in a few days – that's what he said. All safe and sound, he said. He'd done it, he'd fixed it up. Hadn't been easy with Carlo. Know how it is? Up north there, they don't like you monkeying with their women. Trouble over that whore of his. I almost strangled him once, the liar. I swear to God Carlo never touched that woman, never ever saw her even. I was with him the whole time. It was Mammone – and I couldn't do a thing about it. Oh, I talked to the Carabinieri, put in a statement against Mammone. It's right there in the files, I signed it. I accused him. I even wrote for the company records when it was all over. Thought some of those who'd been in the barracks with us, in prison too, they'd remember if I could find them. No one forgets a guy shot like that in cold blood. But they'd lost the records, or that's what they *said.* That was the worst part: I couldn't *do* anything about it and every day I saw Mammone and I watched him swindle his way . . . Well, doesn't make any difference now. It's over and nothing can help poor Carlo.

That's how he died –

Come on, Giulia. There isn't any more to tell. It's time to go home.

TEN

I

Again my diary on yellow paper

Finally the racket is over; today the Basilisks vote. Loudspeakers have been dismantled from party cars and put away for another year, but their messages, brayed at us for so many weeks, ricochet about in our minds. "A vote for the *Democrazia Cristiana* is a vote for Christ!" "Vote Socialist against Corruption!" How often they met and their boomings collided to leave an addled slogan: "Christ for Corruption!" Now the return of silence seems ominous and the tattered political banners that still flap in the breeze are tawdry reminders of man's deterioration.

The peasants streamed out of town toward their fields, walking slowly, heavily, their heads bent and their faces blank like men in an endless funeral procession. The fields and the mountain slopes are preferable to the boredom of another holiday. As I watched them plod, I wondered if they had voted, and if so, how they had arrived at their choice. Bitterness is their most faithful guide. They see nothing to vote *for* and everything to vote *against,* which makes the Socialist's motto a shrewd piece of propaganda. Democracy, like compulsory schooling, has been a disappointing exercise to them. At times they long for the landowner of old who had advantages over the corporate body of today's government. He was homegrown. He had a face and human appetites. He was no bureaucratic Holy Ghost; he could be attacked, stolen from, loathed. No, democracy has not been a success for them. How can it be when it offers them the dregs of "The Italian Miracle" – the land they have learned to detest?

For much of the morning I watched three men sow in a wide undulating valley, studded here and there with hillocks and lone trees. Plows have combed the earth until the fields twist, one from the other, like skeins of coarse, rusty wool. Hour after hour the men tramped along the furrows, swinging their arms wide at the very same instant in an unplanned grace no ballet could imitate. From each hand a spray of seed lofted gently, hesitated and then fell toward the earth. Already the arms had swung back, the hands had closed on another fistful of seed and again the arms swept wide to fan the seed into the furrows. And again and again until the landscape was a peaceful abstraction of dashes and dots – and I knew I had been mesmerized.

Two hours of peace have neutralized some of the mental acidity that has soured these past days. It was more than depression; it was a sense of betrayal, as though I had waited all these years for my southern Italian thesis to be proved wrong. I did not want to be right and am bitter that I am. All right, so the truth is that the Basilisks are born misanthropes, that their cynicism does not simply lead them to self-preservation, but further, to the active, conscious destruction of anyone who appears vulnerable – for the sheer joy of seeing someone else suffer. Their lack of discrimination is brutal. No pity, no compassion. Yet I was the very person who so admired their agility at the *arte di arrangiarsi* – the art of making do – which, when carried to its extreme, wrests advantage from disaster, actual or threatened. *E daiya, daiya, daiya!* Kick him until he falls. Use his belly as a stepladder and then *daiya, daiya, daiya* another time. Watch them fall! Dream of your own glory. Dream and scheme. *Daiya!*

Dr. Dante pricks at their anxiety. And he listens. He is a scavenger. Pale-faced and stiff he sits at his desk and shuffles papers, appearing to do nothing, yet he knows all and he listens. He threatens the Basilisks' self-esteem. To impress him they purge their imaginations of their neighbors' venalities and then, like monkeys, stop to admire their own fetid excrement. They have relieved themselves of another rumor, that night soil of human behavior, and have only to wait to see whose garden it infects.

2

My diary

At noon the Captain of Carabinieri "waited upon" me with all the formality the expression implies. (The Brigadier had been around earlier to announce the visitation.) The *questore* had ordered that I be informed – immediately and by the captain himself – that my delayed departure had only now come to his attention, that, *per carità,* there is no question of my involvement, that I must accept his abject apologies and rest assured that such an oversight will never, never happen again. The good Captain was too overcome with shame to sit down. He paced around, waving his arms and apologizing – for something which was neither his doing nor his fault. Again and again I reassured him that I understood the situation, but to no avail. It seemed the only acceptable denouement would be our falling into each other's arms for a good cry. In the end he accepted a brandy to calm his nerves and left with a smart salute and my promise that I would apply to him should I ever need police assistance.

I have spent the afternoon packing, will do more tomorrow and leave for Rome the next day. Unfortunately I will miss the nomination of the new Mayor, but that is now no more than a formality.* To celebrate my release, if it can be called

* In this I was totally wrong.

that when it was never a detention, I have invited Marina to dinner. She seemed very pleased.

Later

Marina has made me feel guilty for my foul humor of the last weeks. She was charming. Not only was she dressed for a party (no gray flannel – a lovely dark-blue wool overprinted with black baroque scrolls) but she had talked a bus driver out of some red carnations he was to deliver for a funeral in Stigliano! He would accept no money. "They're already paid for. I'll say they blew off the baggage rack." This was the first time in San Basilio she has been invited to anyone's house for a meal. We both know the Basilisks do not ask each other, much less outsiders, but a simple supper became a celebration.

I did not know it, but she has had a difficult time with Dr. Dante. He never waits until classes are out, but asks the principal for permission to call her away, leaving a definite impression that she is deeply involved in Ferri's death. Dante's questions shunt back and forth on one track – What kind of a life is there in San Basilio for a beautiful young woman? Did she come planning to marry here? There are rumors of an engagement, are you, perhaps . . . ? (She smiled at this almost-direct reference to Nicola.) Did Ferri ever try to blackmail her or hint at anything he knew? And so on. Ferri must have blackmailed others before he hit on Donna Giovanna. It seems I had never mentioned to Marina the hold he thought he had over Donna Giovanna. She was surprised and then pensive and finally blank, for the only time in the whole evening. We decided the authorities will close the file on Ferri: accidental death while drunk.

In Matera recently Marina met Dante with his wife: Who, as she said, ever imagined he had one? He does. Small, plump and from Ancona. "Only visiting, Signorina, I assure you. Only visiting. When we were married, I told Emilio if I had wanted to be a missionary I would have gone into a convent. He would just have to get along in these outlandish places without me. After all there is *nowhere* suitable for me to live here, much less all those other things of life – shops, canasta, people of one's own kind. This is the worst yet! Why, it lacks even the simple, civilized necessities – or maybe for you, it's easier. The way I was brought up – *sa* . . ." I had never realized what a mimic she is.

Once started, she went on with her "Provincial Ladies." Anyone who heard us laughing would have been sure we were drunk. I tried to convince her to write about them as she imitates them, but she says she is a reader, not a writer and has known it ever since she read *Madame Bovary,* sitting in the Vasto station after school, waiting for the trolley train back to the village where she lived. She suffered and loved and dreamed as Emma did. She shared every pang, even imagined herself stricken with love for unknown, romantic-looking gentlemen she saw on the street. They were too fleeting to be satisfactory, so she settled her passion on an engineering student who, armed with his charts, texts and slide rule, shared the waiting room with her. They never exchanged a word. When she finally met him years later, she was shocked: he was still an engineering student, too dumb to pass his examinations, but too superior to work. She fell out of love quickly enough, but has not forgotten him or the devoted dreams she wasted on him. Books cast a spell; she is always the heroine, which, she said, is all right now, "but won't it be awful if I'm this way at forty?" It was my turn to change the subject! I have told her to come and take books any time she likes. When next we meet will she be Jane or Tess or Anne Elliot?

So I pack the typewriter once again and tomorrow I leave. The mystery, I suppose, is no longer a mystery. Still, I wish I knew what hold Ferri had over Donna Giovanna. What was so threatening she was roused to movement closely akin to action?

3

Clipping from *La Gazzetta della Lucania* of November 7, 1969

La Gazzetta della Lucania *is the only newspaper that deigns to report local news, so inasmuch as any paper has a following in San Basilio, the* Gazzetta *does. On a sunny day as many as twenty copies may be sold.*

ANACHRONISMS IN THE TEXT OF ELECTION LAWS REVEALED BY ACTION OF CITY COUNCIL OF SAN BASILIO SARACENO

Once again it has fallen to the lot of this correspondent to report an occurrence which cannot fail to scandalize all right-thinking people. A flagrant injustice has been approved by the town council of no less a city than San Basilio Saraceno. It is time, more than time, that such miscarriages be corrected by a full revision of the voting laws.

As my regular readers will recall, I reported some days ago on the communal elections of San Basilio. Voting was carried out in an entirely orthodox manner and the results were clear: the new city council was made up of 9 Christian Democrats, led by the noted jurist Avv. Pancrazio Evangelista; 8 Socialists, the head of that list being Professor Nicola Benevento; 2 Monarchists (1 supporting the House of Savoy, 1 Independent) and finally 1 Reformed Peasant (philo-Communist). Last Tuesday evening the newly elected city council met for the formal designation of the new Mayor, in this case clearly Avv. Evangelista. When the meeting was brought to order, there was an announcement that certain citizens — and I have it on good authority that the group includes some of our largest landowners and even one important figure of the diocesan clergy, men, one would have imagined, of judgment and rectitude until this irresponsible act — certain citizens had requested that the election judges review the eligibility of each neocouncillor, and specifically the proofs of eligibility which they are required to file under the provisions of the elections laws of 1951, Sections II, IV and XIII, paragraphs 6-8-9-22.

What should have been a routine vote of 9 Christian Democrats plus two Monarchists vs. 8 Socialists and a doubtful Reformed Peasant turned into a chaotic exchange of accusations. Last night, after a complete review of the eligibility files, it was announced that two Christian Democrats have been disqualified for failure to file Literacy Certificates, as provided in the above-cited law. And who were the two? None other than Avv. Pancrazio Evangelista and Dr. Mario Galletti, famous throughout the country as one of the luminaries of the operating theater. Can there be any doubt of the literacy of two such men? No. And still it has been the decision of the council and election judges — against clamorous objections from all citizens of that forward-looking city — that these men be disqualified and barred from their legally won seats on the city council.

When the "purged" council voted, it only remained for the Independent Monarchist and the Reformed Peasant to reveal their treachery. To the new Mayor, Professor Nicola Benevento, our best wishes for a fruitful period in office, however brief.

This one outrageous example justifies the existence of that law, much criticized by the Left of course, which empowers the prefect to replace a delinquent mayor with a commissioner of the government's choosing. The prefect has a specific mandate from the central government to protect the rights of every citizen; surely he will not be slow to act in this scandalous affair.

4

Clipping from *La Gazzetta della Lucania* of November 10, 1969

PEASANT OF SAN BASILIO HELD IN CONNECTION WITH MYSTERY DEATH

As the culmination of lightning work and diligence on the part of the Vice-Procuratore, Dr. Emilio Dante, in collaboration with the Command of Carabinieri, a peasant, Rocco Di Luca, resident in San Basilio Saraceno, was taken into custody yesterday in connection with the mysterious death, a short time ago, of Bruno Ferri, a landholder and contractor, resident in the same township.

With his usual exquisite courtesy and precision Dr. Dante declined our invitation to comment, but it is understood from well-informed sources that Di Luca was seen by witnesses at or near the scene of the crime just before the presumed-fatal hour, and further, that from statements filed with the Carabinieri Command immediately after the last war by Di Luca against the dead man, Ferri, it is clear that rancor existed between the two men. Thus, what at first appeared to be a tragic accident, has been revealed for what it is — another sordid vendetta.

5

Letter from Don Anselmo Lanfranchi to A.C.

San Basilio
9 February 1970

Gentile Signora,

You must forgive my failure to appear as announced in my telegram. I was a victim of the weather, one of those sudden manifestations of *forza maggiore* to which San Basilio is so subject: a blizzard. By the time I realized that not even "a miracle of modern technology" could waft me to Rome, the telegraph lines were down and remained so for a week. Now with the myriad duties of Lent, all thought of Rome must be put aside until after Easter. A letter will never take the place of an exchange *a viva voce,* but I have no choice and this may be the best day for writing such a long letter. We are deep in the cotton-wool stage of another sudden snowstorm. Everyone is in hibernation. The schools and shops are closed. There is no water and only an occasional glimmer from the light bulb on my desk – *in somma* one of those drear days without prospect that lead the Basilisks to say God is dead. But He is not; only their hope is.

In the last months I have, upon occasion, wondered if, in

leaving the key with me, you had some purpose in mind other than the safety of your house. Perhaps I have lived in San Basilio too long, but we will let that pass. As you instructed, I have given the key to Signorina Bova whenever she asks for it, which is usually Saturday evening. I am under the impression she spends much of Sunday there. At dusk she reappears, always laden with books, to return the key. In all these weeks she has never said more than the necessary minimum. I presume this is her manner rather than any real suspicion of me, but she examines my most banal remarks for secret meanings she must fathom before she will hazard an answer. She is a very detached and wary young woman who will be drawn out about nothing more personal than your generosity in allowing her to use your library. She must have read all your books by now, still each Sunday she has another armload — a second reading, perhaps.

Fortunately Sabato works on an entirely different schedule. I can expect him on any clear weekday, never Sunday. He potters about in the garden and since three roofs in town collapsed under the weight of snow, he has taken to mounting a ladder and flailing at the tiles with a broom. I say a special prayer for him. He opens the windows and has even lighted the fires, I understand, though I would have to admit that his real concern is the preservation of his hedges. Against all the precepts of nature, he is convinced that *"stanno poppando"* (they are sucking, nursing, as at the breast). He needs understanding more than botany, so I listen and nod wisely. Di Luca's arrest has turned him into a defeated old man. In the only way a peasant knows, he grieves alone, in silence. Words and feelings, as you have sensed, have no common denominator for him. You asked that I help Di Luca. Am I right that you knew the story before his arrest? It is not enough, is it? And yet our intuitions will not hold up against even those fragile proofs the police have been willing to reveal. Di Luca is a prudent man, a man of many, not always popular opinions, which he keeps to himself. He has never joined a political party, never borrowed or owed money. He does not drink, play cards, go to church or molest women. The Basilisks, who have always been uneasy about and with him, are almost content that he has been arrested. The silt of their little pools is settling gently as though it were never really disturbed and beneath it will be hidden Ferri's death and all the suspicions and accusations of the last months. If by "help" you meant evidence, you will understand how little inclined anyone is to discuss the matter. I know of nothing new.

What disturbs me is that Di Luca has neither been charged nor released, a situation which, under your laws, would be impossible, but under ours happens all too often. You have undoubtedly read Rocco Scotellaro's *Contadini del Sud.* Did you know that Scotellaro was impeached as Mayor of T—— and put in prison, where he found, so I have been told, prisoners who had spent their adult lives waiting to be charged for a crime? One, when he was finally released after the war, refused to leave prison because the members of his family had all either been killed or had emigrated. He had nowhere to go. This is the legal limbo into which Di Luca has disappeared. Dr. Dante will say only that the matter is out of his hands,* that it is better that Di Luca be "held" rather than "charged" if he is, as I maintain, innocent. And there the matter has run aground.

Leaving aside other considerations, I had wanted to talk to you about Teresa. At the time I thought that you, or you and I together, might be able to help her. Now I am less sure. I blame us both for shortsightedness. Several days before my decision to come to Rome I called on Ferri's widow. I cannot tell you why. They are not members of my parish, insofar as that influences what I do. I have no particular ties with them, but not to know anything about them, never to hear any comment, seemed strange. You see I usually know what is happening in San Basilio. For whatever reason, I went and

* If after forty days no definite charge has been entered, the files—autopsy, testimony and such—and any persons detained are turned over to the *giudice istruttore,* an examining magistrate of the assize court. He must carry out further investigations and decide what charges should be filed and against whom.

found a group of women relatives snuffling in a room hung with black crepe. The shutters and windows were closed. No wonder the words *incubus* and *incubator* are so similar: the room had the most stifling elements of both. A brazier gave off the acrid dusty smell of a dead fire. I insisted a light be turned on so that I could at least see who was there. The widow's sisters, four of them, the widow and Teresa, all in black with their shawls around them, sat waiting for visitors, for time to pass, for whatever the tradition promises them. Our women are strong enough; they do not waste time. The widow offered coffee, discussed plans, the boys' schooling, their careers. Bursts of tears were social necessities and one sister (you undoubtedly do not know her – she goes to funerals as others go to the cinema and is, in fact, called La Pompa Funebre) could be counted on to console her with wails and hugs. Through it all Teresa sat as though deaf and blind, staring straight ahead with the scowl of black hate on her face that I remember seeing one other time – in an institution of almost medieval horror for subnormal children. She would not look at me. She answered my questions with a shake or nod of the head, and she did immediately all that her stepmother ordered her to do. In other words she was paying attention and she understood.

Enzo, not the eldest, I believe, but the next, came in. (I find it difficult to keep them straight, these arrogant, ignorant little boys – or did you know that, for all Ferri's boasts, they are the plague of the *Scuola Media?* Not one has managed to pass the third-year examinations.* Finally when the sham of education has run its course in futile private lessons and inept bribes and the *Media* is safely behind them, too complacent to go on, which is probably better for the rest of us, and too proud to work, they will sprawl about, polishing the seats of café chairs and sneering at their ex-friends who learned, at least, to plow a straight furrow. I have watched it so many times, this spiral of our defeat. They will gobble those parings their father whittled off for himself, and then be back scratch-

* For their certificate from the "lower middle school," equivalent to our eighth grade.

ing in the dirt and cursing fate or God for what their own pretensions have brought upon them. *Bene.* Here ends the sermon I did not intend to deliver. Now to the Enzo of today.) He came in dressed in some sort of squash-colored suit with tight trousers and a long, triple-breasted coat. His hair was beyond description: Shall we just say it was fashionably long and filthy? I am sure you can sense my revulsion, but it was not entirely brought on by his physical appearance. Alone, in the hen yard, the rooster is a despicable bird. He sneered at the women, calling his mother a *cafona* as though she were deaf and he, of blood other than hers. We, Men, were to discuss matters of importance. (One of them, incidentally, being *free* English tutoring from you this summer: I was to arrange it.)

There was no getting at the root of things, so I took my leave. Teresa was ordered to show me out, which she did as listlessly obedient as before, except that at the last moment she whispered "They're trying to put me out." I turned back, but she slammed the door in my face.

The next day I saw La Pompa Funebre in the market and asked how Teresa had taken her father's death. She shrugged and said, "Who knows? The girl is silent except when she is vicious. We hope an uncle is going to take her. My sister refuses to keep her and *we* feel she is right."

It was after that conversation that I decided to come to Rome and the weather intervened. I wanted to ask you, as I started to ask once last fall, if you could find a place in Rome for Teresa. In such cases an archpriest's possibilities are limited. Nuns come to mind, but they take small children and release them at Teresa's age. My own household is out of the question. You know what would be said and how little that would help her. I tried with the Sanseverinos, but Zi' Gian would not entertain the idea: considering "Teresa's weakness for Evangelista," she felt the mere suggestion out of order. Since you and Nicola were together at the first fight that night, I doubt I need to explain the allusion, though how Zi' Gian ferrets out these things remains a mystery to me. Frustrated by the weather, I decided to write and it is already too late.

Three days ago there was a persistent rumor that Teresa had been put out of the house by her stepmother. To me she denies sending the girl off and says Teresa made a bundle of her clothes and disappeared in the middle of the night. But she did not go far. She has taken refuge with Avv. Evangelista – to be precise in his kitchen, where by day she acts as servant girl and by night she sleeps, more or less supervised by his aged mother who worships her son and recognizes neither fault nor vice in him. In the last two days Teresa has slammed the door in my face twice more. It must be her one act of defiance. Yesterday I managed to stop her on the Corso for a moment. She spat at me like a cornered cat: "Now are you happy? All of you who would not help me!" and she ducked around me. Something must be done – immediately. I turn to you, knowing your infinite kindness to the girl and your understanding of her.

Believe me when I say I am not acting as a bigoted priest, or even as a man who has reason to distrust her protector. The morality or otherwise of the present situation is not my prime concern. If I thought it would ultimately bring happiness, I am practical enough to accept it, but neither this nor the conventional return to the loving arms of her family will lead to anything short of ruin. Teresa is desperate and as she sees it, alone. I fear she thinks she can force Pancrazio Evangelista to marry her. Sooner or later she will realize how little that fits his vision of himself and she will need help. She does not trust me; she does trust you. Can you think of a solution, one which removes her from San Basilio and affords some peace and safety?

Not to close on such a frenzied note, I can report that Nicola flourishes as Mayor. He has been relentless in his attention to detail. He is patient and amused and surprisingly efficient. As you will remember he talked a lot about Fiscal Honesty. When the time came to collect taxes, the Basilisks had either forgotten or assumed *he* had. They showed their incomes as less than last year. Nicola wasted no energy on threats or warnings. He simply had posters printed listing all taxpayers in the township, what they declared their incomes to be and what taxes they had paid. An atomic bomb could not have created more of a furor. No one talks of anything else, even the so-called *cafoni* have read the lists and had, for once, a few days of bitter enjoyment at the expense of their "betters." As Nicola expected, the Basilisks are busy denouncing each other for tax evasion and there is every prospect that San Basilio is entering on a golden era of public works. He is tempted to see himself as a political messiah. I have been rather sharp with him: vanity is a sin and even Cicero knew that "salus populi suprema est lex," so it is hardly a new Socialist ideology. Part of his euphoria comes from another source, I believe. He has not said so, clearly, yet, but he hopes to marry soon. I leave to your intuition the discovery of the lady's name.

This letter is much too long. I have treated it as a conversation and with the passing years I find I am ever more inclined to be verbose. I hope I have not tried your patience. I must repeat, however, that Teresa's situation is very serious and I know of no one else who can help. You are her only hope.

With cordial good wishes,

Your most devoted,
Anselmo Lanfranchi

6

Letter from Teresa Ferri to A.C.

On a lined folder, written in the round disjointed hand of someone who has "done his letters" in school, but is unaccustomed to stringing them together as words and thoughts. There is no question that Teresa wrote the letter herself.

18 February 1970

Cara Signora,

I come to write you these few words to tell you that I am well and hope that you are the same. A few days ago I received your kind letter in which you suggest I come to Rome. I have thought about it and it is not possible. I write also because I want to tell you that soon I will be married. Will you come to the wedding? I would like you for my witness. When you come, there is much I will say to you. I do not write good. Best wishes and kisses from

Teresa

I enclose the 10,000 lire you sent for my ticket.

7

Letter from Don Anselmo Lanfranchi to A.C.

San Basilio Saraceno
24 February 1970

Gentile Signora,

A very brief note to advise you that Teresa Ferri has been temporarily committed to the provincial asylum "after repeated scenes of hysteria, disorientation and violence stemming from an incipient paranoia." The statement was signed by Dr. Mario Galletti. In case the name means nothing to you, he was the *other* town councillor disqualified with Evangelista. The commitment is valid for, I believe, thirty days. Then – if she has shown no further agitation, is not certifiably insane, and no criminal charge has been brought against her – a responsible relative may request that she be released in his custody. If no such request is filed, the commitment renews itself automatically. Neither you nor I are eligible, and no one in the family, so far, is the least bit concerned. You can be sure I will do my best to help. In haste,

Suo Dev.ssmo
Anselmo Lanfranchi

ELEVEN

I

My diary

San Basilio
Good Friday, March 27, 1970

In Rome I tried to imagine what the quarantine of a long winter would produce in the minds of men, for as surely as wheat had germinated in the fields of clay and rock, so had the hatreds and schemes of the Basilisks in the isolation of fog and rain and hunger and boredom that is their winter. Now that I am here, making a further attempt at the book, I find that winter dribbles on, as monotonous at its end as its beginning, but there is a difference: people who approached it with resignation have ceased to expect change, much less change for the better. Their bodies are muffled in mist; their minds, in pessimism. Hope calls for an act of will beyond their strength. They look forward to nothing, and nature with its uncanny gift for revenge is already proving them right. How prodigal I am with the joys and dreams that crowd my mind! In the Piazza, in cafés and shops the Basilisks grumble their annotations of past disasters: the floods of '59, the blizzards of '56, slowly, deliciously back through time to the earthquake of '08. The air is choked with the frowzy, fungoid smells of an interminable winter — of crowded bedrooms, cheap cigarettes, layers of woolens never changed and on the verge of mildew, smoke from sodden, mossy wood and shoes worn too long and too often through the dung of our winter latrines, the stalls. Oxygen is scarce, so the mind works at half speed and silences are long and heavy. No one has seen the almond trees in bloom, and the wheat shoots waving bravely in the wet black earth are only targets for the next hailstorm that strafes through the valley. The Basilisks are so suffocated by the exhaust of their disappointments that I am not even sure they have enough energy and vision left to hate. Easter is two days off, but the Resurrection of Christ, who died for them, will be less a rebirth of hope than a confirmation that the only joy in life is death.

In these last days the house has exuded grief as a swamp, its musty rot. The air is heavy with it. For hours nothing moves, no one breathes. The house might almost be empty. Then abortive sounds, those little noises of retreat: a pan dragged to the back of the stove, a door closing – and silence again. Giulia sits at the kitchen table, her head propped on her hand, her eyes unseeing. When they fill with tears, she shakes her head and sighs. I have tried to talk to her; she listens and then ducks her chin to hide her face in shadow and I am reminded that sympathy cannot penetrate real desperation. She is clumsy, uncoordinated as though suddenly blind, and unable to talk. Hers is the deep, mute despair that spawns loathing – of herself and everything she touches, everyone who is near. She cannot drag herself to consciousness. The night I arrived she made her final effort and only then because I must understand, she said. *She* was with Di Luca the night Ferri was killed. She did not tell me where: in a field, a hut – it makes no difference. I believe her. She left him shortly before I talked to him on the road. Now the truth that she has made her reality is, like a counterfeit, valueless until someone will accept it. The police would not, and Di Luca has sworn her to secrecy and promised he will deny it if she insists on making a statement. When all else is lost, he would save her reputation. He cannot understand that, now, she does not care. For so long she was afraid. She had no reason to believe in love and loyalty and tenderness and she has found out too late. Poor Giulia! She is tragic to watch. Each day the rot of failure and hate eat deeper into her will and the final crumbling is nearer.

Sabato is another matter. Each morning he has come, dressed in his Sunday black suit and fedora, and settled down on a stool outside his toolshed. These are holidays. There is no reason for him to come, so I have watched without disturbing or questioning him. He has spent most of his time shuffling several pieces of cardboard, pausing now and then to contemplate one before going on to the next. Occasionally he gazes off into space or down at the patch of dirt between his own shoes. And the hours pass. I understand that he no longer has any reason to go to the Piazza and nothing to say to the friends who used to wait out the days with him. Their sympathy would be as intolerable as their scorn. Rocco Di Luca sits alone in a prison and Sabato grieves alone in a retreat so private it is unknown even to his wife. The blight of old age is upon him. His face is more than winter pale, like a mushroom. He seems to avoid extra steps and to be content as long as he sits alone, unseen, shuffling his bits of cardboard and thinking. I have not intruded on him. Then late this afternoon he came around to the front of the house, not, I think, looking for anyone, just picking dead leaves out of the hedges and murmuring encouragement to them. For him they are still "nursing" and so delicate. He stopped in front of me to announce, *"Ho deciso."* He willed me to ask what he had decided. I did. "About my tombstone, of course." And he came and sat down beside me to explain it all.

At best Sabato is difficult to follow. He meanders, forgetting or ignoring what his listener does or does not know, changing subjects, decade and venue as he pleases. With excitement the burr of his dialect thickens and improbable words, his own spur-of-the-moment inventions, roll out with such sonorous, onomatopoeic perfection that they should be Italian. Only later do you realize they are not and wonder if you have understood. But it is too late. Sabato is already off to further inspired verbal carpentry, and you must trust your mind's ability to convert sounds to meaning.

He had been considering the matter of death. There was nothing to dread if you *knew* you would be mourned. How can one know? *This* is the problem. Sabato did not explain it quite this way, but after Di Luca's "detention," he feared there would be no one to mourn him, no one who kept his grave, who stood next to it on All Souls' Day, handing out cards with his picture and the inscription from his tombstone printed on it for all to read and remember. He might be there, ignored and forgotten. He would exist as long as people remembered him. Curiosity took possession of his imagination. He found out that the money he had saved toward his and his wife's grave would only rent the plots for ten years; then their coffins would be uprooted and put in a mass burial ground. *Va bene!* He could accept that. He had saved for the graves because one must save for them. That is the way of San Basilio. He was purchasing his own peace of mind, his own pleasure. If that were true, he wanted his grave now. He could not live ten years. Whatever part of his lease he did live out, he wanted to enjoy, so he has paid his money and plans to put up the tombstones and have his own cards printed. He will mourn for himself on All Souls'. *He* will stand by the graves and *he* will hand out the memorials and he will listen to what people say and know he is remembered. Every grave must have a porcelain medallion with a "likeness," rather sepia and blurred, but still a visual reminder in this world where only demographers think surnames refer to actual people. The cardboards Sabato shuffled so diligently were the faded, cracked photographs that document his life: his wedding picture, several snapshots taken by a trembling hand and various identity-card photographs, now mottled and pitted by mildew. He considered nothing taken after 1938, so he will forever be a misty-eyed youngish man with black, drooping moustaches and no tie. His wife is again a shy bride, so the wording he has chosen for her tombstone is a summary not without its own unintentional pathos: SHE WAS A DUTIFUL WIFE. Someone has written it out for him in neat block letters. He admires the spacing; the length is just right. On a second piece of paper, again in block letters, is his own inscription:

SABATO PANTALEONE,

10 AUGUST 1895–197–

ALWAYS A FAITHFUL SERVANT

LIFE WAS LESS CRUEL TO HIM THAN HE EXPECTED

MAY THE LIFE HEREAFTER BE STILL KINDER

He has gone home now, happy. He has decided. He does not pretend to understand the mystic conventions of life and death. He accepts them as he accepts authority. They exist to be circumvented and now that he has ordered what is left of one and has arranged to enjoy the other, he can be happy. He will *know* he is mourned. It is not too much to allow a man who asks so little. Will the authorities be patient or will they exhume some forgotten article of law that states a man cannot celebrate his own death? His is a slender hope – that the life hereafter may be still kinder – they must not take that from him. "The short and simple annals of the poor" have never been rich in hope.

Until I came back I thought my people had all slipped away to disappear in the shadowy monotony of their days. They chose not to act, not to know, and I could do nothing but accept their decision and watch them marching back and forth in the tight order drill of their lives. Now, it seems, I am to know and yet be unable to act. My duty is clear, but my right is not, nor do I have any evidence that would convince a Dr. Dante. How much sorrow would have been avoided had there been any trust, but, of course, trust is a luxury southern Italians cannot afford. Another list of their failings is pointless. We all know them, or if we do not, the press and politicians will enlighten us ad nauseam. The facts of history would tell us why, if only we could pierce that nebulous gray area of the subconscious reserved for subjects judged, with the brutal certainty of youth, to be scholastic tedium. *How* to change is closely guarded material for the exclusive use of the orator seeking office. No one has ever considered putting such idealism into practice. Not really. All in all the southern Italian has no reason to trust and no muscles for the exercise. He must be forgiven if he is suspicious on all levels – with his government as with the fishmonger and the postman. He does not believe in friends, only in mother – and whose fault is that? His sorrows multiply like weeds, and he can slash at them blindly, secretly, never aware that he is spreading their seed.

Today with the random irony that only an impersonal agency can achieve, the mail brought two letters and a package which, though tragic in their own ways, are also documents of trust misgiven or withheld altogether. And now I realize that to trust wisely, both Teresa and Marina had first to know themselves, a pilgrimage we all swear we will make sometime in the future.

2

Letter from Marina Bova to A.C.

25 March 1970

Gentile Signora,

If there had not been the natural break of the holidays, I might have had the courage to talk to you. How often I have tried, only to retreat at the last moment. I was less afraid of what you might think or say than of what I might feel. Strong emotions often have no reality until expressed. I did not want to give mine existence. Now, finally, I have admitted them to myself and all the rest follows as irrevocably as the tides.

Maybe it began with that cone of pickled beans, the ones you called "Marina's forbidden fruit." (Do you remember at the Festa?) Why were they "forbidden"? By whom? It was not hard to decide that the limitations others put on me were only limitations if I accepted them; but I do not have to accept them. It is as simple as that. I must decide what is right for Marina Bova, which would be too obvious to write if I had not just now understood it. To act is harder, but I have made a beginning.

You will have heard of my engagement to Nicola. I can imagine your smile: another appropriate marriage. Nicola is not at fault; I am. If I married him, I would ruin both our lives. Before I left I told him, as honestly and gently as I could, that I cannot marry him — ever. He need not embarrass himself with any blunt announcement. Time will take care of it, for I shall not come back to San Basilio. I have arranged for a supplementary teacher to take my place for the last term and a definitive transfer for next year, should I decide to teach. The truth is I do not like teaching. It is a profession my father considers genteel enough for his daughter, a limitation I no longer accept. Through friends I have found a post in Milan as a translator. With more than six free months in which to try it, I will know by fall whether or not I can really stand on my own. If not, there is always teaching. I can hear you saying that is hardly a good reason to teach, but have you ever considered most of the teachers you know in Italy?

I have one regret about not returning to San Basilio. I will never have had the courage to face you and thank you for your tact and reticence which I have taken to be understanding, maybe even compassion. As you will see it is more than I deserved; no one knows that better than I — now.

This, then, is what I should have *said* to you; still I find it hard to write. Ever since that lonely night I came to your house and found you working, translating something, I have been convinced that you had found the first two notebooks of Marco's diary. Where? I have always wondered. That handwriting is too familiar for me not to recognize it and if I needed confirmation, your sudden curiosity about Marco was more than enough. In time I realized that you were not entirely sure I was the Fantasma. (Marco gave me that name; I always liked it.) Strangely I was not worried about the moment when you would be sure. Perhaps I had finally accepted, at least subconsciously, that not everyone is driven by malice. Does that seem a very small step to you?

During the winter I looked all over the house for the notebooks and never found them, as you would be the first to know. I give you my word, if you are still willing to think it of any value, that I read nothing of yours. The notebooks are not easily confused with letters or manuscripts. I admit that I had thought I would take them, but I am not a courageous person, either in words or deeds, and would undoubtedly have read them and then asked you, as I am asking you now, to give them to me.

You are a fair person. You know that they can never mean as much to anyone else as they mean to me. But I am not simply asking you to accept my statement. In some way I am not sure I understand I must justify to you what I have done in the past and am now doing; you have a right to know the rest of the story. It is in the third notebook which Marco wrapped and addressed to me before he died and which I am now posting to you with this letter. When you have read it, I beg you to send it back to me with the first two, that I may have that much of Marco left to me.

Judge as you must, but not without pity for

your devoted friend,

Marina Bova

3

Marco Santoro Notebook # 3

[And immediately below the notation, the following:]

12 June 1969

I have talked so often of my diary that you have asked to see it. What will you make of it, I wonder, this most recent notebook. I have reread it, relived it too in a way and wish now that you were here with me instead of so far off. I resent mothers' birthdays (I say I resent it, but you had to go. I know) and I resent too the hours lost in classrooms and the courteous, impersonal conversations others force upon us. Come back from Vasto soon. It has occurred to me that without you I am nothing. Come back.

This is the last entry I wrote in the old diary, copied out for you to see and understand:

Nights were never meant for work. Warmed by joy I have walked every night in the last months, through rain, blizzard and fog. My days are half-remembered dreams. I wake with a start to find myself standing before my class. My sentence is lost, my thought knotted in a skein of memories. Faces are smooth as alabaster and as lifeless. I see them in a distant glow. I hear voices not at all. This then is joy. She accepted our meeting as fated. She was glad I had come, but would never have come to me. The hand that touched my arm was steady, but her voice trembled and then slipped into a whisper. We talk of ourselves as we are in this moment of time. Each discovery is a diamond to cut and polish, whose facets, as they deepen, mirror our similarity. We have struggled through different hells to the same conclusion. The unholy future we push off into the black of the night. Only the moment is real.*

April 1969

Spring lures the Basilisks out in their cars to ride back and forth in the soft evenings. They have nowhere to go. They cruise in a mechanized *passeggiata* until the clock says it is time to sleep. We are no longer free to walk; she will not come to the villa even to sit primly in the garden. She insists she cannot. When I press for a reason, she stiffens, but the catch in her voice is a caress that denies her resolution. Her objection is that it would be wrong, not in a moral sense (she insists) but wrong for us. She is afraid of change, afraid that we might lose all that we have now. She always hesitates just there. She is afraid of any decision and change is a decision. She wants the future to wait a few months and begs me to say it can. I have not the strength to say it cannot; we both know there is none really and we both hide in the dark, like two people who shield their faces at the confessional grill. She may be right. We are souls met in the wilderness without past or other present and with no future to fill the vacuum before us. While the stage has none of the trappings of life, the play can be a dream. So our walks are postponed until midnight. They risk being spoiled by the intrusion of the surreptitious, but still she objects. She pleads for time, for understanding. She would soften the break, but I have made up my mind what I must do. Now I must convince her. It will take time and must be

* Marco Santoro did not copy the quotation from Catullus for Marina. [A.C.]

done while we still pace along the road – before either of us is shocked by his own sense of guilt, or worse bound by it.

Pancrazio Evangelista sidled up to me in the Piazza this evening. He thinks he saw me on the road last night – with a woman. The menace in those words sent my gizzard cold. I said, of course, that I take a walk every evening before I go to bed; I often meet people. But he was not convinced. It was after midnight, he insisted, his voice low. He was driving back from Potenza – he had caught a glimpse of us in the lights from the head lamps. He lingered over each word for emphasis. One bulbous eye was cocked up toward my chin. If it seemed strange to him, it might seem stranger still to Uncle. As for the Bishop? and he drifted away, smiling to himself. I could imagine his eyes darting from face to face in search of his next victim. A pinch here, a jab there, a thrust at another. He is a careful vintner who ages for zest and flavor before he drinks. He is just preparing the keg for me.

The end of April. The winter's siege has made the Basilisks testy, like men imprisoned too long together, and spring is still unsure. Only the sun and fresh dry air of summer can lift the oppression of our incestuous familiarity. Until it comes we catalogue each other's pettinesses, and worse, each other's public virtues, as we stand too fed up to talk, waiting in the Piazza. Faults are magnified. Frustration and rage have corroded Don Anselmo's good humor. Nicola is morose. Each day the Bishop is more fatuous and more insistent. Evangelista is so bloated by his prospects that he speaks the language of decrees, each pronouncement a divine revelation.

This evening I left the Archives just at dusk. The sky was black with clouds silhouetted in the fire of the setting sun. Another storm, I thought. Then suddenly the raucous screech of a horn blared the familiar warning of an emergency rush to the hospital. A split second of panic and nausea before the car plunged into sight, skidded spraying dust and rocked to a halt. This time it was too late. A twelve-year-old boy lay curled up, dead, on the back seat, an ax buried in his head. He had ignored the threat of a neighbor who objected to sheep crossing his land and had taken his flock through a field of broad beans once too often. I cannot explain it, but as I looked down at him, his face blurred and became my own. I fled in terror. Thank God tomorrow is a holiday.

1 May — as I remember it now

I woke to thunder across the mountains. San Basilio had disappeared behind a curtain of rain. The shutters rattled and slammed against the house; at times I heard the whip of the cypress. Through the morning and on into the afternoon squalls hammered at the roof and then sailed off, driven by the fickle wind toward some other victim, crouched in the gloom. Through the din I did not hear the knock, but at the sound of the latch, I looked up and was, for an instant, frozen in my chair. Marina* stood in the doorway shivering. Water ran off her clothes. Her face was contorted; her hands clawed at lank strands of hair that covered her forehead. For all the wildness of her appearance, her face was expressionless. Shock. I went to her. She seemed unaware of me, let me take her coat, bring her to the fire. She sat down meekly and looked around, curious, almost surprised at where she was. Her teeth began to chatter.

My own calmness surprised me. I made her take off her rubber boots and went upstairs to get a towel for her hair and a sweater and wool socks. I even remembered to grab up her coat and stopped upstairs long enough to hang it to drip over the tub — all without asking a single question. When I came down she looked like a little girl, sitting with her hands in her lap, her wet boots lined up beside the chair.

I wanted to see if her clothes were dry, but as I reached out to touch her shoulder, she stood up and turned toward me. She held out her arms for the sweater. I slipped it over her head; then her arms came round me and she sobbed the long, strangled sobs of a child who has cried so much he cannot stop.

* A note penciled in the margin: Do you realize that is the first time I ever allowed myself to write your name?

I know I held her, burbling the passionate nonsense that love invents when it would comfort. I stroked her hair back from the temples and pretended to flick raindrops from her earlobes and teased her for getting my floor wet. Finally I just held her until her body relaxed in a sigh against mine and I could feel blood – hers or mine, I do not know which – flood her with warmth. I admit for me there was joy in her anguish. I asked nothing more than to be able to hold her and to feel her cling to me for safety. I would not let her talk. Not until she was warm and sure that she was safe, as she would always be safe with me.

When she did talk, her voice was calmer, already mellow with its floating lilt. She wanted the towel; her hair had begun to "steam." She moved away from me a bit reluctantly, hesitating just long enough for me to hope she would turn back. She did not, nor would she look at me. I made her put on the socks too. She looked very funny in them. I had never seen her so gentle then, so without will of her own, but I sensed she must not be startled and let myself down on the thing closest at hand, the woodbox beside the fireplace. The eerie detachment of her movements suggested a trance; certainly her mind and body were functioning separately and at reduced speed. Only after she had slipped the pins from the bun at the nape of her neck and with an impatient shake of her head brought ropes of gleaming black hair flowing around her face, did she take her eyes away from the fire and look about vaguely. When she saw me, sitting in the shadow of the fire, her face lit with a smile that faded almost at once into sadness. "I must tell you, mustn't I?" was all she said for a long time.

I waited. For the first time in so long she would have to see my face as she talked to me. I think she wanted that, finally. I think she wanted to see me and not just feel that I was there, somewhere near her in the darkness, listening impersonally. And she did talk, splaying her hair out with her fingers for the fire to dry. Occasionally, when she admitted something for the first time, she pulled her hair back and met my gaze straight on.

It was a simple story. She had agreed to meet Nicola in the

Piazza for the start of the bicycle races which were to be the final excitement of the holiday celebration, but the storm had changed her mind. Anyway, the races would be postponed to the following Sunday. After lunch she had settled down to correct papers in her room. At three Signora Cappella knocked on her door with a message that Nicola wanted to speak to her. He had brought the car. He said he hoped she would come with him; it was such a dreary day and he had to go to his uncle's farm on an errand for his father. They would be back in an hour. She had not wanted to go out in the rain, but seeing him so depressed and so obviously in need of company, she agreed. As they left town the clouds lifted, and watching the smoke from my chimney, she had imagined me hunched over my books with the little lamp cocked so the glare shone full in my eyes. Such an accurate picture! Several kilometers beyond the villa Nicola pulled onto a side track, which Marina assumed went to his uncle's and which, she commented, was too muddy for the car to get through. He switched off the motor. No, they were going no further. He had to talk to her in peace. He had made up his mind; she might well say — finally — but once decided he would not change. He would not deny that his family would be difficult. In time they would be reconciled. He had brought her out in the storm to tell her he loved her and wanted to marry her. Marina felt, watching his stiff face, that he had rehearsed the speech so many times that the individual words no longer held any meaning for him. He was reciting hesitantly, as though expecting teacher to correct him at any moment. She was bewildered — I truly believe she was. She had been sure he had given up any thoughts of her and of breaking with his family. In recent months she had seen him seldom. Sometimes he walked home with her. He always offered her a lift to teachers' conferences; once or twice he had met her after mass for coffee. He was friendly, gay, less inclined toward sardonic criticism and above all more at peace with himself, or so she had thought.

She pleaded with me to agree that anything she said would

have hurt him. It was her fault, she insisted. Otherwise he could never have thought, assumed, that once his decision was made, it was settled. But that did not explain the memorized speech. She was confused and thinking out loud, sorting and discarding ideas, grasping at others. In an effort to be kind, she had told him a half-truth: that she could not marry him and be the cause of a family split. She thought to save him the cold hurt of the statement – I do not love you. She was honest too. She admitted it had been easier for her, this excuse, than the brutality of the truth. Nicola had sat in silence, looking away from her out the side window of the car. Minutes passed, five or ten, she did not know how long. Suddenly Nicola turned to her. "There's one way to have their approval." He grabbed her shoulders and for the first time she saw rage in his face. She thinks it was madness. Maybe it was. I believe he had sensed the lie and was driven to know the truth. "Like it or not," he shouted at her, "if you carry my child, they will see us married." His fingers clamped into her shoulders and only as he slung her around with her back to the door, did she realize what he intended. She struggled but slipped further down as his full weight came over on her. Then something gave way behind her – she thinks her sleeve caught on the door handle. However it happened, the door swung open. In the half second before Nicola could stop her, she wriggled out onto the ground and stumbling and slipping in the mud, got to her feet and was off down the road. Her first thought had been to hide, but as cars passed, she realized there was safety in the open and pelted on. The cold and the soaking rain cleared her thoughts. Nicola would not follow her, would not attack her. Even in her panic she knew he might force her, but he would not actually rape her. And so she had come on more calmly to arrive dripping at my door.

That was the basic story; guilt and recriminations have no such clear outline. We talked around and around in circles there in front of my fire. We explored the misunderstandings, the one-sided interpretations, the brief moments when she had seen Nicola. There was no one, unique guilt. She needed understanding, not passion. I tried to comfort her.

By the time the Ave Maria rang, muffled and far off through the fog, Marina was exhausted. Torpor had given way to sorrow and the bells were the final call back to the world of San Basilio.

She must go; but first, could I forgive her? She knew she need not ask; she could see that and more in my face. She pulled off my socks, put on her boots and asked for her coat. I went upstairs to get it and was untangling it from the hanger, when I heard her voice again, nearer, at the foot of the stairs. She had forgotten that her hair was down and now dry, but uncombed. She needed a mirror. There is only one in this house, in the bath. I told her to come up; where to find the switch at her right. I stepped aside to let her pass and as she did, reached out without thinking to touch her hair — just to touch it. My hand brushed her shoulder and she turned and stood, staring at me, her gray eyes wide and iridescent in the half-light. I remember saying "I don't want you to go."

The time of reason was over! For hours, a lifetime, there was no reason, no world, no other living beings. We pinwheeled through our own joy into ecstasy and back again to discovery, to tenderness, to questioning and on until all was lost in the other once more. So it has been for a month and so may it always be. I live in a state of hysteric euphoria, speaking my pompous lines through all the day and laugh at myself and the dupes who are fooled by my public *serietà*. Then rediscovery breathes new life into us — and joy and ecstasy, that word I always thought so overworked. How could I know!

I should not have written all of this. Where has caution gone? But she is away in Taranto on some school outing and I am lonely, was lonely until I captured in my mind, not in these words, something of her and our happiness.

She comes every evening. Sometimes we sit in the garden half planning, half reliving the day before. Other times there is no calm. We cling to each other, but we have not entirely lost our minds. I take her home at a seemly hour, chattering all the way about plans, the future, our future. She laughs and shakes her head, not very seriously, though she still says more often than I like, that it cannot be. It can. I will request my release at the end of the school year – after all I won't be the first to do this. Then we will find other mountains like these and long golden valleys where we can be happy. I will write. I will allow her to make love to me in French to keep her accent up, I tell her. I will be a liberal husband. She laughs at me and tells me to stop. I kiss her neck and we both laugh like idiots.

It amuses me to ignore her in town. She ignores me and yet, she says that every bone and every muscle of her body tingles with the knowledge that my whole being is concentrated on her. I know. Waves of the same possession wrack me from afar as I stand gossiping so calmly. This, then, is joy.

What will you make of it? I wonder. Remembering and reliving these last weeks has been my consolation as I wait for the bus to arrive at ten. I pray you will come, if only for a minute.

5 July 1969

And you came that night, do you remember? We were both so excited we forgot the diary and in the end you never saw it. You came when I had almost given up hope, bringing that wild red sweater you had knitted on the sly. You teased me about my drabness and about my secret life that must include, forevermore, that sweater even if it is saved for damsels in distress. You had been as hollowed by loneliness as I, and together we ignited in a frenzy of gaiety. For once it was you who would not go home, not I who pleaded. Do you remember? For the first time I was sure you needed me as I needed you and I reasoned with you about our marriage, until you stopped me with kisses. Perhaps all would be different now if I had resisted enchantment just one hour more. It was dawn before you left, barely in time for the arrival of the station bus with the passengers from the night train. We joked about rearranging the schedule to suit ourselves. You promised to come that night and you came and we argued some more about our marriage. Do you remember?

Now I am glad I have kept this journal. It is for you. This last part I write *to* you; the rest is about you and will forever remind you that you had no right to choose for two people — only for one. The other had chosen for himself. This is your arrogance — that you knew the only right course for *me*. I had chosen life and you denied my choice out of love and misplaced apprehension.

Only two weeks ago — it seems a lifetime — you came to me saying you were pregnant with my child. You turned aside my joy. No, it was not to be. Now you have broken your promise to do nothing without telling me.

Tonight, standing in the Piazza, I felt the comedy was beginning again. Nicola strolled by with the pretty Albanese on his arm. Uncle chided me for my lack of interest in the land. The way he said it — The Land — sounded more like family gods than family possessions. Evangelista slipped up to murmur in my ear that Signorina Bova had left town early with a special permission — sick leave. Fasano told him it was probably appendicitis. I did not answer and I do not know how much later it was that I heard him refer to his family as the "Counts of Serra." It is full cycle! They are carrying out their destinies; you, your threat. And what of me? Shall I join the well-oiled machinery of living death? Deep in my heart I know the strength of your will. You will rid yourself of my child and of me, convinced you do it for my own good. I have thought in the last days that suffering comes more easily to you than love. You have a desire to punish yourself; there may even be more fulfillment in proving you were not meant for happiness. This torture you can choose for yourself; have you the right to punish me?

I pace the garden, sit in the same chair looking at the town, but I see nothing. I listen for a footstep on the gravel at the gate. No one is there. You never will be there again. I love you with all my being, have no being without you. As surely as you kill my child, you are killing what is alive in me, as you kill that unwanted joy that is within yourself. I pray you may make a happy life. You will love again, perhaps less painfully, less completely, but in a way you will be able to accept. For myself I pray God may grant my only wish – complete death rather than partial life. I can offer you nothing now, but this record of Marco Santoro's struggle against love, his surrender, his joy and his death. All will be worth it if you are happy.

4

Clipping from *La Gazzetta della Lucania* of July 6, 1969

This was slipped inside the back cover of the notebook:

YOUNG PRIEST RUN OVER BY TRAILER TRUCK AT SAN BASILIO SARACENO

Don Marco Santoro, nephew of Donna Giovanna Santoro in Sanseverino, was run over and killed last night by a double trailer truck as it rounded the curve in front of his house. The driver, Giancarlo Miseo fu Domenico of Bari, has been released, but in his statement to the Carabinieri affirmed that because of the grade he was moving only moderately fast and that he had flashed his lights several times before reaching the curve. He saw only a blur of red before he felt the impact of the body against the wheels of his truck. He stopped immediately. He and his helper took the young priest to the hospital where he was declared dead on arrival. Due to his informal attire, a red sweater and slippers, it is assumed Don Marco had gone for a walk and that he neither heard the approaching truck nor saw its lights.

Don Marco, who came of the oldest Lucanian stock, had made himself much loved in the short time he had been in San Basilio. To Donna Giovanna and to the others of the family goes our deepest sympathy.

5

The Second Letter from Teresa Ferri to A.C.

25 March 1970

Cara Signora,

I am writing these few lines to let you know I am well in health and hope the same for you. As I wrote you the other time, I do not write good, but at the moment I do not have another choice and I must tell you two or three very important things. Nothing has gone like I thought. I wanted to come to you in Rome. It was a little after that time you invited me. Don Pancrazio always told me yes, yes. Then he tricked me. He said that we were going to the station for the train when he had me carried here. It is all his fault if I am here. I always believed in what he told me and I ended up here. Even the doctor says I am not crazy, just tired and nervous. They keep me here just the same on his wishes and now I have understood he never meant to marry me either. Just the opposite. He wants to hurt me and if that is the way it is, as I believe, I can hurt him too, only no one believes me in this place, except maybe the confessor, but he is an old man and understands little. I am writing you this letter to let you know that I was in the garden the night he killed my father. I felt sad that day. The Festa did not suit me and because I did not want to explain at home, I sat on a bench there in your garden. I heard all the horns when the Madonna came out and then a little later, I do not know how much later, but a good while, came my father who had drunk a lot, which is nothing new. I was alone but he said I was waiting for someone. First he said is it Di Luca? Then is it Don Pancrazio again? He fixed on him because of what happened those other times, and he yelled at me. I said I wanted to go home, but he went right on about him. All of a sudden we heard a voice. It was really him, Don Pancrazio, and they argued and screamed for a while and then they went down through the trees. A little later he came back and told me my father did not feel good and that it was better that he take me home. Then later he would come back and help my father. And that is what we did. He took me home. That next day when I understood, I thought, you see everything is fixed up right, but nothing has gone like I thought. More than anything I am sorry for Di Luca. He never did anything to anyone. You have to tell it to the police. They can trust you, me no. They say I am crazy and that is enough.

I am well. Here everyone treats me well. They let me clean the floors and then there is television in the evening. I do not have anything else to say to you. A loving embrace from your

Teresa

6

The future is always postponed in San Basilio, and I am impatient. Change is possible. I still believe in eventual justice, but why should we wait any longer? Southern Italians have done nothing else for centuries. Every beginning is feeble. If a few ripples on that gummy, stagnant pond can free two innocent people, then we might try a wave or two. The future cannot be postponed forever.